SAVING JAKE

A PARKER MCLEOD THRILLER

By

A. Hardy Roper

Saving Jake
Copyright 2015 by A. Hardy Roper

West Bay Publishing
www.westbay-publishing.com
Houston, Texas

All rights reserved. No part of this book may be reproduced or transmitted in any form or by any means without permission by the author.

ISBN # 978-0-9840 484-6-5

Acknowledgements

I owe a great deal of appreciation to my friends who helped me through the construction of this book.

I am indebted to the officers of the Vice and Narcotics Division of the Galveston Police Department for their invaluable assistance in helping me understand the scourge of methamphetamine addiction.

I also want to thank Larry Watts, author and friend, who was always there to answer questions and provide guidance through the publishing process.

I thank Yue Xiao, artist and friend, for her creative ideas in design.

I am especially grateful to my editor, Deborah Voorhees, writer, producer and director in her own right. Thank you, Deborah, for your tireless and indefatigable efforts in correcting grammar, punctuation, plot structure and overall construction. Thanks, Deborah. I owe you one.

Of course, I could never complete a manuscript without the patience and encouragement of my lovely bride, Winkie Roper. Thank you, dearest.

Cover credits go to the multi-talented Rich Beer for his creativity and perseverance in designing the scene. Photo credit of the author belongs to John Leech Photographers, Houston.

Other books by the author:

The Garhole Bar

Assassination in Galveston

Saving Jake

Chapter One

A shadow crossed my shoulder. I gazed up into leaden-brown pupils, void of life. Dull-gray blotches covered her drawn face. Stringy, peroxided hair paraded in all directions, shielding inch-long black roots. She was thin as a marsh reed in February, early thirties going on fifty. Faded blue jeans sagged from bony hips, and a T-shirt sporting a picture of a crawfish and words saying "Suck the Head" covered her sunken chest.

"Excuse me Mister, you traveling west?"

The words came through rotted teeth, thin lips too tired to move, her voice like the chirp of a house finch, barely audible, weak, tentative, maximum energy expended with each word.

I studied her face without answering, recalling the instructor's words at an Army Intel course, "If you don't like the question respond with one of your own."

"What do you need?" I asked.

"Just a ride a ways."

She nodded toward a boy, maybe fourteen, slumped at a table across the room, eyes on the floor, wearing jeans, a long-sleeve shirt and dirty ball cap with the initials LSU embroidered in purple on the front. He was thin like his mama with dark, unwashed hair curled up at the bottom of his neck.

Tiny pinpricks goosed my senses, awakening a distant warning siren. Just say no, an inner voice shouted.

"Order for Parker," a call came from behind the counter.

A. Hardy Roper

Captain Billy's Cajun House sits at the base of the big iron bridge over the Calcasieu River in Lake Charles, Louisiana. The cafe is one of those places where pine floors creak under your shoes, and posters picturing mounds of boiled crabs hang on the walls. At the counter where customers order and pick up food, a chalkboard menu lists daily specials.

When I returned with my fried-oyster breakfast, the woman was back at her table, hands wrapped through the straps of a small duffel bag, feet pointed toward the door. The boy stood and reached for two small backpacks. I left my food on the table and ambled over.

"Are you hungry?"

The woman glanced at the boy. Faster than a blink, a flicker of hope flashed in his eye, then quickly vanished, retreating to some long familiar respite of what seemed like despair. But the woman, reading the signal, responded with a nod of her head.

I didn't have to get involved. I had just walked out of the casino into a hot, gray morning, and stopped at Captain Billy's for something to eat. I was tired and hungry, facing a four-hour trek home. I could have simply bought the woman and boy a meal and left.

Maybe I stayed because helping them provided some level of atonement after celebrating my birthday by drinking until dawn and losing a week's income in an all-night poker game. Maybe I hoped playing the Good Samaritan to these poor souls might somehow redress a night of empty wantonness. Or maybe it was just the way I'm wired...me, Parker McLeod, proprietor, The Garhole Bar, Galveston, Texas.

Nothing on the menu suggested breakfast so the woman ordered an extra-large Coke and bowl of gumbo for herself and fried crawfish for the boy. She finished the Coke and returned for a refill. The woman picked at the gumbo, but the boy scarfed every morsel on his plate. Then he reached for her bowl of gumbo and scooped it clean.

We piled into my pickup, the boy in the middle, the woman claiming the passenger seat. She'd called the boy, Jake and said her name was Joy. She didn't ask my name, and I didn't offer it.

I stashed the backpacks in the truck bed with my gear. Joy kept the duffel on her lap, both hands tight on the straps as though the bag might form wings and fly out the window. We crossed the Texas line an hour later, her grip on the bag white knuckled tight.

We passed through Beaumont chugging along just under the speed limit. My twenty-year-old Chevy pickup ran well, but the salty Gulf Coast air had eaten away most of the finish leaving alternating patches of paint and rust, something like the hide of a giraffe. With the air conditioner not working, we rode with the windows open. Jake leaned forward trying to grab the air passing through the cab. Joy held a cloth to her cheek absorbing the sweat collecting on her face while attempting to hide the intermittent quivering of her lips.

I glanced at the boy and said, "Kid, it's going to get hotter. If you want out of that long-sleeve shirt, I'll stop, and you can get something cooler from your backpack."

Jake moved his head side to side with the energy of a turtle. He wiped his forehead with his hand. The boy had not uttered a sound in the restaurant or the truck. I was starting to wonder if he was mute.

When we reached the exit off Interstate 10 for the town of Winnie, I slowed to the right lane and took the off ramp. Joy had indicated she wanted to go west, but she hadn't spoken since leaving Lake Charles. I assumed her destination was Houston an hour ahead on the Interstate. I planned to turn at Winnie and drive Highway 120 to the Gulf and Bolivar Peninsula, then travel the coast highway through the small

A. Hardy Roper

towns until I reached the ferry for the short hop across the open bay to Galveston Island. That would be adios time, good deed for the day coming to an end. I pulled to the stop light beside the overpass, leaned in and spoke to Joy.

"I'm heading south here. I'll drop you across the street. You can pick up a ride to Houston at the Valero station."

Joy squirmed in her seat, opening and closing her hands on her duffel with a nervous twitch. She glanced out the back window, then turned back and studied the gas station. She gestured toward the underpass and said, "You can get to Galveston the way you're going, right?"

So much for the best of plans. I tried again and pointed at the freeway. "The Bolivar beaches are crowded this time of year. The wait at the ferry can be hours. It's faster to take the Interstate to Baytown. You can pick up a ride there, south to Galveston."

She fidgeted again, viewed the Valero for a moment and then pivoted to check behind us.

"We'll stay with you," she said.

When the light changed, I turned under the freeway. An elderly man driving a pickup followed behind. As we cleared the overpass, a 10-year-old black Pontiac with dark-tinted windows filed in behind the old man's truck. Not having seen the Pontiac at the intersection, I assumed it had come from behind the Valero.

I motored through the small town of Winnie, the pickup and Pontiac following behind. A few minutes later, free of traffic, I pushed the old truck to the speed limit. The highway stretched out straight and flat, the oncoming lane clear as far as we could see.

The closer we got to the coast, the more desolate the area became. Empty marshland framed both sides of the highway. Out in the prairie, potholes, filled with water, dotted with various cranes and waterfowl, broke the endless line of salt grass. On the power line beside the road, a red-tailed hawk sat stone-like waiting for an unlucky field mouse to leave its burrow. It was a normal, steamy, August day on the Gulf Coast. Except, it wasn't normal at all. I just didn't know it yet.

On this lonely stretch, a driver could easily overtake several cars in a single pass, yet neither of the vehicles behind me seemed interested. I checked the mirror. The old man in the pickup appeared harmless, so I focused on the black Pontiac. Something about the car bothered me. I don't like people hiding behind dark walls. Maybe it was just my training...but whatever it was, I didn't like it. And Joy's increasing nervousness didn't help, tongue flickering—darting over her lips, jumpy eyes constantly checking the outside mirror.

I slowed below the speed limit to encourage the truck and Pontiac to go around. The old man in the pickup didn't appear to be in a hurry. He closed the gap behind us but elected not to pass. The Pontiac kept pace behind the pickup. I glanced at Joy, her face taught, hands looped tight on the duffel, eyes peeled to the side mirror.

Jake had dozed off, leaning into me. I had a strange feeling there was more than his weight against my shoulder. It was as though the boy was transferring the burdens of his world.

A mile later, the pickup slowed and turned onto a dirt road leading to an old cow barn on the prairie. The Pontiac closed in on my rear bumper; the driver, with a scowl on his face, gunned the engine. Then I saw the gun. He waved the weapon out the window. The gesture made it clear he wanted us to pull to the shoulder and stop. Fat chance.

I pushed the pedal to the floor and surged ahead. At 75, the Chevy began to shake and rattle, the steering wheel vibrating in my hands. Trying to outrun the beast behind me, I

A. Hardy Roper

pushed the limits of the old truck hoping the engine wouldn't blow. The Pontiac closed in again.

Ahead, the high bridge over the Intracoastal Waterway rose like a Phoenix out of the bleak horizon, looming tall and narrow, tight, like a vise closing in. The Pontiac pulled into the oncoming lane, its nose at my rear bumper and gaining. We're close to eighty and the bridge is upon us. I'm thinking the idiot driver wants to get us on the bridge and force my truck into the railing.

I slammed the brakes at the last second and veered sharply onto a sand road beside the bridge, hands tight on the wheel, attempting to keep the truck from sliding sideways into the marsh. The Pontiac missed the turn and roared up the bridge.

At the bottom of the lane, a barbed-wire fence stood as the only barrier between my truck and the Intracoastal Waterway. I pumped the brakes hard hoping they'd hold. The Chevy fishtailed right then left. Last chance...I jammed the brakes again. The truck slid sideways, slamming into the barbed wire, crashing me into Jake, both of us into Joy, and Joy into the door. I regained my balance, glanced back and spotted the Pontiac at the top of the lane.

I reached across the boy and grabbed my Colt 1911 .45 automatic out of the glove compartment. The fence blocked the passenger side of the truck. I yanked Jake out the driver's side and half-dragged him toward one of the cement pilings supporting the bridge. He stumbled to the ground. I tugged him by the arm and kept going. Joy hung on our heels carrying the duffel.

The Pontiac hurtled down the sand road and screeched to a stop thirty yards away. A beefy, dark-skinned man with a heavy mustache wearing jeans and a dirty baseball cap leaped out firing a handgun. Two shots ricocheted off the bridge piling flushing a flock of cowbirds out of the marsh.

Saving Jake

I huddled with the kid and Joy behind the piling and let loose a volley at the attacker. My rounds missed the shooter, but several pinged into the metal of his car. The attacker hustled behind the Pontiac, opened the passenger door, slid across the front seat and fired twice more out the driver's window. His gun clicked empty. My .45 held seven rounds to his revolver's six, but how many times had I fired? I ripped back the receiver to an empty chamber, cursing for leaving my extra clip in the glove compartment.

Gambling he didn't have extra rounds, I slammed the receiver shut and stepped around the piling, moving toward his car, steady, purposeful, weapon extended, as though I intended to close without stopping and put a bullet in his brain.

But then, either out of panic or hoping the gun had only misfired, he snapped the trigger again, click. And again, click. Now his hand dropped the gun to the seat and found the gearshift. He jammed the Pontiac into reverse and powered the old car back up the sand road, clearing the lane, fishtailing up the highway toward Winnie, trailing a cloud of black smoke.

A. Hardy Roper

Chapter Two

Jake sat crouched behind the bridge piling, eyes wide, taking in the scene, Joy behind him, her body shaking, her face the color of white chalk.

"What the hell?" I screamed at Joy, adrenalin peaked. "Who was that maniac?"

Not waiting for an answer, I scurried to the truck, grabbed an extra clip from the glove compartment and quickly reloaded my .45 in case the mad man returned. I cranked the engine and pulled away from the fence waving frantically at Joy and Jake to hurry.

I goosed the old pickup, pedal to the medal, and raced over the Intracoastal Bridge toward High Island, the small town just before the beach road to Bolivar Peninsula.

Joy clutched Jake's hand but kept her eyes pasted to the side mirror anxiously scanning the road behind us. We pushed through High Island without slowing, my eyes alternating between the road in front and the scene behind.

"We'll stop the first cop we see," I blurted out.

"No...don't," Joy said, eyes red, tears building.

I glanced at the terror on her face and at Jake almost catatonic beside me. I blew out a big breath trying to calm myself, shuffling the last few minutes through my consciousness. Joy was right of course, flagging a cop meant hours spent explaining the incident, plus having to defend carrying and firing a weapon without a gun permit. There were no witnesses and no injuries. All I wanted was to unload this woman and kid and get back to Galveston. I had a bar to run.

A. Hardy Roper

We turned onto Bolivar Highway heading west and approached the small bridge over Rollover Pass, the man-made cut across the peninsula that fed water from the Gulf to Galveston Bay. As we slowed to maneuver the tight lanes, Joy turned in her seat to scan the road behind us. At the top of the bridge, she sighed heavily and lowered her head as if in prayer, tension lines in her face dissipating, color returning to her cheeks. She released Jake's hand, closed her eyes and put her head against the seat.

"My boyfriend," she said.

"What?"

"He figured we was going to Galveston. Knew we could turn at Winnie or go straight. He must of waited for us at the Valero where he could watch the freeway and the exit."

"Why Galveston?"

"Got nothing else."

"What's there for you?"

"My poppa."

If it's true that bad things happen in threes, and if the stupidity of picking up a woman on the run followed by a shootout with her ex-boyfriend are two of them—what happens next? The thought of something else lurking out there was more than I wanted to consider. I pushed the thought to some dark, hidden part of my brain, and focused on the road before me, long and straight.

To the left along the shore, summerhouses built on 20-foot pilings lined the beachfront. To the right lay open fields dotted with cattle. We drove through the village of Crystal Beach passing the usual small town businesses: a gas station, a real estate office, a seashell shop. At the local grocery store, I watched a truck driver unloading several cases of beer. The store was stocking up for the throng of visitors expected over the last few days of summer.

Saving Jake

A few minutes later, we reached the ferry, relieved to find a deckhand motioning us forward. Several more vehicles entered behind us before the steel ramp slammed shut, clanking hard and final, the boat full.

It wasn't a conscious decision, the move purely reactive, spontaneous—but whatever the source, whether imbued by twenty years of Army training or some primordial instinct for safety and protection—I glanced behind us, eyes straining, searching for the dark Pontiac. When the boat's huge diesel engines powered up and pushed the ferry away from the dock, I exhaled a long stream of air, relieved we were safe, at least for the moment.

Jake raised himself from a crouched position, and I motioned for him to get out and follow me. We left Joy sleeping in the truck and made our way to the stern of the boat to watch kids feeding the seagulls hovering overhead. As a young girl held a piece of bread in her outstretched palm, a bird fluttered close and snatched the crumb away. Jake's eyes widened at the sight.

"You like birds?" I asked, wondering if the kid could talk. He pulled the ball cap tight over his forehead and stuck his hands in his pockets.

"Guess so," he answered.

Finally, I thought...ice broken. A few minutes later we arrived at the Galveston terminal. The deckhand lowered the dock board, and we rolled off the ferry.

"Where to?" I said to Joy.

"Go to the seawall, I'll show you."

We followed Ferry Road to its intersection with Seawall Boulevard, the wide street bordering the beach. Vehicles of all description, from pickups to convertibles and classics, inched along, jamming the lanes. Tourists strolled along the seawall, their bodies red and hot from too much sun. Across the boulevard, restaurants facing the water were crammed to capacity with customers devouring fresh seafood, laughing and drinking cold beer.

Out over the water, a southerly wind pushed dark clouds heavy with moisture toward the shoreline. The approaching summer squall churned the water into a white-capped tempest delighting the surfers riding the waves to shore. On the beach, families with small children gathered under brightly colored umbrellas protecting themselves from the coming rain.

Jake missed nothing. His eyes darted left and right like those of a wild animal trapped in a cage and dropped off in new territory. Joy rotated her vision between the side roads and furtive glances behind us. Her nervousness had increased. She was more jumpy, her eyes flittering like a trapped bird.

The protective seawall ended at the edge of the city, and the road descended to sea level.

"Now where?" I asked.

"Just keep on down the island," she mumbled.

The western segment of Galveston Island narrows like the jagged shape of a hand-sculpted pre-historic spear that gradually diminishes to its pointy end. The area is bordered on the south by the Gulf of Mexico and on the north by a shallow body of water known as West Bay, which separates the island from the mainland.

Along the 20 mile drive between where the seawall stops and isles end, a number of housing developments stretch across the island. I know them all well, along with every crossroad, liquor store and beer joint besides my own. But there was no reason to let Joy know that. The quicker I dropped her and the kid off the better.

A few minutes later, we passed through Pirates Beach, the first large-scale sub-division past the seawall. Rows of houses built high on pilings lined the shoreline. Across the highway, canals snaked through the development providing boat access to West Bay. Joy didn't indicate a turn, so I continued driving west.

By the time we reached Jamaica Beach, the next large development, Joy's nervousness had increased five-fold, eyes bouncing all over the road, body rocking, mouth twitching, tongue constantly darting over her lips. It was almost as though a horde of invisible insects were biting and chewing their way across her frail body.

"How much farther," I asked, ready to dump her and the kid at the next intersection.

Joy said nothing. When we reached Sea Isle, my pulse danced hard. The cutoff to my watering hole lay only a few miles ahead. We were running out of island. Where was she going? An uncomfortable tingle crossed the back of my neck. My little piece of heaven loomed ahead, and we were getting too close to The Garhole for comfort. If that third bad thing I mentioned was coming up, I sure didn't want it to happen in my back yard.

And then, out of nowhere, without prompting, she blurted out, "Bay Harbor, just up the road. You know it?"

I said nothing, but of course I knew Bay Harbor, a cluster of weekend houses built on stilts, one of the oldest subdivisions on the west end. There were a few canals and homes on the bay side, but the majority of the houses were landlocked on what the locals termed "Kansas lots." Development began in the 1950s as a cluster of wooden structures designed to be washed about by hurricanes and then rebuilt. Most of the houses were completed before federal flood insurance and the state windstorm pool combined to change the landscape from fishing camps to the Mc-Mansions now crowding the beachfront.

We turned in past the line of tall palm trees guarding the entrance and cut over to the last street in the subdivision where the row of houses bordered the marsh. We stopped at a

A. Hardy Roper

paint-bare house built atop wooden pilings. A rusted chain-link fence surrounded what appeared to be various beachcomber treasures. A seashell collection glued to plywood leaned against the fence. Two lifesaving rings with ships names stenciled on the canvas hung from a clothesline next to a large pile of driftwood. In the middle of the yard, sitting on a battered trailer with flat tires, was an old wooden fishing boat with an ancient outboard motor perched on the stern.

I stopped next to a sun-bleached station wagon parked outside the fence. As we got out of the truck, the wind stiffened and a light rain pinged the top of the cab. The coming summer storm gave me a good excuse to quicken the pace and get the hell out of there. I hustled Joy and Jake out of the truck and grabbed their packs out of the back. As I put my hand out to open the gate, a German Shepard the size of a small lion bounded around the corner of the house. The behemoth pounded against the gate barking and growling as though he'd cornered an escapee from a POW camp.

Up on the porch, a white-bearded old man wearing a tattered wife-beater shirt and resting a beer can on his huge midsection, glared down at the scene. He called to the dog.

"Buster, come."

When the dog didn't respond, the old man yelled again, "Buster get your ass up here!"

The German Shepard trotted tail down toward the stairs. With rain pelting her tired face, Joy turned to me, eyes averted, blotched lips quivering as she spoke.

"Thanks, Mister Parker."

"You know my name?"

"They said it at Captain Billy's."

I managed a quick glance at her tormented face and thought about her name...wondering if the poor, bedraggled human being before me had ever known happiness or even peace, much less *joy*.

Saving Jake

I locked eyes with Jake for the first time. He didn't speak but his eyes reflected something I thought could have been gratitude. It was as though he was giving me the benefit of the doubt for being a member of the human race. I also glimpsed something else...something I tried to deny, to push away, something I didn't want to see. But there, mirrored in Jake's lonesome countenance, I saw a reflection of myself.

A. Hardy Roper

Chapter Three

Of course, I should have known better. Officer Candidate School had taught me success involved making good decisions. So what was I thinking, picking up a hitchhiking doper and her waif kid? I had asked myself the question a thousand times since leaving Louisiana and still couldn't answer why. It was the perfect ending to an already lousy weekend.

I came to a stop at the exit to Bay Harbor feeling an immediate release, the shiver in my neck dissipating, and my heart rate heading south toward its normal sixty-five beats per minute. I was almost home—ready for *island time*—the easy pace of taking each day as it comes.

I drove past the marsh bordering Bay Harbor and a half-mile farther to the barbed wire fence that marked my property's boundary line. I turned on to the sandy lane to the bar and stopped. A quick glance back at the top of the palm trees left me with a strong sense of foreboding. I had dropped Joy and Jake off less than two miles from my house with nothing in between but a few splotches of salt cedars and tangles of cord grass. Close...too damn close.

I eased down the lane and stopped in the oyster-shell parking lot. Before me, the faded, cedar planks covering The Garhole reminded me I hadn't painted the exterior since the last hurricane pushed five feet of water over the island. The storm surge had inundated the bar trapping piles of mud on the concrete floor. Even now, four years later, my olfactory senses revolted at the remembered stench of thousands of dead organisms rotting in the summer heat.

A. Hardy Roper

I shook the thought away and noticed the large opening at the front was closed, and it was past noon. The front door was locked, so I moved around the side of the building to the rear.

I slipped in the back door, popped two cold Shiner Bocks out of the cooler and ambled out to the dock. Joe Stubbs sat in his wheelchair casting a plastic shrimp into the bay, his thick chest accentuated with each throw by the tight fit of a Go-Army T-shirt. Coal black hair dropped below his neck and a heavy beard heightened the intensity of his steel gray pupils. Two gnarled, white stumps stuck out from cutoff jeans giving the appearance of a double-barreled shotgun guarding the dock from unknown intruders.

Joe let the shrimp sink and then reeled in slowly giving the line a quick jerk every few turns of the handle. I sat his beer on the arm of the bench close to the wheelchair and watched for a moment.

"Any luck?"

Joe reeled in the bait and stuck the handle of his pole into a rod holder mounted on the bench, the plastic shrimp dangling below the tip. He sipped his beer and stared out over the bay.

"Water's too hot," he said.

I followed his view to the heat waves shimmering off the bay water and couldn't hold back a sarcastic quip. "Yeah, well, it is the middle of an August afternoon on the Gulf Coast."

Joe offered a glancing frown and said, "Parker, I knew I wasn't gonna catch any fish when I came out here. I just needed to throw out a line, okay?"

"Sure," I said, regretting the wisecrack. "Why didn't you open the bar?"

"Just having a bad day, I guess. Sorry."

I knew he was referring to his own set of demons and not anything about the bar. I let the comment slide.

"Any business yesterday?"

"You didn't miss nothing. Two fishermen, six beers and two bowls of gumbo."

When he asked about my trip, I hesitated, considering how much to divulge. I had acted stupidly picking up the woman and boy and had already beaten myself up enough without getting more grief from Stubbs. Then I decided risking Joe's wrath was better than keeping it bottled up. I recounted everything that had happened and without waiting for a response, I crossed the concrete apron and entered the back door of the bar.

I heated leftover sausage and tortillas and moved to a table. Joe rolled in the back door. He took a huge bite out of the wrap and aimed the rest at the two-foot long skeleton head of an alligator gar hanging above the back counter. Rows of razor sharp teeth gleamed down on us.

"You're about as smart as that goddamn gar head," he said, shaking the sausage as he spoke. "Trying for nookie or what?"

I gave him a hard look. "Come on, Joe...don't do this. I almost didn't tell you because I didn't want to hear your bitching."

He ignored my plea and continued. "Well, I mean holy crap, Parker. Blasting away with your .45 like some drunk cowboy."

"What did you want me to do? Get shot? The son of a bitch was shooting at me, for Christ's sake. And there was a woman and a kid."

"How many times did you fire?"
"Emptied a full clip."
"And didn't hit nothing?"
"Put a round or two in his car."
Joe frowned.

A. Hardy Roper

"This wasn't TV. The guy was a hundred feet away and I was firing a handgun at someone shooting back at me."

Joe shook his head. "You need to go to the range," he said. He finished the tortilla and wheeled away from the table, yelling over his shoulder, "You were just lucky the bozo ran out of ammo."

I was tired of Joe's sniping, but his harangue had made me think about my intentions. Was I really trying to hit the guy or just scare him off? The more I thought about it, the more I realized I couldn't answer the question. In the end, everyone had gotten away safely, and thinking about it now, I was glad I missed. The last thing I needed was to get tied up in someone else's squabble.

With the heat index hovering over a hundred, I shifted to the front of the bar to unlock the front door and raised the large opening I had cut out of the wall. I hoisted the wall section using ropes and pulleys and secured the heavy window covering to the ceiling. The prevailing breeze off the Gulf quickly invaded the room pacifying the stifling heat.

I let Joe know I had opened the bar for business and left for a run hoping to sweat out what remained of last night's alcohol. I jogged up the sand lane, crossed the highway, and maneuvered along a trail that wound past prickly pear and sand dunes.

When I arrived at the beach, a hundred yards out in the water, several trawlers worked their nets along the shoreline. It was the time of year when shrimp migrated into shallow water to spawn. The surviving larvae then worked their way along the beach until they could enter the bay and grow up. One of the boat captains was a Garhole regular, and I anticipated putting a few of the extra-large shrimp on the barbecue pit.

I stood for a moment at the edge of the beach trying to decide which way to run. Two miles to the left was the entrance to Bay Harbor where I'd just left Joy and Jake. A right turn meant a trip toward the end of the island and the bridge over San Luis Pass.

I jogged toward the pass dodging mounds of seaweed and dead jellyfish washed in with the tide. The farther I went, the faster I ran as if exertion alone would throw off the images of Jake's tired face and hopeless eyes. The vision tugged at my humanity, as though I alone could assuage the injustice. I knew better, but couldn't seem to let the feeling go. I circled the bridge and continued along the beach back to the trail entrance. I maneuvered along the path and arrived back at The Garhole, sweat-soaked and panting like a hunting dog.

A black sedan occupied the space next to my truck. Inside the bar, Special Agent Maurice Matthews sat at a table across from Joe Stubbs. Matthews, tie tucked inside his shirt, was busy shoveling in a pile of boiled shrimp. He wore his gray hair, long and combed straight back. With his perpetual dark tan and suspenders looped over his shoulders, he reminded me of the famed lawyer, Clarence Darrow or maybe Matlock on TV. Matthews was in the home stretch of a thirty-year FBI career, the last 10 as agent-in-charge of the Houston office.

Off the job, Matthews, nicknamed the Silver Fox, was a well-known ballroom dance instructor, spending his time giving tango lessons to upper crust blue-haired patrons of Houston's finest dance studios. Each summer Matthews spent his vacations cruising the blue waters of the Caribbean, working as the lead dance host on several of the larger ships. A few years ago, he foiled the largest jewelry heist in the history of cruising when, while performing the mambo with the wealthy widow of one of the world's largest Hedge Funds, he noticed one of the onlookers slipping something out of the woman's purse that she'd left at the table. Matthews and the ship's security officer later opened the man's room safe and discovered thousands of dollars' worth of stolen jewelry. The tale spread rapidly across the industry making Matthews the number one pick among available dance hosts.

Stubbs and Matthews had met a year earlier when Joe volunteered to help the FBI trap a couple of red-neck survivalists planning an insurrection on Bolivar Peninsula. At least that's what everyone thought in the beginning. Turns out, the red-necks were the foils in an elaborate assassination plot hatched by Fidel and Raul Castro. I had gotten involved when the assassin, a Cuban spy, murdered a friend of mine, Bernice Bentzel, an innocent eighty-year-old lady whose passion for saving sea turtles had put her in the wrong place at the wrong time. My involvement ended with the spy floating in the current at Rollover Pass.

I met Joe during the Cuban spy caper and after learning he had also served in Iraq, I encouraged him to move to The Garhole and help me run the bar. He bought a new mobile home with the FBI reward money and set the trailer up next to the dock.

"What brings you to Galveston," I said to Matthews. "In between cruises?"

"Used up all my vacation," he answered, wiping his mouth with a paper towel. "It's back to work for me—bank robbery, stock manipulation, wire fraud, money laundering. The beat goes on."

Matthews sucked in more shrimp while continuing to talk. "The VA has a new procedure. Thought I could convince Joe to check it out, but he's playing the hard ass."

Matthews turned to Joe hoping for a response, but Joe turned his head aside. The only sound in the room was the slow creaking of the ceiling fan. After a few beats, Matthews pivoted back to me.

"The process involves implanting a shaft of titanium into the medullary canal of Joe's upper leg."

"Medullary canal?"

"The inside of the femur," Matthews continued. "The bone grows around the implanted shaft. When it's all healed, the prosthesis is screwed to it. Joe could be walking again."

"Titanium my ass," Joe chimed in. "Sounds like *Star Wars* to me."

"Come on, Joe." Matthews fired back. "I'm just talking about going in for an evaluation. You may not even be a candidate. I'll even meet you at the VA."

"Never happen," Joe said, waving his arms. "They're looking for a guinea pig, and it ain't gonna be me."

Joe turned toward the door and rolled out to the dock. Matthews grunted and shook his head, showing his disappointment while he continued to scarf more shrimp.

I knew Joe's reluctance. Change in the status quo involved risk. And Joe couldn't bring himself to chance failure. What if the VA couldn't make the procedure work? Joe had told me stories about other amputees who'd tried various prostheses and many had failed. He was fighting hard to lift himself out of depression and accept life as it is. The mobility of the wheelchair had at least given him a sense of continuance without risk.

I slipped two beers out of the cooler, gave one to Agent Matthews, and waited while he wiped his mouth and pushed his plate away. I decided not to mention the assault on the Winnie highway because I knew as a law enforcement officer he'd feel obligated to report it. I could have told all and then asked him to keep the attack confidential, but I didn't want to put him in the position of compromising his integrity. Instead, I talked around the problem.

"Tell me something, Maurice," I said. "What do you know about *ice* and *coke*?"

Matthews swallowed some beer. "I assume you're talking drugs," he said.

"A friend of mine might be having problems. High anxiety, fidgety, blotched skin, abnormally thin. What do you think?"

The slight crinkling around Matthews' eyes told me he suspected I was more involved than I had indicated. He hesitated. Then he relaxed in his chair and pursed his lips, no doubt thinking about his reply. I read his movements as a signal he wasn't going to push the issue and play cop.

"Well, I'm not an expert on drugs," he said. "But if you're thinking illegal substances, it could be almost anything from cocaine to a prescription drug habit. You spent twenty years in Army Intelligence. Didn't they teach you anything about drugs? I know you were in Germany most of your career chasing spies, but..."

"Like the FBI," I shot back, "the Army has its specialists."

"If it's someone you're trying to help, I can put you in touch with a good treatment facility."

"Thanks, but—"

"Why don't you check with the Galveston Police Department? The local guru is Sergeant Martinez head of the Drug Enforcement Division. He knows his stuff."

Chapter Four

Clementine Garza sat by the open window of her second floor office suite in San Antonio, Texas staring at the garbage cans in the alley below. Today, she'd tallied nine cats, a record. Clementine was no expert on the feline species. In fact, this was as close as she cared to get, ever since, at the age of four, one of the neighborhood mama cats had taken a hunk out of her hand. But Clementine loved the species lifestyle, their independent nature, beholding to no one. She smiled remembering what her dad, retired Army Master Sergeant Felix Garza, had told her when she decided to become a cop. "Any big organization is a dysfunctional, bureaucratic mess," he liked to say. "Like herding cats."

The image stuck with Clementine. She'd witnessed its execution daily during her days as a beat cop with the San Antonio Police Department, political correctness taken to the extreme, personal initiative stifled by regulations designed to placate the public instead of protecting the officers.

Every time she thought about the absurdity in the rules of engagement, she knew she was lucky to be alive. The sergeant reminded her daily, "You'd better be sure the perp has a weapon," he'd say, "or your ass will be reconstructing the scene in a six by ten cell for the next twenty years."

At five-four and a hundred twenty pounds, Clementine had barely squeaked by the department's recruiting requirements. She had joined the force, eyes open, knowing she'd have to prove her metal on the beat time and time again.

A. Hardy Roper

That's where her baton had come in handy. She preferred the telescoping type. The 10 inch long collapsed version fit comfortably on her belt. A quick flick of the wrist extended 20 inches of steel, a solid tip at the end. In most confrontations, just hearing the click and seeing the baton expand sent the adversary into quiet submission.

One night, Clementine and her partner responded to a domestic dispute on the south side. On arrival, they found a naked woman on the front lawn with a man astride her lashing her back with a rider's crop hollering "giddy up bitch, giddy up." Blood oozed from the woman's neck and back.

Clementine leaped from the still rolling police unit and without warning, lashed the baton down hard on the man's backside. He fell sideways, hands raised in defense. Clementine whipped the baton across his arms, shredding his shirt, blood streaking from his body. The Incidence Report quoted a bystander as saying, "That bitch cop, she done beat the shit outta that po' bastard. Lucky for both of 'um the other honky fuzz pulled the bitch off."

When Internal Affairs decided she had used excessive force, Clementine turned to everyone in the squad room and yelled, "Screw this job."

Then with all aplomb, she went into the ladies room and checked herself in the mirror. She hoped she'd done the right thing coloring her hair so light, wondering if her natural dark hair looked better against her Latin skin. She couldn't decide. She applied fresh lip-gloss and fluffed her short blond hair. No roots showing yet, she mused. She took one last glance at the mirror and decided she never looked better.

She marched into her sergeant's office, flung badge and radio onto the middle of his desk, and unbuckled the heavy black belt holding a flashlight, mace, handcuffs and 9mm automatic. She dropped the eight-pound bundle into a chair and exited the room before the sergeant could get off the phone leaving everything but the baton she'd purchased with her own money. She would have stripped her uniform, but she had nothing else to wear. In front of an entire shift of cops, she strode out of the station wailing Martin Luther King's mantra, "Free at last, free at last. Thank God almighty I'm free at last."

No more wasted days completing paperwork to cover the department's rear. No more tolerating her fat-assed sergeant hovering above her desk sneaking a peek inside her blouse. Although sometimes she'd allowed a look just to torment the little dough boy. Size 36D was a nice rack, and Clementine knew how to use it. But the sad part was there were days when she thought if he'd only lose a hundred pounds, he might get more than a cheap look-see.

And now, each day while gazing out the window of her office, she reaffirmed her decision to flee the insanity of the police force and hang her shingle as a private investigator.

The beginning had been tough. Building a clientele from scratch wasn't easy. Still, she'd rented two offices, and the small reception area in front begged for an assistant. Clementine had high hopes.

She reached for her pack of no-name cigarettes and lit up. The building was non-smoking, but that didn't bother Clementine. She wasn't about to let the inane ban compromise her autonomy. She blew one puff after another out the window, amused by the thought of someone seeing the smoke and calling the fire department.

Just then a homeless man entered the alley carrying a broomstick. He took a swing at a shorthaired calico. Thankfully, he missed, the cat scrambling back into the bags of stacked garbage. Clementine grabbed her baton off the desk, flicked it open and slammed down hard on the windowsill.

"You swing that stick again, I'll come down and whack your knees off." She stood, banging the baton ever harder. "Get your tired ass outta there and leave my cats alone!"

A. Hardy Roper

When the man took off, Clementine crushed the cigarette into the wooden windowsill and flicked the half-smoked butt out the window. She was sick of the cheap, generic brand, the tobacco raw in her throat, smelling like it'd been grown in a chicken coop.

She returned to her desk, glanced over the stack of unpaid bills and focused on the 5,000 dollar Crime Stopper reward. She picked up the check and breathed in the fresh, pungent scent of the ink. She balanced the check across her index finger, both sides hanging over, testing its weight. She enjoyed the smell, the feel, wanted to keep the check another day. But bills were bills. The madness never ended—clothes, hair, nails, cosmetics, utilities, cell phone, wine, cable, food.

A sharp pain crossed her forehead and settled just above her eye. She pushed the stack of bills away and for a fleeting moment considered calling the department. She reached for the phone, but the thought vaporized when she visualized her sergeant announcing her attempt at reinstatement around the squad room and all the jerk-offs laughing their asses off. Ugh! No way. Her eye throbbed and the old familiar rumble in her stomach returned.

She gritted her teeth and reached for a pen and checkbook. She paid a month's back rent on her office and apartment and a token amount on her overdue VISA bill. She took in a big breath and blew it out. What now?

The only smart thing she'd done was order several cartons of Vogues online. Now she just had to wait for their delivery. No more suffering through chicken dung generic cigs. Vogues were made especially for the female gender, thin, long, and colorful. She'd discovered the little beauties watching Madonna smoking one in an early video. Madonna—the quintessential liberated woman. Clementine wasn't a Madonna groupie. She just liked her music and admired the fact Madonna didn't give a crap what anyone thought.

Clementine rubbed her eyes. The pain seemed to dissipate. She sealed the envelopes and was about to head for the mail slot when the telephone buzzed.

"Garza Investigations."

"Yes, Ms. Garza?"

"Speaking."

"Please hold for Mr. Stanford?"

The phone clicked and a male voice spoke.

"Miss Garza, this is Reginald J. Stanford. I am calling to discuss retaining your services."

Clementine noted the sophistication in the caller's voice, the carefully enunciated words and deliberate phrasing, indicating an educated background. His accent was from somewhere north of the Mason-Dixon Line. The slight nasal twang pointed to New England.

"Sure, go ahead." Clementine answered, determined to keep her voice noncommittal, almost disinterested. Play it cool, she told herself. But desperate for business, her stomach turned butterflies. She reached for one of the tainted cigarettes and lit up. She sucked in a lung full of smoke and blew it out, holding back a cough.

"My assistant showed me an article in the San Antonio newspaper about your recent success in finding those two little girls."

"I got lucky," Clementine said.

"Please, Ms. Garza. Your attempt at false modesty belies your obvious talent. You somehow managed to perform when the authorities could not. Your efforts show zeal, fortitude and most importantly...courage. All traits I admire."

The story had flashed across every radio and television network in San Antonio. The abductor was the mother's boyfriend, a known child molester. The FBI sent in a special team, but after 48 hours with no results, the desperate mother called Clementine, her old high school friend.

A. Hardy Roper

Working quickly, Clementine located the kidnapper's uncle, another pedophile. She tied him to a chair and lashed him repeatedly with her baton until he gave up the boyfriend's location, a farmhouse 60 miles outside San Antonio in the mesquite country of South Texas. Clementine rescued the girls, killing the woman's boyfriend in the process. She never disclosed how she located the farmhouse, and the uncle she had strapped to a chair left town without ratting out what Clementine had done to him.

She pulled a notepad and pencil close. "What can I do for you, Mister, uhhhh, Stanford?"

"Tell me Ms. Garza, how did you manage to find the farmhouse and know the girls were there?"

"Is this a test?" Clementine asked.

"Excuse, me?"

"You know my work is confidential."

"The answer I wanted," Stanford said. "I believe confidentiality is the most important attribute in a business association. Do you agree?"

"If you want me to work for you, you're going to have to trust I can keep my mouth shut. How about I send you a vial of blood and a thumb print."

"I don't appreciate your impertinence, Ms. Garza. I have neither the time nor the inclination."

The cigarette sent Clementine's stomach into a vortex of discomfort. She held her hand over the phone, turned her head and burped.

When Stanford didn't continue, she said, "Okay, let's cut the bullshit. No games, huh? Tell me what you need."

"Indeed," he said, answering with a huff. "I received a call from a police officer in Del Rio, Texas who informed me my son Morgan has been murdered and that his body is in the county morgue."

He spoke the words, but Clementine detected no feeling of grief or even sadness in Stanford's voice. He could just as easily have been reading a page from the congressional record.

"I am sorry for your loss," she said.

"Yes...well, you see...the thing is...I assumed Morgan died years ago."

Clementine's first inclination was to find out why Stanford had lost touch with his son, but she knew this wasn't the right time to ask.

"I am offering to engage your services to go to Del Rio and find out what you can. Bring closure to the matter."

The matter, thought Clementine? That's the best this Reginald J. Stanford, could do? Who was he, anyway? She didn't appreciate the man's attitude, but she also knew the Crime Stopper reward money was half spent and even with the publicity from the case, the phone wasn't ringing off the wall.

"I will be glad to help you, Mr. Stanford," Clementine said. "Shall I meet you at the airport?"

"No. That will be quite impossible, Ms. Garza. I must prepare for a board meeting this week."

Clementine thought about the strange nature of the P.I. business, how one never knew what the next case would bring.

Where is your home, Mr. Stanford?"

"Boston."

"I'll call you from Del Rio," she said.

A. Hardy Roper

Saving Jake

Chapter Five

Sleep never comes easy for me, and last night I had the extra burden of trying to reconcile stupidity. Getting involved in a shootout—dumb and dumber—and escaping the fiasco without killing or getting killed—pure luck.

I finally dozed off only to be awakened at daybreak by intense squawking coming from the deck outside my bedroom door. A dozen seagulls sat on the railing, sounding off at their accomplices circling over the water. I flung a tennis shoe against the railing scattering the invaders.

I needed sleep, but knowing the birds would return, I slipped on shorts and T-shirt and sauntered out to the top deck to locate the cause of the turmoil. Abnormally hot weather had created an oxygen shortage in the water, causing a fish kill, not an uncommon occurrence during the steamy, late summer days of August. Thousands of dead menhaden floated with the tide just off my dock. The stench from the rotting baitfish saturated the air while a hundred or more seagulls scooped the remains. I hustled down the stairs hoping the scavengers would finish the banquet before customers arrived.

I found Joe on the dock in his wheelchair hosing salt off a stack of crab traps. I nodded and turned toward the bar.

"You have a visitor," he said.

Jake sat at the counter, sipping a Coke and wearing the same dirty LSU ball cap and long-sleeved shirt as before. A warning tingle shot across my shoulders, the same sting I'd felt back at Captain Billy's when I'd first met Jake and his mother. I hadn't heeded the warning then, and with Jake in front of me there was little I could do about it now.

"How'd you get here?"

"Walked," he said, eyes averted. He pushed his long hair back over his ears.

I grabbed a cold Shiner from the cooler, raised the beer to toast the gar head hanging over the counter, and sucked in a big swallow.

"Why'd you do that?" he asked, his voice soft.

"A show of respect. The species has been around since the dinosaurs."

"How big do they get?"

I pointed my beer toward the skeleton head. "That one was huge, six foot, maybe two hundred pounds. I found the carcass washed up in the marsh after a storm. I bleached its head white and hung it there."

"Why?"

"Needed a name for the bar. Plus, before Joe moved in, when fishing was off and customers weren't around, the gar head was good company."

Jake scrunched his forehead, as though wondering if I was kidding. He sipped more Coke.

"Gars are tough creatures," I said. "They ask nothing but to be left alone to wallow in their holes. They take care of themselves, forage their own food and mind their own business."

His eyes floated up to mine. "Kind of like you," he said.

I sensed no sarcasm or judgment in his voice. Coupled with the great sadness in his eyes, his demeanor came across as more of a plea, a longing.

"What do you know about me?" I asked.

He hesitated, then looked away. He finished his drink with a slight slurping sound. I recognized the tactic—stalling,

Saving Jake

buying time to formulate a reply. When he was ready, he raised his eyes.
"My grandpa knows about you," he said. "Told me where you lived."
"The old man on the porch?"
Jake nodded. "He said you were a loner."
I ignored Jake's admonition and said, "What's your grandpa's name?"
"People call him Slim."
"Slim?"
"I guess he used to be."
"I don't know him," I said.
"Grandpa said to stay away from you."
"Really," I said. "So why are you here?"
Jake didn't answer.
I waited.
He studied the gar head for a moment and then focused his eyes on mine.
"He said you killed a man."
The way he spoke sounded more like a question than a statement. I was trying hard to read between the lines. We stayed that way for a moment, eyes fixed on each other. I was the first to blink.
"What else did he tell you?"
Jake looked away. "Nothing."
I took in a big breath and blew it out. "The man I killed was evil, full of hate. There was a big storm, a hurricane. We were trapped at The Garhole, couldn't get out, wind and water tearing everything apart. The bad man came to kill people I cared about."
"What did you kill him with?"
I nodded at the gar head.
Jake studied the beast again, rows of razor sharp teeth staring down at him.

A. Hardy Roper

"How'd you feel afterward?" Jake asked.

"I don't think anyone ever feels good about something like that."

Jake bit his lip. "I think...sometimes it's okay," he said. "Sometimes people deserve to die."

A palpable tension filled the room, something I hadn't intended, the conversation leading somewhere I hadn't expected and didn't want to go. I straightened and moved toward the back door.

"Come with me," I said. "Something I want you to see."

I cranked the old truck and drove along a sand lane out into the marsh. Wild lantana bushes lined the road, their orange and gold blossoms sweetening the air. The morning seemed quiet and peaceful, yet I knew somewhere out in the thick carpet of salt grass surrounding us, a diamond-backed rattler slithered through the weeds. Whether exploring unmarked terrain or the unknown haunts and fears of a person's mind, one could not be too careful.

A quarter-mile into the marsh, I stopped the truck, and we climbed to the top of a berm just before a small pond. A large blue heron, startled by our arrival, lifted his giant wings and lumbered toward the bay.

Jake looked over the pond and said, "I came by here on the way to your place."

He said he had walked, but I assumed he'd come down the highway.

"You went through the marsh?"

"I found a trail behind Grandpa's house."

"It's dangerous in the marsh, Jake. "Mud holes and snakes. You could have been hurt."

Jake shrugged.

I removed my binoculars from the glove box and pointed to a wooden bench.

Saving Jake

"Take a seat and focus on the group of scrub oaks on the other side of the pond."

Jake pressed the lenses close to his eyes. "Never seen trees grow like that before."

"When the trees are in a clump like that, it's called an oak motte. The wind off the Gulf keeps a steady pressure on the limbs until the trees lean and grow in the same direction. It takes years for the wind to build a formation like that. My grandfather used to tell me it reminded him of a bunch of old women huddled around each other, gossiping."

I smiled at Jake hoping for a response to my humor but got nothing from him. I waited a beat, then said, "Focus on what's in the trees."

I laid my hand lightly on his shoulder trying to improve his direction. He shrugged my hand away. He leaned forward increasing the distance between us and pressed the binoculars harder against his eyes. I stepped back, realizing I had invaded his space, uninvited.

"Lots of birds," he said. "Different kinds."

"Song birds migrated up from Central America," I said. "They fly across the Gulf of Mexico in the spring and land here. The majority goes farther north, but some stay."

Jake kept the field glasses steadied on the trees, relaying the color and size of birds, allowing me to identify each one from memory—warblers, painted buntings, a scarlet tanager. Jake lowered the binoculars to wipe sweat from his brow.

"What's with the long sleeve shirt?" I asked.

As though he hadn't heard me, he adjusted the binoculars sweeping his vision across the pond. It was obvious Jake wasn't ready to open up. It was as though he'd had no experience in trusting another human being. I needed to back off, see what developed. I decided talking was better than the pressure silence brings.

A. Hardy Roper

"My grandfather used this land as a cattle ranch long before you and I were born. There was no fresh water, so he dug this pond with a team of mules. The mules drug the sand from the hole and piled it where we're sitting. Then he scraped the land around the pond and added more sand to make this hill bigger."

"Why'd he do that?" Jake asked keeping the field glasses glued to his eyes.

"If a hurricane flooded the island, some of the cattle could bunch up on top this berm. Those that made it might not drown."

"Don't see any cows now," Jake said.

"He died when I was thirteen. We had to sell the cattle to pay the taxes on the land."

Holding the glasses with one hand, Jake pointed to a stand of cattails at the opposite end.

"What's that," he said. "Looks like a wooden box or something."

I followed the line of his arm. "An old duck blind," I said.

"Can we see it?"

We hiked around the edge of the pond to a spot directly above the blind.

"Never seen one like that in Louisiana," he said.

Four steel stanchions set in concrete held the shooting stand in place. Jake and I stepped onto the platform.

Jake looked down and said, "What is that door to?"

"Open it," I said.

Jake lifted the heavy metal door. The concrete vault below was as wide as the blind and several feet deep.

"Wow," Jake said. "What is that?"

"I always thought my grandfather was an avid hunter, but he fooled me. There was a time when making and selling liquor was illegal. It was called Prohibition. A friend of my

Saving Jake

Grandpa known as Big Gus used to row out in a skiff from San Luis Pass and meet Cuban rumrunners. Buyers met Gus at the beach and took delivery. Sometimes my grandfather let Gus store the extra booze in the duck blind."

Jake bent to examine the hole. "No foolin'," he said.

"No fooling," I said.

We arrived back at The Garhole to find a beer truck pulling out of the parking lot. Joe sat on a stool at the counter reviewing the delivery slip.

"See some birds?" he asked.

"Yeah," Jake said, "and that ain't all."

Joe glanced at me acknowledging that he knew Jake had seen the duck blind. He slipped off the stool into his wheelchair and motored toward the back door.

"Better get you back to your mom," I said. "She probably wonders where you are."

"I doubt it," he mumbled.

We approached the house in my pickup, and from a block away, we could see Joy circling the deck, her head twitching in all directions. She was patting the railing with one hand and swinging the other arm like an airplane propeller, never slowing.

"She won't stop for a while," Jake said. "Not 'till she comes down. Could be hours."

Jake opened the door and hopped out. He slammed the door and stared at me through the open truck window, his eyes projecting a silent plea as though he didn't want to go in. I didn't want him to go into that snake pit either. It was obvious his grandfather was a boozer, and his mother was on some kind of drugs. I turned my head and cranked the engine signaling there was nothing I could do. I watched as Jake cleared the stairs and passed his mama without looking at her. He entered the house, the door slamming behind him. Joy didn't seem to notice. She never stopped moving.

A. Hardy Roper

Chapter Six

The day broke hot and steamy. I slipped on a clean pair of jeans and my only laundered shirt for our meeting with Sergeant Martinez and hustled downstairs to answer the telephone.

"Garhole."

"Major McLeod?"

"In another life."

"This is Maggie, Doctor Kennon's nurse. We miss you around here."

"I miss you too, Maggie but not the trips to Houston or waiting around for treatment. You ever get more help up there?"

"You know better," she said. "Our country sends boys off to war, but when they come back crippled, the government seems to have amnesia about their sacrifices."

"What can I do for you? My treatment program is finished."

"Not exactly," she said. "You know we worry about you. How about coming in for a tune up?"

I hesitated, coming close to taking the bait and scheduling an appointment. The last few nights the headaches and sleeping problems had resurfaced, reminding me I'd quit the treatment program early.

Thousands of soldiers returning from the Gulf War suffered from ailments the doctors couldn't explain—everything from blurred vision to nerve pain, liver damage and even memory loss. The VA finally had to admit something had happened over there so they invented a name, Gulf War Syndrome, a convenient label meaning nothing in its self.

"No response, huh," Maggie continued. "Okay, enough about you. How about getting Sergeant Stubbs out of the rack and make sure he hauls his buns in for today's appointment."

"Agent Matthews was here yesterday pounding Joe about new legs. You two have a conspiracy going?"

"Shhhh," she whispered. "This line may be tapped."

After a good chuckle, I terminated the call with Maggie and found Joe rolling down the ramp from his mobile home. I informed him about the call from the VA and told him about the appointment.

He screwed up his face and screamed, "What appointment? I don't have no stinking appointment. Matthews and Doc Kennon been teaming up on my ass."

Trying a last minute appeal, I said, "Canceling at the last minute is not cool."

"Ain't going," he screamed again. "And quit bugging me about it."

Rather than argue, I called Maggie back and told her I'd tried, but Joe didn't seem to care that the new titanium prostheses might change his life. She expressed disappointment and terminated the call.

I can't say that I blamed Joe. I know what it's like to give up, feel abandoned, unappreciated. Sitting day after day in a VA ward surrounded by dozens of other injured veterans can do that to a man.

Joe rolled past me in his wheelchair yelling over his shoulder. "We're late for our appointment with Martinez. We'll take my truck. I ain't gonna ride in that coffin of yours and show up at the police station soaking wet and smelling like dead fish."

Saving Jake

"Suits me," I said. "I'm not getting the air in my truck fixed just because you're worried you may stink. I like it hot and natural."

Joe opened the door to his truck, and with one hand on the wheelchair and the other on the truck seat, he used his massive arms to lift himself from the wheelchair to behind the steering wheel. He hit a switch and the arm of a small crane in the truck bed swung around until it hovered over the wheelchair. He attached the crane's straps to the chair, pushed the button again, and the crane arm returned the chair to the bed.

When he cranked the engine, a blast of cool air hit my face. I closed the vent and cracked the window to let in fresh Gulf air hoping he wouldn't notice. He operated the hand controls and powered up the lane to the highway.

We arrived at the Galveston Police Station and met Sergeant Martinez coming out the front door. I knew Stubbs and Martinez were in high school together so that put Martinez's age around thirty, the same as Joe's.

Joe and Martinez greeted each other with hugs and Joe introduced me. Martinez almost broke some bones with his powerful grip. His massive chest and powerful arms indicated a strong workout routine.

"You guys are late," Martinez said. "Cost you lunch."

With Joe rolling his wheel chair beside us, we scurried across the street to *La Estacion,* a local favorite. A stream of men and women from the police station and jail entered at the same time. Martinez scooted around and grabbed a back booth. I vied for the seat against the wall, but Martinez beat me to it.

"You like the Wild Bill Hickok seat too," he said. "Back against the wall."

"An old habit," I said thinking about my Army Intel days.

A. Hardy Roper

Joe slid in the other side of the booth. I folded his wheelchair, sat it against the wall and moved beside Joe. The waitress brought chips and salsa. We ordered drinks and the restaurant's specialty, three bowls of *caldo de pollo*.

"I don't have much time," Martinez said. "Tell me what you need to know."

I leaned in, keeping my voice low. "Okay," I said, "If I know someone who might be on drugs—"

Martinez waved me off, "Don't we all," he said. Then he noticed the surprised look on my face. "Don't worry," he continued. "I don't need the name. If we locked up all the crank heads, we'd have to build a stockade like the POW camp the government built here during WWII. We're looking for bigger fish to fry."

I went into detail about Joy's appearance—the rotted teeth, blotched skin, pupils void of life. Then I described her behavior on the deck, moving incessantly, flailing her arms like a mad woman.

"Sounds like a tweaker," Martinez said.

"A what?"

"A meth addict. Users call it tweaking when they're on a high. The bad teeth indicate m*eth mouth*. They crave sugar. Spend all day sucking on soft drinks. Was she flicking her tongue around?"

"I wasn't close enough to see," I said.

"Probably a good thing," he said. "If you'd approached her, she'd probably have taken you inside and screwed your brains out."

Joe's mouth fell open in surprise. He gaped at Martinez. I fell back against the seat.

"Tweaking and horny seem to go together," he said, munching a chip. "We hear stories about marathon sessions. Some of them can't seem to get enough of it. Never satisfied. Makes me want to put a rock in the wife's morning coffee."

Saving Jake

Martinez laughed at his own joke. Joe and I smiled.

"So how do they ingest the stuff?" I asked.

"Different ways. It's often sold in a crystal like form. They crush the rocks and smoke them in a water pipe. Or they melt it and shoot a vein. Sometimes they swallow the stuff. It's the most addictive and dangerous drug on the streets today. One hit and they spend the rest of their lives trying to duplicate the same high again. Never happens, but they keep trying."

"How do they get started," I said.

"Pushers try to get them young. Start with marijuana or prescription drugs. Then they trade up, have a customer for life. We watch the schools closely."

The waiter arrived with lunch, and we dove into the bowls of steaming chicken soup. While Martinez and Stubbs reminisced about high school, I thought about Joy, wondering how long before she was either dead or in jail.

Joe and I turned off 61st street onto Seawall Boulevard heading west toward The Garhole Bar. Tourists crowded the beach, broiling their bodies. The windless surf lay flat, not even a ripple. In late August, the early cold fronts weakened as they reached the coast. The island blocked enough of the north wind to allow the surf to quiet, which in turn cleared the water. Clear water meant good fishing. And good fishing meant increased business for The Garhole Bar.

Joe pulled into Walmart, so I could restock the kitchen. After picking up the basics, I moved to the clothing aisle and selected two medium, short-sleeved shirts.

We drove for a while, each to our own thoughts. Halfway to The Garhole, Joe slowed for a stoplight at Jamaica Beach. Two teenage boys carrying fishing rods crossed the highway headed for the beach.

"Where are you going with this Jake thing," he said.

"Jake thing?"

"Yeah, the kid," Joe continued. "The shirts are too small for you."

"Can't I buy a kid a shirt without comment? I'm not going anywhere with this *Jake thing* as you call it. I have enough grief putting up with your tired ass. The kid needs clothes. That's all. I'm going to call Martinez as soon as we get back and tell him about Joy. Dump it all in his lap."

"Sure," Joe said, smirking. "And when they haul Jake's mother away, what then?"

I waved Joe off and turned my head toward the window, signaling the conversation was over. As we passed a large field, a flight of mourning doves landed in a group of salt cedar trees a hundred yards out. I had hunted the birds often in my youth. But then one day someone told me doves mated for life. I couldn't imagine it, didn't know it was possible for birds or people. But I never shot another bird.

The nuclear family...something that had passed me by. And from the looks of things, Jake as well. Joy had said boyfriend, which I assumed meant the weasel who shot at us wasn't Jake's father. But someone had planted Jake's seed. I wondered if Joy even knew his father's name.

I didn't know what I was going to do. Maybe instead of calling Sergeant Martinez, I'd do nothing. Wasn't my business anyway.

Chapter Seven

The eight-foot pirogue Luther Bourdain poled through the swamp had been hand-hewn by his grandfather from a hundred-year-old cypress tree. The old man's carved initials marked the bow. Luther was proud of the boat. He knew sculpturing a tree-trunk was a lost art.

Most of Luther's neighbors now plied the bogs with skiffs made from plywood or fiberglass. Luther tolerated the manufactured pirogues with contempt. He liked the old ways of the bayou people. Many still spoke the patois French of their grandmothers. They earned their living fishing, trapping alligators for their skins and meat, and guiding duck hunts for wealthy New Orleans oilmen. Luther admired the laid back lifestyle, but not their pitiful existence, poor down-the-bayou Cajuns who seldom accumulated more money than they needed for cigarettes and beer.

Luther's future had been on the same track, but his fortunes changed in high school when he met the local drug pusher. It wasn't long before Luther graduated into selling dope himself. Now at 26, he owned his own production facility and fancied himself the main supplier of crystal meth for the entire parish.

Each time Luther's pole struck the swamp's mud bottom, the boat moved forward the distance of its length, pushing aside the water lilies clogging the trail. The plants sprung back as soon as the boat passed, closing the path as quickly and efficiently as quicksand devouring an animal. Along both sides of the dark water route, huge cypress and tupelo trees erupted like centurions of old, guarding against unwanted and unwelcomed visitors. Above him, the sun dipped past the tops of the trees. Long shadows acknowledged the last flickering vestiges of light.

Luther's breathing accelerated as he cursed his late start. He needed to reach the cabin before nightfall or risk getting lost. He'd built the lab so far back in the swamp, the cops couldn't find it with GPS coordinates. Even local swamp dwellers didn't know about the small island.

To house his operation, he'd built a one-room shack with plywood and tarpaper. He placed camouflage netting over the wooden shingles on the roof so nosy helicopter pilots couldn't spot the cabin. The outside walls were a series of large plywood shutters Luther opened to ventilate the shack when the cooking started.

Luther worked solo, bringing in supplies and ferreting out the finished product. He cooked only at night, lessening the chances passing locals might hear the generator or smell the foul, sulfurous odor of rotten eggs.

Luther's chest filled with pride thinking about his newest creation—the special infusion of dye that brought the crystals to the prettiest blue he'd ever seen. The new brand he called Royal Blue created such a rippling sensation, Luther began to demand advance payment for each new batch. His fame spread quickly, attracting the attention of a pair of New Orleans dealers.

But Luther had a problem...he liked to gamble. He bet on anything and everything from blackjack to football to horse racing. He couldn't help it; he liked the action. And now the $50,000 payment he'd received from the two New Orleans brothers was gone, lost to bookies and the Lafayette horse track.

Even worse, the batch of Royal Blue the dealers had paid for was missing. He'd caught up with the skinny bitch who'd stolen it, but he'd had to bolt after running out of ammo. How stupid of him to forget extra bullets. He'd never do that again. Luther figured he had two options: go after the bitch again and recover the meth or cook another batch before the dealers arrived. But Luther knew, even working all night, he couldn't make a dent in the amount of *ice* the whore had stolen. He only hoped he could cook enough now to stall the brothers until he could cook more. It was all he could do.

Luther reached the island just as a curtain of darkness enveloped the swamp. He stashed the pirogue in a thicket of palmetto plants and began carrying the supplies to his plywood shack. Two days of rain had softened the earth. His 250 pound frame sank several inches with each step. Halfway to the lab, with one foot into the muck, he stopped to wipe sweat from his cheeks and swat away the cloud of mosquitoes, attacking his face. He cursed and moved on.

A fire pit contained the half-burned remnants of hundreds of packages of cold pills and decongestants—any over the counter medicine containing ephedrine, the magic elixir—the one essential ingredient for making crystal methamphetamine. The labels on the discarded cans and bottles indicated the range of goods he'd used while experimenting to create the perfect product: acetone, lye, hydrochloric acid, mineral spirits, bleach, car battery acid, starter fluid and even gun cleaning solvent.

Luther had studied the cooking process carefully. One could not be too vigilant; the risk of fire hung in the air like an early morning swamp fog. Except fog was visible and vapors weren't. Only last month a meth head in the next parish had stupidly lit a joint in the middle of cooking and blown his face off.

When Luther first starting cooking, he preferred the *Nazi Method,* the nickname meth cooks had given the process that the Germans used during the war to keep their soldiers lit up through long days on the battlefield.

The Nazi recipe required ephedrine, red phosphorous, iodine, lithium and anhydrous ammonia. Local cooks gathered the phosphorous from matches and the lithium strips from cut-down flashlight batteries.

Luther had been heavy into his third batch when he learned ammonium nitrate, the chemical used in fertilizer, had been the main ingredient in the Oklahoma City bombing. He didn't understand the connection between anhydrous ammonia and ammonium nitrate, but the pictures he'd seen of the destroyed Federal Building sent shivers through his body.

Looking for a better way to cook meth, he stumbled upon the *Red, White and Blue Method*, replacing anhydrous ammonia with ether and methanol. He didn't know much about either chemical but to be safe, fearing a spark; he placed the gas generator outside the shack. For light, he ran a cord from the generator to a string of bulbs along the building's ceiling.

Darkness came early in the thickly wooded swamp. Luther hoped the generator would run better tonight. Last time he'd had problems with the engine almost dying, then suddenly speeding up again, which had the effect of pulsing inconsistent current to the lights. He cranked the engine, pleased at the generator's gentle purring sound. He went inside, flipped on the lights and opened all the windows. On a plywood bench, he placed three plastic jars, coffee filters, an eyedropper, a glass dish and a funnel.

As he worked, a heavy wind came upon the island tossing loose limbs and plants into the air. Rain followed, dropping the temperature. Dressed in a T-shirt and shorts, he closed the shutters to ward off the debris filled wind and moisture ladened air.

Saving Jake

Always the careful cook, Luther knew the process well. He washed the cold pills in ether to remove the red color, crushed the pills into powder, put the powder into a jar, added methanol and shook the jar for 20 minutes. The ephedrine separated from the wax and other additives and floated to the top. Luther inserted a coffee filter into the funnel and poured the ephedrine into the glass dish, careful not to include the waste material. Later he would add iodine, HCL, and red phosphorus, shake some more, heat the product to evaporate the liquid, and then add the dye ending up with beautiful blue crystals of pure *ice*.

The generator had started to sputter again causing the overhead lights to flicker. Luther cursed, hoping the engine wouldn't quit throwing him into total darkness. He knew he should stop and fix the generator, but because the process was at a delicate stage of manufacture, he had no choice but to continue.

The next step was to separate the ephedrine and methanol by burning off the alcohol. He had run out of masks, and the fumes were making him nauseous. Good thing though, because the sick feeling reminded him to open the windows to clear the vapors before he fired the burner.

He stepped to open a shutter, but as his hand reached the latch, one of the overhead electric bulbs burst from a surge of current. The spark ignited the alcohol vapors, sending a fireball roaring high above the tree canopy, setting off the phosphorous in hundreds of match boxes and blowing open quart jars containing thousands of cold pills. The jars exploded like hand grenades tossed into a bunker, the glass shards ripping apart anything in their path.

A. Hardy Roper

Chapter Eight

Clementine Garza eased to a stop at the intersection, relieved her fifteen-year-old Honda Civic had held together for the three and a half hour drive to Del Rio. With her newfound money, she'd already decided to trade the old heap for something more in line with her self-image, but the call from Stanford had put her on the road before she'd had time to check the want ads.

She hit the eject button on the console and removed the Madonna CD that she'd been warbling along with since leaving San Antonio. She'd made the tape herself and included all Madonna's greatest hits—*Like a Prayer, Take a Bow,* and her favorite, the one that always got her juices flowing, *Like a Virgin.* Clementine smiled at the thought of putting the words virgin and Madonna in the same sentence. The whole concept reminded her too much of herself.

Her mind drifted to the night of her seventeenth birthday when she'd lost her cherry in the bed of a hay-filled pickup to some big football player, who couldn't keep his mouth shut. He might as well have been a cheerleader using a megaphone. Even talked about her ass, the finest he'd ever seen he said, one of those protruding kind you could rest a beer can on. At the time, Clementine hadn't objected to the characterization. She was proud of her butt. She knew all the boys ogled her behind as she sashayed down the halls. But that was then. Now she only wanted to find a way to stop its perennial growth.

A. Hardy Roper

When the light turned green, Clementine sucked in one last drag off a pink Vogue. Her new cigs had arrived just before she left town, and she'd already puffed through the first pack. Fortunately, she'd brought two additional packs, one green and one blue. She blew out the smoke, smashed the butt into the ashtray and looked both ways. She knew the intersection well. Go right to the center of Del Rio and the hospital or turn left and cross the bridge into Mexico.

In her college days, Clementine liked nothing better than to cruise in from San Antonio and have lunch at Crosby's, her favorite restaurant in Ciudad Acuña, the sprawling Mexican city across the Rio Grande. The routine never changed. She and her friends crammed down 10,000 calorie lunches of tortillas and cheese, inhaling *grande margaritas*, all followed by a rousing night of bar-hopping, capped by several rounds of tequila shots. More often than not, they'd run into some University of Texas hard dicks down from Austin. She'd awaken the next morning with cotton mouth and an unknown hairy leg wrapped over her thigh.

In those days, the closest thing she ever saw to illegal drugs was a bottle of Benzedrine tablets. Two bennies popped at midnight insured an eight-hour cram-fest before an early morning exam.

But the drug cartels had changed all that. A gringo, male or female, would be insane to even consider going over. Bodies piled up in the border town like horse flies on a pile of manure. The Mexican police seemed to find new multi-grave burial grounds each week.

Clementine turned right toward the police station. She parked, entered the main entrance and asked for Detective James Scruggs. A moment later a fortyish man, tall and slim, dressed in kakis, western shirt and snakeskin cowboy boots bounded out from the hallway.

Saving Jake

He extended his hand in greeting. "Ms. Garza, I'm Jimmy Scruggs," he said shifting a wad of something in his cheek as he spoke. "Come on in and sit awhile."

Clementine noted the ruggedness of Scruggs' outdoor face and the feel of his leathered fingers as they shook. She also noticed his naked ring finger. She released his hand thinking maybe she should spend the night.

Clementine entered the detective's office pausing before several photographs of Scruggs in his younger days riding bulls and bareback horses.

"Was on the rodeo circuit a while," he said. "Until I got too busted up to ride."

Clementine turned in time to see Scruggs spitting a wad of tobacco into a paper cup.

"Got an extra chew," she said, a playful grin on her face.

Scruggs laughed waving Clementine to a chair. "Nasty habit, I know," he said. "I've got a small spread outside of town. Have a hard time separating ranching from the office. What can I do for you?"

Clementine positioned herself slightly sideways in the chair so the cup of her bra bulged out farther than if she'd sat head on. She regretted not wearing something more revealing.

"You were the investigating officer in Morgan Stanford's death," she said pushing a business card across Scruggs' desk. "His father hired me to look into the situation."

Scruggs studied Clementine's card. "The *situation* as you put it, Ms. Garza, is that someone beat the hell out of Morgan Stanford. Left him in an alley with the cats licking on him."

Clementine smiled, "Good line," she said. "*Cats licking on him.* What movie is it from?"

Scruggs looked taken aback. He hesitated, smiled broadly, and said, "Okay, you got me. I don't know if it came from a movie or a book. I read a lot of detective novels."

"Pretty hard boiled. Sounds like something from John Ross McDonald or maybe even Raymond Chandler."

"Could be," Scruggs said. "I like them both." He got up and walked to a coffee pot in his office. Poured a cup. "Want some?" he asked.

Clementine declined, then wondered if Scruggs was talking about coffee or—

"Had Morgan lived in Del Rio long?" she asked.

"He never lived here. He had a place across the river in Acuña. Morgan Stanford was a druggie. Autopsy indicated he was full of heroin when he died. And like a lot of users, he'd turned to dealing to support his habit. We knew he was smuggling drugs across the border, but we hadn't been able to catch him in the act."

When he finished speaking, Scruggs paused as if he'd said something shocking. But Clementine didn't respond. He glanced at the package of Redman tobacco on his desk.

Clementine noticed an ashtray on Scruggs' desk. "Mind if I smoke," she said.

Scruggs nodded and shoved another chew in his mouth. Clementine lit up a pale-green Vogue.

"Something had probably gone wrong," Scruggs continued. "Maybe Morgan was slicing off the top and short-changing the dealers in Del Rio. Whatever the reason, we feel sure the cartel decided to teach him a lesson. Probably took it too far and he died. The way we look at it, one more doper off the streets is not the worst thing that happens around here."

Scruggs reached for the cup and spit. His cell phone buzzed. He looked at the number.

"Gotta take this," he said. "The little woman is out at the ranch tending to a sick calf."

There goes the evening's entertainment, Clementine mused. She snuffed out the Vogue in the ashtray and stood.

Scruggs spoke into the phone, "Just a minute, hon," he said. He looked at Clementine. "Might want to check with Doc Dussair over at the hospital. My sister says he and Morgan were roommates in medical school."

"Your sister?"

"Yeah, Lou is married to the Doc. Del Rio's a small town, Ms. Garza."

"What medical school did they attend?" Clementine asked.

"University of Texas Medical Branch in Galveston. They call it UTMB."

Clementine entered Dr. Dussair's suite and talked the receptionist into letting her wait in the doctor's office while he was in surgery. The woman seated Clementine but made sure she left the door open. Clementine studied the family photo on the desk. Dussair appeared mid-thirties with a strong chin, crystal blue eyes, and loads of dark, wavy hair. His wife, Lou, was a perfectly coiffured blond with a nice smile and bright eyes. Three perky kids, two boys and girl, grinned happily in front of them.

A moment later, Dussair hurried in wearing a green surgical cap and gown. Tall and slim, the doctor towered over Clem's five-four frame. Clementine rose to greet him.

The doctor smiled and extended his hand, "Sorry, I'm late," he said. "Emergency surgery. I'm Kurt Dussair."

She accepted his extended hand and felt the smoothness of his delicate fingers.

"Clementine Garza. Everything okay?"

"Car accident," he added, moving behind his desk. He removed his cap and motioned for Clementine to sit.

"Thank you for seeing me," she said.

"Yes, well, Ms...uh, Garza, is it? I don't have much time. You're a family friend of the Stanford's."

"Not exactly," Clementine said, sliding a business card across the desk.

Dussair picked up the card. "Private Investigator? I don't understand," he said, the smile disappearing. "You didn't mention that to my nurse when you asked for the meeting. I thought you were here to claim Mr. Stanford's body."

Clementine noted the change in Dussair's demeanor from friendly to suspicious. Her senses went to alert.

"Morgan's father, Reginald J. Stanford, asked me to look into the situation."

Dussair pursed his lips and sighed as if collecting unpleasant thoughts. He straightened in his chair and leaned into the desk. "Have you checked with the police?"

"Yes, I spoke with your brother-in-law, Detective Scruggs. He sent me to you."

"Okay, well, I'll tell you what I know. It isn't much. I was on duty when they brought Mr. Stanford into the E.R. He was in bad shape."

"So he was alive when he arrived. Any conversation?"

"No, whoever attacked him tore his liver in the assault. Mr. Stanford bled out internally before we could save him."

"Why do you keep calling him Mr. Stanford?" Clementine asked. "Scruggs indicated you and Morgan Stanford were buds at UTMB."

Clementine studied Dussair's face looking for any sign of surprise or reticence.

Dussair didn't answer. He fidgeted as if searching for a way out. And then his pager went off. "I'm needed in the ER," he said, standing. "Have a safe trip home, Miss Garza."

Chapter Nine

The early cold front had stalled over the island, calming the surf. I made a quick trip to the beach to confirm my expectations and found green water lapping at the shoreline. The clear water brought trout and the trout brought fishermen. A row of pickups and SUVs sat at the water's edge while fifty yards out in the surf, anglers waded waist deep, tossing live shrimp into the mouths of hungry trout.

Back at the bar, I peeled shrimp, chopped okra and onions, and made a rue of flour and bacon grease. About the time I got it all in the pot, Stubbs rolled through the back door in his wheelchair sniffing the air.

"Man, I could smell that gumbo from my bedroom."

Over the next couple of hours, fishermen in wet clothes filleted their catches at the cleaning table on the dock. The pungent scent of fish entrails mixed with salt water, wet jeans and sand-laden boots, wafted through the air. The regulars knew the drill—clean the fish and drop the remains into the washtub for crab bait—then go into the bar for gumbo and cold beer.

The clear water at the beach had provided one of the best business days of the summer. I knew most of the locals, but the exceptional fishing had brought in a few new customers.

By noon, I had run out of gumbo and started frying shrimp and potatoes. At times, hungry customers filled all four tables. While I cooked more food, Joe moved around in his wheelchair serving beer and emptying trash.

A. Hardy Roper

After everyone left, I cleaned tables while Joe washed off the dock with a hose. We finished the chores and moved to the bench by the bay to rest. I raised a beer and clinked bottles with Stubbs. "Good day," I said.

Out in the bay, a flock of white ibis lumbered across the water low and steady like bombers on a run. They crossed in front of us and flew in over the marsh. Behind the birds, a fishing boat sped by. People I'd never seen before waved as though we were old friends.

I waved back at the folks in the boat, but Joe ignored the gesture. He seemed distracted, sipping his beer all the while fidgeting and squirming in his wheelchair. I'd seen the behavior before and waited for him to vent.

"I don't need a daddy," he said.

"What are you talking about?"

"Matthews didn't have any right to go to the VA. Now they're hounding me to come in for an evaluation."

"And?"

"Going in this afternoon. Probably a waste of time, but what the hell..."

"Get some new legs, you could wade-fish again."

"Oh that's great, Parker. Salt water will probably rust the damn things and strand me in the bay unable to move."

"You could always do the polka at the American Legion Hall."

"Yeah, sure. Better than calling bingo, right? Don't piss on my back and tell me it's raining. I'm goin' in, all right. Anything to keep you and Matthews off my ass."

After Joe left, I went back into the bar and looked out through the front opening. The wind had shifted to the south. By tonight, the increased wave action would dirty the water sending the trout away. Tomorrow, business would be slow again.

Saving Jake

I turned to the empty room wondering why Jake hadn't come by today. Something in me stirred. The thought of his bleak future tore at my gut. I sat at the bar, sipping a beer, staring at the gar head for company, remembering my own life at fifteen, knowing I had to do something.

A. Hardy Roper

Chapter Ten

Luther woke, a thousand needles stabbing the burns on his arms and cheeks. He blinked, adjusting his vision, the glare from the overhead light bouncing off his eyes. Everything gleamed white...the ceiling, the walls, even the metal frame of the bed. A strong scent of antiseptics and bleach filled his nostrils.

Bandages covered his right arm past his elbow. He pushed up in the bed, his arm collapsed, and he fell back to the mattress, moaning. He tried again—swung his feet to the floor—steadied himself and eased to a mirror in the bathroom. A white, gooey cream covered his cheeks and forehead partially disguising his blistered face. He touched his cheek and recoiled from the tenderness. All the hair from his face was gone, mustache, eyebrows, eyelashes, the front part of his scalp shaved to the skin.

Breathing hard, pulse pounding, Luther stumbled to a chair trying to recall what had happened. He was obviously in a hospital or clinic, but he had no idea how he'd arrived. He remembered working in his lab, the process going well and then...nothing...a total blank. He realized the lab must have exploded. But how? He'd always been so careful. And how had he gotten here? Had someone found him on the island and brought him in? What about the cops? What did they know?

He gritted his teeth as another wave of pain hit, trying hard to think through his options. Whatever had happened wasn't his main concern now. He had neither money nor his precious product. He had to escape the clinic, and soon, before the brothers heard about the explosion and tracked him down. He pictured the brothers looking for him, checking his house, driving the roads. The brothers had connections, knew people. Every hour he wasn't on the move increased the chances they'd find him. And in a small town, the news of this type of accident got around quickly. Time to go, now!

A soft rap came on the door and an elderly man entered, a white-cotton coat hugging his knees, his white hair and mustache mirroring the starkness of the room.

"Surprised you're awake," the doctor said, smiling. "We had to drug you for pain. You shouldn't be out of bed."

"How did I get here?" Luther asked.

"Darned lucky," the doctor said. "One of the local boys found you in a boat next to the levy. Your burns are unusual, as if something exploded on you."

Luther moaned and dropped his head to his hands.

"We don't even know who you are," the doctor continued. "You carried no identification of any kind, a half-naked man floating in a hard-carved pirogue." The doctor smiled again. "What's your name, son?"

"My name is...oh, Christ...I don't know," Luther cried. "Oh God, help me, doctor."

The doctor laid his hand on Luther's shoulder. "Don't worry, son," he said. "Temporary loss of memory is common with trauma. You'll be fine."

"How long have I been here?"

"Maybe twenty-four hours. The sheriff came by to talk to you but you were asleep."

Luther moaned again. The memory ruse had worked, but he hadn't exaggerated the pain. The needles jabbed hard, and he could almost feel blisters popping out on his face.

"We're a small country clinic," the doctor said. "As soon as the sheriff comes back, I'll have you transferred to the burn ward at Thibodaux Community Hospital. For now, let me help you back into bed."

The doctor grabbed Luther's good arm, giving him no option but to comply. "Just rest awhile," the doctor said. "I'm going to my office to call the hospital."

When the door closed, Luther eased to the floor. He found his pants and shoes in the closet but no shirt. Probably burned in the explosion, he thought. He used the hospital gown for a top, tucking the lower part inside his pants. He cracked open the door, spotted a red exit sign and slipped out to the hallway. He sure as hell wasn't going to be around when the sheriff returned.

A. Hardy Roper

Chapter Eleven

Clementine struggled through her office door with an armful of packages. She'd spent more than she'd anticipated, but the summer sale was just too good to pass up. She checked the bags: two pair of shoes, three blouses, matching pants, and even a dress just to have something really sexy in case the moment arose. Good, she thought. A single lady had to be ready.

She tossed the goodies on the couch, grabbed a green Vogue from her purse and hurried across the room. She lit the cigarette on the run inhaling deeply as she moved, barely getting the window open in time to blow out the lungful of smoke.

Clementine didn't live in a vacuum. She knew tobacco ravaged the body. She'd have to quit smoking one day, but today wasn't it. Cigarettes calmed her nerves, helped her think. Smoking also helped keep her weight down, and that was good for her ass. It was big enough already.

Two cats in the alley below she'd never before seen were scrounging around the garbage cans. She grabbed a sack of treats from her desk and shook the contents down to the new arrivals, welcoming them to the neighborhood. Three more appeared. She watched the scramble until all the morsels were gone.

She finished the cigarette, returned to the couch, and withdrew the charge slip for the clothes. She screamed out loud, "Get control you stupid hussy."

She felt both triumph and torment about the shopping spree. She considered the clothes a just reward for acquiring a new case. The guilt came from thinking about how she was going to pay for them. She recognized the tug of war with her conscience as a never-ending battle usually soothed only by a drink. Or maybe two.

Clementine crossed to her desk. She removed a bottle of Vodka from a drawer and poured a glass half full. She sipped from the glass, trying to think of something else to do to stall off the call to Stanford, but nothing came to mind. She'd delayed the call because she couldn't stand the old goat's stuffy-assed demeanor. She'd also not called because she wasn't pleased with the results of her trip to Del Rio. The exercise had gone down too quickly without so much as a night's lodging or even a good margarita to tack onto the bill. The Stanford case was her best opportunity for an extended job since hanging her shingle. And right now it was her only case.

She sipped more Vodka, leaned back in her chair and propped her feet on the desk. She made a steady motion of lightly tapping her leg with the baton, careful not to flick open the shaft of tubular steel that could cut to the bone. Clementine shuttered, remembering the cuts and streaks of blood when she'd lashed the man's back who had assaulted his wife in the front yard.

She reached for the Stanford file and reviewed her notes. Jimmy Scruggs, the police detective in Del Rio, had told her Morgan was a heroin addict who was murdered because he'd double-crossed a Mexican drug cartel. Clementine knew in order to learn anything more about Morgan's drug history she would have had to cross the river into Ciudad Acuña. And that wasn't going to happen. She wasn't going to risk her life in Mexico for Reginald J. Stanford or anyone else for that matter. Besides, she thought, even Detective Scruggs had all but admitted the Del Rio police department was through with the case. "Just another doper off the streets," he'd said.

She thought about her conversation with Doctor Dussair including his sudden change in attitude when she'd brought up the fact that he and Morgan had been friends in medical school. What was that all about? She wanted to pursue the mystery further, but that depended on old hard ass up in Boston. All she could do now was report what she knew and see what Reginald baby wanted to do about it.

Clementine stared at the telephone. She'd stalled long enough. It was time to find out if she'd be working tomorrow. Act or get off the pot as her dad used to say.

Just as she reached for the receiver, the line buzzed indicating an incoming call. Glancing at the packages on the couch, Clementine crossed her fingers hoping for a new case.

"Ms. Garza?"

The voice seemed tentative as though the caller wasn't sure she should be calling.

"Yes, this is Clementine Garza."

"My name is LuAnn Dussair. My brother, Detective Scruggs, told me you spoke with my husband, Kurt Dussair."

Okay, Clementine thought to herself, the intrigue about the good doctor Dussair's strange behavior in Del Rio deepens.

"Of course, how can I help you, Mrs. Dussair?"

"Please," she said. "Everyone calls me Lou. What did Kurt tell you about his relationship with Morgan Stanford?"

"My work is confidential, Lou. I can't—"

LuAnn interrupted, "I understand," she said. "You may want to contact a woman named Mary Ann Barnes in Galveston. She knew Morgan's girlfriend. Mary Ann was studying to be a Physical Therapist. I checked with UTMB. She received her degree the year Kurt graduated. I don't know if she's still around, but she was a B.O.I, *Born on the Island*. Kurt used to say most of those people wouldn't leave Galveston unless it sunk into the ocean."

"Why are you interested in Morgan's girlfriend?" Clementine asked.

There was no response for several moments. Clementine waited.

"My brother, Jimmy, used to hunt with Kurt," LuAnn said. "One day when Kurt was drunk out at the deer lease, he told Jimmy that Morgan dropped out of medical school and left town in a hurry without saying goodbye."

"Did he say why Morgan left?"

"No," LuAnn said. "Kurt told Jimmy that he and Morgan more or less shared the same girlfriend if you know what I mean. I have never told Kurt that I know about his *ménage à trois* or whatever you call it. I want to know what happened that caused Morgan Stanford to leave so suddenly. I will pay you for your time."

Clementine knew she couldn't have two clients on the same case. But before declining the offer, she thought she'd take a stab at the mystery.

"I appreciate the offer," Clementine said. "May I ask how it concerns you?"

A moment of silence, and then, LuAnn said, "I'd rather not say in case I'm wrong."

"I see," Clementine said. She waited a beat and continued, "I'm afraid I can't help you, Lou. I already have a client in this case, and two would create a conflict of interest."

When the call ended, Clementine considered what she'd just heard. There was no doubt Lou Dussair suspected something. But what? Clementine figured it must be tied in with Kurt Dussair's sexual dalliances in med school.

She immediately called Stanford and related her findings about the results of the autopsy report and the fact that Kurt Dussair, Morgan's friend from medical school, had coincidentally been on duty in the ER and tried to save him. She finished her report recounting Detective Scruggs' suspicion that Morgan was killed by a Mexican drug cartel.

After a brief silence, Stanford said, "Thank you for your service. I'll arrange to have my son cremated. Please send me your bill. My assistant will be most prompt with payment."

"Hold on, Stanford. There's more."

When Stanford didn't immediately respond, she figured she had the old snot's attention. She'd make him sweat. She casually picked up the pack of Vogues, shook out another green cig and lit up.

"What is it, Ms. Garza?" Stanford asked, impatience zinging through the line.

Clementine said, "I think Morgan may have quit medical school because of his girlfriend."

Clementine puffed the Vogue, waiting.

Finally, he said, "Morgan was my only child. His mother is dead, and I thank God she didn't live to see the disgrace he brought to our name. There are no other heirs, and as you may suspect, I am quite wealthy. My estate will go to charity as I had planned before I learned of Morgan's death. In any event, my son was a drug addict, a scourge on society. So, as you can see, Ms. Garza, I certainly have no interest in a possible girlfriend. Our business is concluded"

"I also got a call from Dr. Dussair's wife," Clementine said, trying to keep the conversation alive. "She gave me the name of someone who knew Morgan in medical school. The way she talked, I got the feeling something happened there that severely impacted Morgan's life. There is more to his story. Give me a day to follow this up in Galveston."

No response. Clementine waited. She heard nothing but the anemic noises of an old man breathing.

And finally Stanford said, "Good day, Miss Garza."

A. Hardy Roper

Chapter Twelve

Luther parked under the big oak tree in his driveway feeling lucky no one had connected the abandoned Pontiac at the levy with finding him burned and unconsciousness in his pirogue. Neither the doctor nor the sheriff knew his identity.

Now he only had to worry about the brothers. He didn't know how they'd found his house so easily the first time, but just thinking about their influence reaching this far down the bayou sent shivers through his spine.

He sat in his car thinking through his next move. With the lab destroyed, the only way to square it with the bros was to find the bitch Joy and get his goods back. And time was running out. He needed to grab his emergency money stash inside the house and get on the road quick.

He turned in the seat, looked around, and seeing nothing suspicious, he focused on the house. The old cypress-wood shack on the edge of the swamp wasn't much, but it hadn't cost him anything. When his father went to prison for molesting a 10-year-old neighbor girl and his mother died of an alcohol-ravaged liver, the place became his. He studied the paint-bare siding and sunken porch looking for any sign that someone unwelcome had come by. He saw no movement, nothing out of place.

He had a thought and almost laughed. After retrieving the meth from Joy, and squaring things with the brothers, he'd be on a roll. Maybe he'd return and burn the shithole down for the fun of it.

A. Hardy Roper

Luther stepped on the broken porch wondering why the doorknob turned so easily. Had he forgotten to lock the door or was Joy back with her worthless kid? That's it, he thought. The slut actually missed me. He gave a half grin.

As the door swung inward, a powerful hand grabbed Luther's bandaged arm, twisting him around, slamming his 250 pounds of heavy bulk hard to the floor.

Luther screamed, holding his arm. It was as though a thousand angry hornets were attacking his body.

Luther was taller and heavier than Vinnie Calzone, but no match for Vinnie's well-muscled arms and gym-sized chest. Vinnie looked even bigger than the last time Luther had seen him and a lot more menacing.

Vinnie wore a skintight, V-neck purple pullover. His pumped-up deltoid and pectoral muscles stretched the cloth to its max. The pullover melted down to a trim waist covered by matching purple dress pants. He finished the look with Italian mauve-colored loafers. He kept his hair dyed coal black and slicked back with grease. A neatly trimmed dark beard camouflaged a pocked complexion. Out of habit, Vinnie patted his hand against his scalp, ensuring every strand remained in place. He followed the movement by running finger and thumb across his lower cheeks and chin, smoothing his beard. Against the dark beard, his teeth showed white as bleached bones. Vinnie Calzone was *the man*.

Luther scooted to the couch, winching in pain. He leaned back against the cushion. He knew better than to try and get up.

Vinnie pulled a chair in close and leaned toward him. "One time, Luther," he said. "Don't make me ask again. What happened to you?" He slapped Luther's burned arm with the palm of his hand.

Luther yelped and turned away, moaning, his arm on fire, lightning bolts raining down. "Damn it, Vinnie," he cried out. "You don't have to do this." He squeezed back into the couch. "My lab blew," he said. "Almost killed me. Made me look like a freak."

Vinnie laughed, teeth gleaming. "You were always a freak, Luther, you dumb coon ass. If anything, you look better now."

Tommaso Calzone, not wanting to sit on Luther's filthy couch, came in from the kitchen, dragging a chair. Tomas, as he preferred to be called, was two years older than his brother Vinnie and several inches taller. He styled his hair in a high pompadour, swept upward on the sides. A black-silk shirt, with the figure of a gold-colored pelican embroidered on the front, covered a bulging stomach and sunken chest. He wore black pants and black alligator shoes. On his left pinkie finger was a two-caret diamond ring. A thick-braided, yellow chain with a fifty-peso gold coin encased in a bezel hung from his neck. Tomas had bought the coin from a dealer who'd told him it was a genuine first edition *Centenario*, minted in 1921. Tomas didn't care much about that. He liked the coin because the woman on the front had a nice rack. He liked to rub the woman's chest for luck. Tomas had always considered himself a tit man.

He scooted his chair close and opened a large knife. He ran it across his forearm, dropping bits of shaved hair on the floor in front of Luther.

"Where is our order, Luther?"

"I have it. I have it," Luther pleaded, holding his hands out to protect himself.

"Well, it's not here, Luther. We looked. All we found was this," Tomas said, fanning a role of bills he'd pulled from his pocket. "Kinda stupid, Luther. Leaving money in your freezer. First place anybody would look."

Tomas stood and splashed the bills across Luther's chest. Luther swallowed hard, his emergency stash scattered around him.

Tomas screamed, "Luther you shit. Where is the meth?"

"That bitch Joy stole it. But I'll get it back. I promise."

Tomas shook his head and sighed. He turned to Vinnie. "He's all yours," he said and left the room.

Vinnie leaned into Luther's seared face, screaming, "Where is Joy?"

Luther raised his hand to protect against another slap. He cowed down against the couch. Without looking up, he whispered, "She's...in Galveston."

Tomas came back into the room waving the knife. "Now listen close Luther," he said. "We have obligations. A big convention in New Orleans this weekend. Bringing in lots of working girls. Customers need their *crank*. You understand?"

Luther cowered against the sofa. "Don't worry, don't worry," he said.

"Oh, I'm not worried, Luther," Tomas added. "But you should be. You've got 24 hours to deliver the *ice*. Meanwhile, we'll take the advance money back until you deliver. Get the money for us now, Luther."

Luther slinked down closer to the floor, hands raised in front. "I...I don't have it."

Vinnie slapped Luther's hands away. He yanked him off the floor, held him with one hand and punched his nose hard with the other. Luther slumped back onto the couch.

Blood trickled from Luther's nose. He wiped the blood with his hand. "I lost it at the track in Lafayette," he said.

Vinnie screamed, "All 50,000!"

Luther nodded, eyes swollen. The needles in his face zinged worse, maybe a million stabbing him now.

Vinnie put his nose at Luther's ear and whispered, "Call me when you get to Galveston. And again when you've got the goods. Don't jack us around, Luther. Keep us informed, got it?"

Luther nodded. Then he saw Vinnie's hand closing toward his swollen face again. He gritted his teeth as the slap hit, sending searing pain racing across his face.

He fell over on the couch, wanting to pass out, his only avenue of escape. But then he felt Vinnie's hot stale breath on his cheek.

"Twenty-four hours, Luther. Got it? Twenty-four hours."

A. Hardy Roper

Chapter Thirteen

Late in the afternoon, Joe called from Houston saying he'd agreed to spend the night for more tests. The opportunity of a night without his continual carping came with great relief. I climbed to the deck outside my bedroom and stretched out in my favorite Adirondack chair. Out past the marsh, the tall palms at the entrance to Bay Harbor stood like beacons beckoning me forward.

My mind flashed to Jake. What was I getting myself into with this kid and his mama? Just turn it over to the law, I kept telling myself. It's not my problem. Sure, not my problem.

On my way in to the store to replenish supplies, I found myself turning into Bay Harbor. As soon as I'd parked in the old man's driveway, Buster the German Shepard rushed the fence. He pounded the wire, snarling and flashing teeth. I grabbed a bag of jerky from the truck and tossed a piece over the fence. Buster grabbed the treat and scurried away.

The old man stepped out to the porch wearing ragged shorts and no shirt, a blob of stomach folded over his waistband. He stared down toward the fence and seemed to recognize me.

"What the hell do you want?" he yelled.

"I came for Jake."

The old man rubbed his hand across the white stubble covering his face. "He didn't tell me nothing about it."

"My name's Parker McLeod and—"

"I know who you are," he blurted out. "Run that bar down the road. You got no business here."

A. Hardy Roper

Jake marched out the front door wearing the same jeans and the long-sleeve shirt that he'd worn before. He mumbled something to his grandfather and hurried down the stairs. When he got to the truck, I asked Jake what he'd said to his grandpa.

"Told him I was hungry," Jake answered. "Ain't nothing to eat in the house."

"Where is your mom?"

"In the bedroom doing something to herself."

"What?"

"Sex stuff. She always does it when she's on a high."

I remained quiet during the drive to the store waiting for Jake to open up more, but he didn't say anything. We stopped at *Red's*, a quick market with gas pumps out front. While I shopped, Jake watched bugged-eyed at the steady line of teenage girls in skimpy bikinis traveling in and out. Every boy with a fake ID carried a sack of beer. When the last of the group piled into a topless jeep headed for the beach, Jake and I started back to The Garhole.

"You have a girlfriend back in Louisiana?" I asked.

Jake shook his head. "Girls don't have nothing to do with me. They know about my mama."

We stopped at the bar to unload the groceries and fill Jake with French fries and leftover shrimp. Then we drove to the oak motte. A variety of cranes stalked around the pond. I settled Jake on the bench and returned to the truck for the Walmart bag.

"Got something for you," I said, handing Jake one of the folded shirts.

His eyes grew wide.

"School is starting soon," I said. "Thought you might like a new shirt."

Jake rubbed his hand over the soft cotton.

"Try it on," I said.

He set it on the bench. "I...I'll do it later," he said.

I didn't know how to follow his comment. We sat without speaking. After a moment, Jake picked the shirt up again. He squeezed his eyes shut, his face in a tight grimace as though he was holding something in that was trying hard to get out. When he opened his eyes, they were swollen and red. But there were no tears, just something else—resolve, defiance.

He put his head in his hands, not moving. Finally, he straightened, removed his long-sleeved shirt, and stood before me. Now I understood, saw it all. Burn marks along his arms and torso, some healed, some fresh, red and inflamed.

I choked back the anger building in my throat. "Who?" I asked. "Your mother, grandfather?"

"Luther," he said.

"Luther?"

Jake lifted his eyes. "The man you shot at," he said. "I wished you'd killed him."

"Jake...Jake," I said. "What did the bastard burn you with?"

He gazed past me, the fear gone, replaced by what veterans know as *the thousand yard stare*. Jake stood robotic like, as if in a trance.

"He...he said I was his ashtray...flicked ashes and put cigarettes out on me. And mama...she just watched."

I held still, afraid to move—afraid he would retreat back into his protective shell. I swallowed hard, "Your mom was there?"

"He only did it when she was there. When she needed the meth so bad she would do anything. And Luther would say, 'Don't want me to stop do you, Joy. You like this, don't you Joy. You need this don't you, Joy.' And Luther, he'd burn me again."

"Jesus Christ," I said.

A. Hardy Roper

Jake blinked several times. He turned toward me. "Jesus Christ?" he said. "No, Jesus wasn't there. It was only my sweet mama."

A piece of my heart chipped off, but I was determined not to show pity. I understood now. Jake had lived through the worst kind of childhood and come out the only way he could, tough, resolute...a survivor. At least on the outside.

I unfolded the new shirt and handed it to him. He slipped it on and pressed the sides down to smooth the wrinkles. When he thought it looked good, he tucked the tail in his jeans and refastened his belt ignoring the burn marks showing on his lower arms. He picked up the old shirt and began ripping it apart. He threw it to the sand and stomped. Then he took a stick and dug a grave into the soft sand beside a prickly pear bush and buried the remains.

From somewhere deep in his being, right on the precipice of being lost forever, Jake had crossed a threshold. His eyes announced the passing, steady and sure. Maybe for the first time in his life, Jake had taken a risk. He had begun to trust.

We piled into the truck and started back to the bar, neither of us speaking.

About half way, Jake said, "She's getting worse."

"Your mom?"

Jake nodded. "She's high all the time now. No sleep. Screaming and throwing things. Can't stop herself. Grandpa says he's gonna kick us out."

I focused on the road ahead. "Where is she getting the stuff?"

"Brought a whole bag full with her," he said.

"The duffel?"

Jake nodded. "Luther's coming back...I know it."

Jake's lips quivered. He began to tremble, almost as if having a seizure. There was something in his eyes I never wanted to see in a kid...terror...abject fear.

"Why do you say that?" I asked.

"Mama stole the bag from him."

I eased ahead on the lane. Neither of us spoke. As we approached The Garhole, I cut the truck's wheels toward the highway to take Jake home.

He glanced at the bar and then back toward the highway. "Can I stay here tonight?" he blurted out.

I hesitated, feeling the weight of the moment, realizing letting Jake stay the night would put me deeper into the tangle of his life—a crazy grandfather and drug addicted mother. I liked life simple, cooking food for hungry customers, sitting on the deck at night watching the moon rays bounce off the water. No wrinkles, plain vanilla, uncomplicated, attachment free. That was the whole reason I came back to West Bay. No Army regulations, orders, required routines. I did what I pleased here; the captain of my one-person ship. About as few responsibilities as a man could have.

Jake turned and met my eyes. I saw no desperation, no pleading. He had proffered a simple request, one night of peace, a few hours of relief from dysfunction and chaos.

A. Hardy Roper

Chapter-Fourteen

Old-man Stanford hadn't approved Clementine's trip to Galveston, but she'd gone anyway. She had a hunch. Others may call it women's intuition but to an ex-cop turned P.I., it was a hunch. And she wasn't about to let a crotchety, old stuff-shirted, Yankee Blue-Blood stand in the way of following her nose.

Clementine reached the crest of the Galveston Causeway doing 70 mph with the top down. She had fallen in love with her bright yellow Mustang at first sight. And a convertible was so *her*. She'd used the last of the reward money for the down payment and financed the remainder with the car lot owner. He'd kept the title but so what. She knew how the game worked. One payment missed and the guy's goons would steal it back the same night.

She drove with abandon, sunglasses pressed against her eyes and hair blown back in the breeze, singing along with Madonna.

"Don't put me off 'cause I'm on fire
And I can't quench my desire
Don't you know that I'm burning up for your love."

A car full of raucous college kids heading for the beach pulled beside her in a new Firebird. The boy in the front seat stuck his head out the window and rolled his tongue around his lips. As the bird sped by, the kid in the back howled in laughter and chugged his beer.

A. Hardy Roper

Clementine ignored the group and focused on a patrol car at the bottom of the causeway. A cop holding a hand-held radar gun motioned for the Firebird to pull over. Clementine moved to the middle lane. When she passed the Pontiac, the cop had his back turned but the kids were facing her. She slowed, raised her hand in a one-finger salute and rolled by.

She stopped at the first convenience store and bought a tourist map to orient her to the city's layout. Popular tourist attractions were outlined with caricatures and bold print. The street off the causeway had become Broadway Boulevard, running straight through the city to the beach at the east end of the island. Tucked away on quiet streets were many of the fine old Victorian homes she'd seen featured in magazines. To the right of Broadway lay the beach, the Gulf of Mexico and a mixture of residential and commercial areas that ended at Seawall Boulevard. To the left was the downtown business area along with the Strand, a tourist street where island visitors shopped for fudge and T-shirts. Past the Strand were the dockyards and cruise ship facilities.

Clementine entered a telephone booth outside the convenience store and checked the directory's white pages hoping for a long shot. There was no listing for Mary Ann Barnes. She turned to the yellow pages and quickly scanned the names of Physical Therapists. There were eight listings for individual therapists but none for Barnes. She noticed most of the therapy clinics were located close to UTMB, the city's main hospital. She ripped the listings out of the phone book and tucked the pages in her pocket.

Thinking the larger the office the more therapists, she started at the largest clinic and worked her way down. She stopped across the street from each clinic and called on her cell phone. Halfway through the list, a young receptionist, friendlier than most, answered the phone.

"Island Therapy."

"Mary Ann Barnes, please."

"Who?"

"Mary Ann Barnes."

"I'm sorry," the girl said. "We don't have anyone by that name."

"Well, thank you—"

"We do have Mary Ann Sloan."

At the mention of the name, Clementine left the Mustang and started across the street.

"Oh, that's right. Mary Sloan," Clementine said as she approached the clinic. "May I speak to her please?"

"She's in therapy. Are you a patient?"

"I'll call back," Clementine said.

Clementine watched the receptionist replace the receiver and turn to a patient at the counter. She entered the waiting area and strode past people reading magazines and watching television. The wall beside the reception desk displayed the therapists' pictures and bios.

Clementine scanned the group and quickly found Mary Ann Sloan posed in glamour shot, one of those photos taken in a studio following an hour of makeup and hair treatment. Clementine almost barfed. She knew no one looked that good. The picture reminded Clementine of the photos posted on dating sites she'd skimmed—hair glued still, lipstick overdone and teeth as white as a polar bear's fur.

Still, Clementine thought, depending on when the photo was taken, Mary Ann Sloan appeared to be about the right age. And the bio underneath the photo indicated Sloan was graduated from UTMB about the same time as Dussair. Clementine stepped to the counter.

"Excuse me Miss, please let Mrs. Sloan know Clementine Garza is here to see her?"

The receptionist checked a sheet in front of her and handed the card back to Clementine.

"I'm sorry. I don't have your name listed on the appointment calendar."

"Just please tell Mary Ann that Dr. Dussair asked me to call on her."

The girl relayed the message. "She'll be right out," she said.

Bingo, thought Clementine. A moment later, a well-coiffured blond with caked makeup came out a side door wearing a white coat. As she approached, Clementine noted the overly tight eye sockets and stretched skin around her temples. She wore large rimmed glasses, the attached cord fitting loosely behind her head. She was taller than Clementine and thinner. Her hands were long and slender and void of rings.

The woman removed her glasses and peered down at Clementine. "I am Mary Ann Sloan. Dr. Dussair referred you?"

Clementine noted Sloan's condescending tone, but with a forced act of decorum, she made a calculated decision to withhold her usual sarcastic retort.

"Yes, that's right," Clementine said. "Do you have a few moments, Ms. Sloan? It's important."

Clementine sat in a hard metal chair in Sloan's tiny office at the rear of the clinic. She shifted and squirmed, for once thankful for her otherwise obtrusive *Gluteus Maximus*.

Sloan's desk appeared neat and clean and noticeably void of family photos. The walls were bare except for a diploma mounted in a large frame. The name on the diploma read Mary Ann Barnes. Clementine slid a business card across the desk.

Sloan glanced at the card, then at Clementine, a look of suspicion in her eyes. "Garza Investigations?"

"Didn't mean to appear so mysterious, Ms. Sloan. May I call you Mary Ann?"

Sloan didn't respond. She raised a hand in a gesture of impatience, glanced at the card again and said, "I don't have much time...Miss, uh...Garza. What is this about? Has something happened to Kurt?"

"No, not at all," Clementine replied. "Doctor Dussair is doing fine, the perfect life. All American family—a beautiful wife, three great kids."

Clementine delighted in pushing the dig to the pompous bitch across the desk. She watched with glee as a flicker of disappointment flashed across Sloan's face. It was obvious Sloan and Dussair had been more than friends. But somehow the medical school tryst hadn't succeeded. Along the line, Barnes had become Sloan, and judging from her bare ring finger, that union hadn't succeeded either. Too bad, Clementine thought.

"I am a private investigator," Clementine continued, "employed by the father of an old acquaintance of yours...Morgan Stanford."

Clementine noticed a slight tick in Sloan's lips. Sloan rose and shut the door. She returned to her seat.

"Okay...Miss Garza. What is it you want?"

"Morgan is dead," Clementine said.

Clementine watched Sloan's pupils expand as if taking in more light, then recover quickly.

"I am sorry about Morgan," Sloan said. "But I have neither seen nor heard from him in fifteen years. What does Morgan's death have to do with me?"

Clementine let it all out, relating Morgan's drug history, that a Mexican cartel had beaten him to near death, and that Dussair had treated Morgan in the E.R. She watched Sloan carefully during the entire disclosure looking for any sign of empathy in her eyes or even acknowledgement that she and Morgan had once been friends. She saw nothing.

Sloan glanced at her watch. "I have a patient waiting."

Clementine had seen this phony act of impertinence many times before, both as a cop and as a P.I. It was calculated to throw her off her game, but Clementine didn't bite. She felt a twitch of sadness instead. Here was a once attractive woman, only in her late thirties, who was so insecure she'd let a butcher carve her face. And then there was the phony routine of pretending to be a queen dressing down a handmaiden. The bitch obviously thought her role in life was more important than Clementine's and probably more important than anyone for that matter. But Clementine knew the woman had her own *Come to Jesus* every time she removed her makeup and watched all that fake confidence melt like wax from a burning candle. Clementine smiled inwardly reviewing the ghastly sight in her mind.

As much as Clementine wanted to reach across the desk and slap the wax off Sloan's face, she had a job to do. As Sloan rose from her desk to leave, Clementine stepped to the side blocking her exit.

"Please, just one moment," Clementine said, a new softness to her voice. "Morgan's father is heartbroken. You can imagine the loss of a son. I'm trying to piece together Morgan's life, get closure for the old man. Anything you can tell me will help."

Sloan, sighed, exhaling a large breath. "Well I really don't know—"

Clementine broke in thinking it was time for a little white lie, the kind in every PI's handbook. "My client, Mr. Stanford, hadn't spoken with Morgan since he left Galveston. He knows Morgan had a girlfriend here, and he wants to find her. You understand, don't you Ms. Sloan. I need the girlfriend's name. That's all. And if you know her whereabouts."

Sloan winched, followed by an uncomfortable expression as if she was deciding whether or not to go forward.

At first, Clementine had read Sloan as a cool customer, someone so in control she probably took laxatives twice a day.

But Clementine knew she was getting to her now. She just needed to keep pressing until the cold fish in front of her exploded.

Sloan blew out another big breath. She glanced around the room as if trying to stay in control. Her face reddened. She finally lost composure sending her words out in a hurried rush.

"I haven't seen that bitch in fifteen years," she said, her voice rising with each word. "When Morgan disappeared, she hung around his apartment because she didn't have any place to stay. She was a slut, a working girl...a common streetwalker and cocaine addict. I have no doubt she got Morgan into drugs."

Finally the queen was on a roll, Clementine mused. She just needed to keep her going.

"What was her name?" Clementine asked.

Sloan put her hand to her head as if trying to recall. "I can't remember," she said. "After Morgan left, it came out that the hospital was investigating Morgan for stealing drugs. But there was no proof. The slut's father was a janitor at the hospital. The hospital accused him too and forced him to quit. He lost his pension."

"What was his name?"

"You expect me to remember that?" Sloan said, exasperated.

"Please try," Clementine said, boring in.

Sloan scrunched her forehead. After a moment she said, "Green, I think. Henry Green. Now if you'll excuse me..."

Clementine stepped aside, and Sloan strode to the door. She held the door open waiting for Clementine to leave.

Clementine hesitated. She knew once outside the office, Sloan would disappear, and Clementine wasn't finished yet.

"What happened to the girl?" Clementine asked.

"I don't know and don't care," Sloan said, impatience growing. She shifted from one foot to the other.

"You said Morgan was already into drugs when he was in school here. Do you think it was possible he *was* stealing drugs from UTMB, and he left town because he was afraid he'd get arrested?"

"I don't know why he left," Sloan said.

"Any guesses?"

"I really must go," Sloan answered.

"Just one guess?"

"I always thought maybe Morgan had knocked the little whore up."

"Was the girl pregnant?"

"I have no idea," Sloan said.

"Morgan left medical school because of that?"

"He was flunking out anyway. Morgan was a weak soul...good looking, but fragile," Sloan said. "His father was an absolute tyrant. Morgan never had the courage to confront the old bastard. Probably the reason he escaped into drugs. And if the bitch was pregnant, Morgan probably chose to run rather than embarrass the family.

"His mom and dad were the charity ball king and queen of Boston. The Sunday society section wasn't complete without their mug shots dominating the pages. Old-man Stanford is the top of the hill, a billionaire. By far the richest man in Boston."

"Old money?" Clementine asked.

"Ancient," Sloan replied. "Slave and whisky trade from the 1700s. Make old Joe Kennedy's rum-running escapades look tame. Of course now, the Stanford machine is legit...banking and real estate. I should have made a play for Morgan myself..." she said, hesitating. "But there was..."

"Kurt Dussair," Clementine said, finishing Sloan's thought.

Clementine knew Sloan had gotten on a tear and gone too far, but she couldn't resist the last dig, "I don't blame you for trying, Ms. Sloan," she said. "Kurt was quite a hunk."

"Get out of my office!" Sloan said, exploding.

"Of course, Ms. Sloan. Sorry to have kept you. Just one last question. You claim the girlfriend was a hooker and that she hung around the apartment after Morgan left because she didn't have a place to stay. Kurt and Morgan were roommates. Is it possible they were dipping their spoons into the same honey pot?"

"You're disgusting," Sloan said, an awful sneer on her face.

Clementine scooted past Sloan into the hall. Sloan pulled the door shut behind her, locked it and stomped away.

A. Hardy Roper

Chapter Fifteen

Clementine hustled out to her car, checking her watch on the way. Three o'clock and she hadn't eaten since breakfast. She pulled through the window of a KFC and ordered spicy wings, mashed potatoes and gravy, a fresh baked biscuit doused with a butter-like substance and a large Coke. The thought of a week's worth of calories inhaled in less than five minutes flashed through her mind, but hey, she was working. She needed the energy. And she'd burn it off in the gym next week...maybe.

She drove to the beach and parked along the seawall. She raised the top of the Mustang and sat with the windows lowered. The breeze off the Gulf cooled the car's interior while she munched on the chicken. Down on the beach a young couple walked barefoot along the edge of the water holding hands, their shoes tied over their shoulders. The couple stopped and kissed.

Scenes from her life flashed by—high school, college. Clementine couldn't remember a single moment of such intimacy. She squirmed in her seat and looked away.

She sucked the last of the Coke out of the cup and burped softly, lady like, all the while stealing a quick glance to the sidewalk hoping no one walking by had noticed. She wrapped the naked chicken bones into her napkin, put the napkin into the sack and dropped it on the passenger side floorboard.

She rested her head on the seatback and closed her eyes thinking about Mary Ann Sloan. It was obvious to her

Sloan hadn't gotten over Kurt Dussair. And Clementine could tell beyond the heavy makeup and botched repair job, Sloan had been a real looker fifteen years earlier. Any man would have made a play for her. Yet Dussair had moved on. Clementine knew it had to have hurt. She knew about rejection. But carrying the pain on her sleeve all those years couldn't have been healthy for Sloan. Unrequited love, a woman scorned...not fun stuff. Clementine felt a sudden pang of empathy for Sloan but quickly pushed it away.

Clementine wondered if Sloan had also made a play for Morgan Stanford. She said she hadn't, but Morgan was the rich one after all. The truth was, after being trampled all his life by an unrelenting father, Morgan probably didn't think *he* was good enough for Sloan. Clementine figured Morgan's self-esteem must have been lower than a whale's bottom. And Sloan probably never noticed it.

Clementine straightened in the seat. She lowered the sun visor and noticed small cracks beginning to form at the edges of her eyes. She slammed the visor back and opened a new pack of cigarettes, pink ones this time. She lit up and blew the smoke to the side all the while squirming in her seat. Time to call the old goat, she thought. Can't put it off any longer. She dug her cell phone out of her purse and punched in the numbers.

"Mr. Stanford, please. Clementine Garza calling."

The receptionist transferred the call. A moment later the phone clicked and a voice said, "This is Reginald J. Stanford."

Clementine felt her blood pressure soar. Stanford was acting as if he'd never spoken to her before. The phony indifference was almost more than she could stand. But then she remembered her car payments.

"I arrived in Galveston this morning and met with Mary Ann Sloan, an old friend of Morgan's," Clementine said.

Saving Jake

"Our business was concluded at our last phone call," Stanford snorted. "I didn't authorize the trip."

Clementine ignored the remark. "I need a few days," she said, hoping the open-ended statement would at least garner a response. She took in a deep lung full of smoke and waited.

"For what reason?" Stanford replied.

Clementine blew out smoke and said, "There is more to this than I thought."

"Yes," he said.

"Morgan had a girlfriend in Galveston. He may have left town because she was pregnant."

More silence, not even a gasp or a chortle.

"Did you hear me, Mr. Stanford?"

"And what has this to do with me?" Stanford said.

Clementine fumed at Stanford's obstinacy. The old man seemed to be in a perpetual bad mood. She pictured Stanford sitting in his chair with an ax handle up his ….

"The answer is obvious, Mr. Stanford," Clementine answered. Then she paused for effect. She wanted the next statement to be as dramatic as she could muster. "You may have a grandchild."

Stanford stammered through the phone. Clementine hoped his blood pressure was spiking through the top of his phony-assed head.

"I...I warn you Ms. Garza," Stanford said, his voice rising an octave. "Do not attempt to swindle me. I have more resources than you can imagine."

Clementine's pulse raced. She exhaled a slow breath to calm herself. But nothing worked. She'd had enough. She flicked the cigarette out the window and cranked the car's engine.

"Look, Stanford," she said. "I don't need this grief from you. You hired me, remember?"

"And the task has been completed," Stanford answered.

Clementine slammed the phone to the seat beside her. She breathed in and out in a measured pace until she felt her pulse slow.

So far, her hunch had only cost gas money for the trip from San Antonio to Galveston. But now questions had evolved that she couldn't let go of: Kurt Dussair's sudden change in attitude, the mysterious phone call from his wife, Lou Dussair, and the new information from Mary Ann Sloan. The plot had definitely thickened, she thought.

Sloan had said the father of Morgan's girlfriend was a janitor at the hospital, and his name was Henry Green. Clementine punched in numbers on her cell phone and waited.

"Information," the voice said.

"Number for Henry Green, please."

A few beats later, the voice said, "We have no listing for Henry Green."

Clementine terminated the call wondering what had happened to Green. Had he moved away? Died? Maybe he still lived in Galveston and didn't have a phone. Then she remembered his long tenure at the hospital.

Clementine drove to UTMB and rode the elevator to the fourth floor. A sign on the door read "Human Resources." She pushed on the door but almost slammed into the glass when the door failed to open. She stepped back and read the office hours: nine to four. Her watch read 4:05.

Inside the office, a young Hispanic woman walked by the receptionist desk, grabbed her purse and started to move away. Clementine knocked on the door to get her attention. The woman pointed to her watch. Clementine rapped again. The woman shook her head.

Clementine whipped out her phone on the way back to her car and called her answering service. Nothing. No business calls, personal calls, nothing at all. Her only choices were to return to San Antonio and hope for a new case or spend the night on her own nickel and pursue the Green lead.

She decided to trust her instincts, take the gamble, see what she could learn and hope Stanford would be interested enough to continue the case...and pick up the bill. She hoped she had enough credit left on her Visa card for a room. And maybe a good seafood dinner and a drink or two.

A. Hardy Roper

Chapter Sixteen

Luther awoke after midnight, curled on his couch. His stomach turned from the stink of rancid cigarettes, marijuana and stale beer. He lit a joint, sucking the smoke into his lungs and holding it as long as possible, letting the weed do its trick. One or two good long puffs should do it. A good toke always calmed his nerves, allowing him to think more clearly. He sank back into the worn out cushions of his filthy couch waiting for the magic to hit his brain.

He rolled his head around his shoulders, letting the high build. Then he sucked in one last lungful, pinched out the fire at the end and slipped the remaining joint into his shirt pocket. Luther knew just how many puffs to take and when to stop, quit before the paranoia came. But he was tired and worried. He hoped he hadn't smoked too much. He needed to make a plan while he still had the smoothness of the hit, before the worst of it grabbed his brain sending him into that magic place where nothing mattered and all was lost.

Vinnie Calzone had given him 24 hours to retrieve the goods. Not much time. He'd smoked too much weed, trying to kill the pain from the burns and had stupidly fallen asleep, wasting several hours. He stepped out to his car and retrieved a map from his glove compartment. He went back inside and spread the map on his kitchen table.

He traced the map with his finger from Thibodaux down bayou La Fourche to his house. It appeared the drive from his shack to Lake Charles was three hours and another three hours to Galveston, six in total. Adding six more for the return trip meant he'd still have plenty of time in Galveston to locate Joy and get the goods. That is, if she was still there. If she was still on the run and had left Galveston, he may never catch her. And he'd be out of time.

But what other options did he have? He considered robbing a bank in Thibodaux, but doubted the teller cages contained 50,000 in cash. That meant he'd have to rob two. And what did he know about robbing banks anyway? Nothing. And he sure didn't have time to learn. Besides, the Calzone brothers didn't want cash. The brothers planned to unload the entire batch over the weekend at a huge profit. So cash wouldn't work, he needed the meth.

And then it came to him, his main competition, Waylon Fontenot, an old high school buddy. Luther had deer hunted once with Waylon at his camp deep in the woods. You had to have been there or you'd never find it. He hadn't seen the little puss since high school, but he remembered the geeky horn rim glasses, pimply face, greasy hair and skinny-assed body. Waylon wouldn't be much of a threat. Luther figured he'd just waltz in and make Waylon a deal. Give him some bullshit promise about repaying the stash he needed and blow out of the place. Good plan, Luther thought. If Waylon had enough *ice*, it would save him a trip to Galveston. He'd deal with Joy later.

Even in the dark, Luther managed to find the dirt road that tracked back into the deep woods. He stopped at the entrance to the road, lifted the Smith and Wesson .38 Special off the seat and opened the cylinder. Six 158-grain bullets all tucked in neat and proper. He closed the cylinder and opened the box of cartridges on the seat, 10 rows of five each, less the six bullets in the gun. Luther smiled. He'd never be short of ammunition again. If he'd had extra bullets with him when he'd cornered Joy and that jerk-off at the bridge, he wouldn't be in all this trouble now. Stupid. And who was that dickhead with Joy anyway, he wondered. Probably some redneck the bitch had hustled on the run from him. No matter. He'd deal with that peckerwood the same way he would with Joy. A permanent solution.

Luther eased down the dirt road, trying to remember the cutoff. The trees were thick and tall, the woods the darkest he'd ever seen. Every half-mile or so another side road cut deeper into the woods. So far he'd not seen a living organism of any kind, no people, no animals, not even a bird. An eerie place, he thought. Not like the comfort of the swamp, something he was used to.

Luther racked his pot-filled brain, trying to remember the turnoff. Right or left? "Come on, Waylon. Help me," he murmured. "Where are you?"

He drove on, slowly now, hoping he could find the cabin in the dark. And then he saw the big, spreading tupelo tree. Biggest damn tupelo in Louisiana Waylon had always said. The tree was there when Waylon's grandfather had built the hunting camp 50 years earlier. Filled with green leaves, the tree didn't look the same as when Luther had first seen it in the fall. The leaves were all red then with streaks of yellow. It was the most beautiful tree he'd ever seen.

It was almost 10 years earlier, during high school, when Waylon invited him on a deer hunt. They shot everything that moved that weekend: deer, rabbits, birds. Even a skunk they'd found under the cabin. Waylon had actually shot the skunk, but Waylon's grandfather blamed Luther. Waylon said the scent had stayed in the cabin for weeks afterward, and Luther was never invited back.

He turned left just past the tree, remembering that the lane dead-ended at the camp. He slowed. "Be careful," he mumbled to himself, thinking the little pissant could have a dog or even a guard. Maybe a camera in a tree.

A. Hardy Roper

Luther backed his Pontiac into a small break in the woods beside the road, facing out, ready for a quick getaway. The shack was just as he'd remembered, one large room made from split logs, the windows covered with rags to keep out the mosquitoes and flies. Luther thought the coverings looked like the same rags he'd seen 10 years earlier during the hunting trip. A single light bulb lit the interior, casting a soft glow against the rags.

A spanking clean, new Harley Davidson sat out front. Luther eased to the bike and glanced at the nameplate—Road King Touring Model. Luther didn't know much about bikes, but with all that chrome, he figured the thing had to cost 20,000 or more. "Nice," he mused. "Business is good, huh, Waylon."

He untucked his shirt to cover the .38 stuck in his waistband and approached the door. He heard a noise inside. Best be friendly, he thought. No sense scaring old Waylon in the middle of the night.

Luther stepped to the porch and called out, "Hey Waylon, you in there? It's Luther."

He heard someone moving. He waited, yelled out again, "Hey Waylon, it's your old buddy, Luther."

Luther heard footsteps outside the cabin. He turned toward the voice.

"Hey, Luther. Long time no see," Waylon said from the side of the porch. "What you doing out in the middle of the night?"

Waylon had gone out the back and circled around. Luther had a hard time making out all Waylon's features, but he did recognize the sawed-off, double-barreled shotgun pointed at his chest. Waylon stepped into the porch light. Luther noticed Waylon hadn't changed much. He was still skinny with greasy hair and a pimply face. He also wore the same thick glasses.

Saving Jake

"Jesus, Waylon. Put that thing away. I just came by to see your place. Maybe do some business."

"Sure, Luther. Just keep your hands where I can see them."

"Look, Waylon. Can we just go inside and talk? I got a business deal for you."

Waylon motioned Luther inside with the shotgun. The room looked the same, a small table with benches sitting on a pine wood floor. A battery-operated lamp hung from the rafter replacing the old-kerosene lantern Waylon remembered. The only difference was a wall full of two liter soda bottles, all empty...waiting.

Luther pointed to one of the bottles filled with a foaming liquid sitting on the table.

"So you're taking the easy way, huh, Waylon. Shake and bake?"

"I'm just a small-time operator," Waylon answered. "Not a sophisticated manufacturer like you. But then from the looks of you, maybe I made the right choice."

Luther inadvertently touched his face. The pain shooting across his cheeks reminded him of how pitiful he must look.

"You're right," Luther said. "My lab blew. But I still have my customers. Cut me a deal so I can fill an order that's pressing, and I'll pay you double as soon as it's delivered."

Waylon laughed hard, almost dropping the shotgun. "You kidding me, Luther," he said. "You're out of business, and I'm the only other local supplier. I can't even imagine how good my business is going to be."

"Look," Luther said, gesturing with his hands. "How much product can you make with shake and bake? I mean really, Waylon, one little order at a time? Get real. You can't grow. Tell you what, we'll partner up. You help me now, and we'll combine when I get my lab working again. We'll run it 24 hours, switch off shifts. I got more business than I can handle, and I've got more smurfs than you. Probably stole some of yours."

"You didn't steal my smurfs, Luther. I'm smarter than that. I don't need a bunch of dopers running around buying Sudafed anymore. Cops are gonna turn one of your smurfs, take you down."

"How you getting the pills then?" Luther asked. "The law says you can only buy 300 a month."

"Yeah, Luther, but that's a federal law. Goddamn it man, we're in Louisiana. You know how folks along the bayou feel about the feds. Most of them coonass a-holes still fly the Confederate flag, wear white sheets over their heads on Saturday night. I get mine straight out the back door of a couple of drugstores. Besides, shake and bake is safer. I got no interest in cooking it like you do and blowing my dick off. Sure don't wanna look like you."

"What you talking 'bout, man. Heard shake and bake will blow too. But maybe you know something. Show me how it works."

"Why should I?"

"Cause I got me a pipeline to the New Orleans' crowd. You do local. If you're so good, maybe we'll use both ways when we team up. Look at the cash we can make that way. I can't do it all. Show me."

Luther watched Waylon's eyes begin to waver. Slow now, he thought. Don't blink.

Waylon gestured with the shotgun. "Get your fat ass next to the wall," he said.

Luther moved across the room. Waylon gathered supplies with one hand while holding the shotgun with the other. He set the shotgun on the table with the barrels facing Luther. He snapped the lid off a drink bottle and poured in lighter fluid. Then he removed the lithium strips from two AA batteries, rolled the strips into small balls and dropped the balls into the bottle.

"Can't have any water around or even sweat on your hands," Waylon said. "Moisture at this stage could cause a fire."

Waylon emptied and measured several teaspoons of beads from a cold pack and added it to the bottle. He looked at Luther.

"You use anhydrous ammonia. We use ammonium nitrate, the stuff they put in the instant cold packs jocks and hikers use. It's a lot safer."

"Safer my ass," Luther said backing closer to the wall. "They make bombs outta that shit."

Waylon shrugged. When the chemical started to react in the bottle, he added the pseudoephedrine. Then he added lye pellets from a can of Drano.

"This is the tricky part," Waylon said. "You don't release the pressure at the right time, it will blow." He shook the bottle, watching carefully. He quit suddenly and released the cap.

"Now we let it sit for a while. Let's go out for a smoke, and I'll show you the rest after the batch cooks."

Luther couldn't believe Waylon left the shotgun on the table as they walked outside. They both lit a cigarette.

"What's left to do?" Luther asked, blowing out smoke as he spoke.

"Several steps. We still have to make a gas bottle. I'll use a plastic tube and some aluminum and muriatic acid. Some of the same stuff you use."

"So it takes an hour or so to make a batch?"

"If you're careful."

"You're right," Luther said. "Simpler method, but I don't know if it's safer. So how much is that batch worth?"

"I'll get a thousand dollars for the crystals out of this jar."

"How many do you do in a day?"

"Depends on the orders. I don't keep stock. Just shake a batch when needed."

This wasn't sounding good, Luther thought. He relaxed his posture and started gesturing with his hands again wanting Waylon to get accustomed to the movement.

"Oh, so you don't have any on hand now?"

"Only what I'm making tonight. Sold a batch this morning."

Luther quickly did the math. At a thousand a batch he needed fifty batches. Even with a gun to his head, Waylon couldn't produce anything close to that in 24 hours.

Luther glanced at Waylon's Harley. "Tell me about your bike," he said.

When Waylon turned toward the Harley, Luther whipped out the thirty-eight from his pants and shot him between the shoulder blades. Waylon collapsed into the dirt. He rolled to his back squinting up at Luther. Luther looked down, a nasty grin on his face.

Waylon struggled for words. "Luther you..."

Luther fired two more rounds into Waylon's chest and walked away. "Never liked you, that's all, Waylon. Just never did."

And then Luther mumbled, "dumb ass," and went back inside. The reaction in the bottle was cooking as expected but Luther was now so afraid of an explosion, he just wanted to haul his buns out of there. He'd wasted two hours and Galveston was no closer.

On the way out, he stopped at the Harley and climbed onto the seat. He grabbed the handlebars and mimicked the sound of the engine racing. He saw himself roaring around a curve, his long hair flaring in the wind. He got off the seat and ran his hands over the saddle bags. Nice and smooth. He could take it now and leave the Pontiac. But he'd never ridden a bike that big before. Besides, Waylon's camp was so well hidden, the bike would still be there when he returned. What's the rush, he thought.

A. Hardy Roper

Chapter Seventeen

I slept late and ambled downstairs into the bar. I opened the big window at the front, turned on the ceiling fans, made a pot of coffee and toasted the gar head with a cup. I was about to check on Jake when the door to the mobile home opened, and he came out rubbing his eyes.

After a breakfast of scrambled eggs and bacon, Jake went out to the dock while I cleaned the dishes. I found him sitting on the bench looking out at the bay.

"Feel like working, making a little money?"

"Really?" Jake said.

For the first time, I noticed Jake's mouth curl up at the edges as he spoke. I smiled back and said, "We need help running the crab traps."

I grabbed a sack of fish heads from the freezer and dumped them into the washtub. While Jake loaded the tub into the boat and untied the bowline, I cranked the motor. We puttered along the shoreline of the bay until we came to the first trap. A Styrofoam ball connected to a nylon rope floated on top the water. The other end of the rope snaked down to a wire trap lying on the mud bottom. Jake pulled the trap into the boat. I unfastened the wire door and shook the crabs into a bucket. Jake filled the bait trap with fish heads and dropped the trap back into the water. He peered into the bucket checking our catch.

"What's that orange sponge stuck to the bottom of some of the crabs?"

"Egg sack," I said. "We can't keep those. It's illegal to take female crabs when they're spawning."

We sorted out the egg-bearing females along with the smaller crabs and dumped them back into the bay. By the end of the line, we had captured several dozen large blue crabs.

With the sun blazing directly overhead and sweat dripping off our noses, I passed Jake a cold Coke and opened a Shiner for myself. I took my hat off and ran my fingers through my hair and shook out the accumulated sweat. Jake pressed the Coke can to his cheek. We caught each other's eye and nodded.

On the way back, Jake drove the boat while I sat in the bow facing him. The motor hummed smoothly.

"Think you could do this by yourself," I said.

"You mean it?"

"It's an everyday job. You can start tomorrow if you want."

"Tomorrow is my birthday."

I smiled. "Congratulations. Day after tomorrow then?"

Jake grinned. "No, no. Tomorrow's good."

"Great. When school starts you can come before or after."

Jake looked puzzled. "School?" he said.

"Yes," I said. "A couple of weeks from now."

Jake docked the boat, and we unloaded. I filled a crab pot with water, dumped in seasonings and fired the propane cooker. Jake leaned over the pot and sneezed.

"Red pepper," I said.

He watched as I ripped the back off the crabs and washed out the bodies. We tossed the empty shells into the bay. A single seagull appeared out of an empty sky and squawked a signal. Within minutes a dozen more arrived and dove into the remains.

Saving Jake

We dumped a dozen cooked crabs on an outside table. I taught Jake how to break the bodies in half and extract the meat, soft and juicy, filled with the aroma of cloves, paprika, thyme, oregano and garlic. When the birds left, the only noise was the gentle lapping of bay water against the dock.

An hour later, I pulled the old Chevy to a stop in front of the gate to Slim Green's house. I scanned the yard and the deck, nothing moved. The windows and front door were shuttered as if the house was abandoned. Jake looked worried.
"You want me to go in with you?"
"Grandpa's station wagon ain't here," Jake said. "It'll be okay."
"You go and check," I said. "Wave at me. Let me know everything is okay."
Jake got out and opened the gate. I craned my neck out the truck window.
"Where's the dog?"
Jake glanced around the yard. "Grandpa must have him."
He climbed the stairs to the deck and entered the house through the unlocked front door. A moment later, the door flew open, Jake screaming, "Help, Mr. Parker, help! It's mama."
I raced up the stairs and found Joy sprawled on her bedroom floor totally naked, emaciated, ribs pushing against mottled skin, her cheeks drawn and taunt. She couldn't have weighed a hundred pounds. I checked for a pulse and found no beat.
I locked my elbows over her chest and started rapid compressions trying to keep the heart pushing blood, oxygenating her brain. One and two and three and four—fast paced and deep. Ribs cracked. I knew there was a chance I had punctured a lung, but it wouldn't matter if she didn't survive.

Jake bent over her, shouting, "No, mama, no."

"Call 911," I yelled to Jake, continuing compressions, talking to myself, trying to keep the rhythm. "One and two and three and four and—"

"We...we don't have a phone."

"Go to a neighbor, pound on the door." I yelled again, "Call now!"

Moments later, Jake raced back in, out of breath. "There're coming," he said. He went into the bathroom, came out with the duffel and slid it under the bed.

EMS arrived a few minutes later. The paramedics connected an automatic defibrillator. After the second shock, Joy's heart began a normal rhythm. They started oxygen and connected an IV pushing in fluids. They rolled Joy onto a stretcher and wheeled her down the stairs into the ambulance.

Jake and I jumped into my truck and chased the ambulance into the city, across town to UTMB. We parked, caught the ambulance as the paramedics unloaded Joy, and followed behind until a nurse shuffled us out to the waiting room.

Jake took a seat at the end of a row along the back wall. He stared at the ER desk, not moving or speaking, another thousand-yard stare. I sat beside him saying nothing. His eyes were puffed and red, his cheeks flushed. He looked as if were about to bust open. But there were no tears. I thought about Jake back at the bird pond stomping that shirt into the ground and figured he was past crying. He leaned back in the chair staring at the ceiling. The words came out so softly I strained to understand him.

"If only I hadn't left her...gone to your place..."

I wanted to console him, tell him it wasn't his fault—that his mother was an adult, responsible for her actions. I wanted to say all that and more, but instead, in an attempt to temper his remorse, I went another route.

I leaned down to him and said, "Let me tell you a story, Jake."

When our eyes met, I continued as softly as I could, compelling him to focus his attention so that he could hear me.

"When I was about your age, I moved out with my mother to West Beach and built a bait shop. My grandfather had died and left her the land, but we had no income. She wanted to sell, but I begged her not to. Every morning I was out before dawn slopping bait shrimp to fishermen, so tired at night I fell asleep on the dock."

Jake said, "What happened to the bait shop?"

"I changed it when I got out of the Army."

"Oh, The Garhole," Jake said.

My story seemed to take his mind off his mom, so I continued. "When I turned sixteen, my mother ran off to New York City with a museum curator." I turned to catch Jake's eye.

He looked at me. "She left you by yourself?"

I nodded. "Two months after she moved to New York, she stepped off a curb and a taxi making the corner hit her. She died at the scene."

"You were alone," Jake said.

"Didn't like it," I said. "But I had to learn to live with it. And even with her leaving me, I still felt the guilt."

"Guilt?" Jake said. He blinked several times.

"Yes guilt," I said. "Do you know what that is?"

Jake shook his head.

"Guilt is the feeling you get when something goes wrong and you feel like it is your fault. Maybe something you did or said hurt someone. It weighs on you, drags you into a funk. I felt bad for a long time. I thought if only I would have stopped her from going, she'd still be alive. Maybe if I'd have begged her not to go."

I shifted a little in my seat. Let the words sink in.

"You think you could have stopped her?" he said.

I waited a beat and said, "No. I realized later I was just a kid, and she was going to do what she wanted to. Kids don't have control over what grownups do."

I sat quietly, letting the thought sink in.

The nurse at the ER station called out a name. A man and a woman in front of us went to the window. After the nurse spoke, the couple turned, despair lining their faces. They returned to their seats and waited.

I leaned back in the chair and closed my eyes to take the pressure off Jake. He shuffled in the seat.

"How did you get over it?" he asked.

I stayed relaxed, spoke with my eyes closed. "Took a long time. Had no one to talk with about it. Then a judge appointed, a lawyer, Harry Stein, as my guardian. Harry helped me understand it wasn't my fault. She was an adult, and I was a kid."

He straightened in the chair and said, "Do...do you think your mother loved you?"

"I don't know, Jake. She never told me she did. I know I needed her to love me. Later, when I was older I tried to remember moments—searched for signs. It used to bother me a lot, still does sometimes."

Jake lowered his head, eyes downcast. "Wasn't she supposed to?" he asked.

I nodded. "Things don't always work that way, Jake. The only thing I knew for sure was that Harry Stein cared about me and that was enough to get me through it. Harry made me see there were good people in the world. I look for people like that all the time, Jake. But it takes courage to trust."

After a long, anxious wait, a physician came out of the ER and motioned us to a small private room off the main area.

"She's stabilized," he said.

Jake sighed heavily, put his hand over his eyes and looked away.

The doctor motioned me aside. "Worst OD I've seen in a while. Lucky you were there."

I nodded.

"She needs to stay here through detox," he said. "It'll take several days."

I nodded again not knowing what to say. The doctor turned and strode out of the room.

A voice bellowed, "What the hell happened?"

Slim Green stood behind us, panting heavily, his face flaming red as though he'd run the 20 miles from Bay Harbor on foot. People in the E.R. stared at us. I raised my palms to quiet him.

"Overdose," I said.

He blew out a breath. "Damn," he said. Then he recovered and faced me. "What are you doing here?"

Jake stepped between us, defiant. "Parker saved her," he said. "Where were you?"

"At the store," Green said.

"Buying beer?"

Slim ignored Jake and said to me, "I'm here now. You can take off."

"No. Mr. Parker stays," Jake said. "And I'm gonna stay here with Mama."

Slim grabbed Jake's arm. "You'll go home with me and stay there," he said. "Your mama will be all right. She's done this before. I'll come back later and pick her up."

I broke in, "She's going to be here a few days. The doctor wants her to detox."

"Won't do no good," Green said. "She'll be right back on it."

Jake twisted away. I stepped in front of Green, pushed Jake behind me, and spoke softly trying to keep the situation as calm as possible.

"We'll stay here awhile," I said. "And then Jake will go home with me."

"No he won't," Slim growled. "I'll have the cops on your ass for kidnapping."

I moved to his face, and whispered, "And I'll have you arrested for that bag of rocks in your house."

People stared and the nurse behind the counter spoke into the phone. The standoff continued chests inches apart, puffed and ready. In the background, two security officers stepped off the elevator.

I pulled Jake aside, and whispered, "Does Slim know you weren't there last night?"

"Doubt it," Jake said. "I keep my bedroom locked. He probably thought I was in there if he thought about it at all. I'm sure he passed out in his bed with a beer in his hand like he does every night."

As the officers approached, Slim said, "You're going home with me Jake. We'll come back later and get your mama."

I started to object, but Jake put his hand up and said, "It'll be okay, Mr. Parker. Thanks for your help."

I didn't like it but decided this wasn't the time to challenge the old man. I left the hospital and stopped at a local dive a couple blocks from Seawall Boulevard. Somehow I just didn't feel like giving up the day yet. The bar inhabited the bottom floor of an old-corner grocery store long abandoned to the Walmart's and Kroger's of the world. The windows were covered and painted black. It was one of those places you would pass by swearing it was closed.

The inside was as dark as midnight except for a few beer signs on the walls and a small light over the cash register. The bartender, about sixty, thin with a day-old beard, a large bulbous nose and bags under his eyes, was too busy reading a newspaper to look up as I entered. There was no one else in the place, no music or sound of any kind. I took a stool at the far end of the bar, ordered a Shiner Bock and settled for a Budweiser. The bartender served me without comment and went back to his newspaper.

A roach scurried across the counter. The thing stopped midway and turned toward me; its antennae twitching as though it had noticed a presence and was checking out the threat level. For some reason, I raised my beer and toasted the pest. The roach twitched again and scurried away. I could have reached over and smashed the thing, but I didn't. I figured it wasn't any different than me. Just trying it's best to get through the day.

My mind floated to Jake, his mother, his grandfather, and their pitiful life at the margins of existence. And then I thought about my own, and my stomach turned at the comparison. What was the difference, really?

The bartender brought a bottle of some cheap brand of whisky from under the counter and refilled a small glass. He took a drink and went back to the paper.

The taste of malt and oak passed my tongue thinking about the half-full bottle of scotch under the counter at The Garhole. I decided to find a new bar before I weakened. I had come too far, tried too hard, to cave in now.

I needed someplace where people moved and talked, a place where I could witness life, maybe verify my own pulse. A new feeling for me, wanting that, and I didn't understand it.

I drove along the seawall to a restaurant with an outside deck that overlooked the Gulf. I ordered a beer and a hamburger and sat at a table by the edge where I could watch the beach. Couples strolled hand in hand along the top of the seawall. Children played in the sand. Around me, people laughed and ate and drank. The hamburger came, and I ordered another beer. And then several more.

A. Hardy Roper

Jake's circumstances had brought feelings I had pushed away most of my adult life. Emotions no one should have to endure, much less a child. Life was tough enough without having to suffer through the abandonment and rejection caused by those who were supposed to love and care for us. I knew every touch of loneliness and despair Jake was grieving with. I wanted to go back and rip him away from the burdens life had dumped upon him. I wanted to...but I didn't.

Chapter Eighteen

Luther Bourdain drove the entire Bolivar Peninsula under the speed limit. Unusual for Luther, but he didn't want to get stopped by a cop. Not the way he looked, all burned up, fried like a damn crawfish. And especially not with the .38 in the seat.

He was also on a raging high fueled by continuous joints consumed on the trip from Louisiana. His car reeked of burning pot, a sign any cop would notice. And paranoia had arrived, squeezing his conscience like a vise, demanding attention to his enemies who were coming in an ever-growing number.

Luther knew he had to quit toking soon. But the buzz was a double-edged sword—the risk of going to jail versus keeping the pain at bay. The tokes kept the needles from stabbing his arms and face and lessened the relentless throbbing.

He took one last drag, held it in briefly, exhaled and tossed the butt out the window. Don't drive too fast or too slow, he reminded himself. The cops look for that.

He drove past houses built on pilings, some of the homes so old and weather-beaten they reminded him of the Louisiana bayou country. He noticed that the beach ran the entire length of the peninsula, offering miles of playground for visiting families and the perfect spot for a little recreational drug use.

A. Hardy Roper

And when summer ended and winter arrived, what then, he wondered? Not as isolated as the Louisiana swamps, but still, during the entire drive, he'd not seen a single cop.

And away from the beach on the other side of the highway, he'd noticed large patches of undeveloped land and lonely roads meandering across the prairie to the Intracoastal Waterway. Lots of good areas to find a new hidey-hole for a meth lab.

Thirty minutes later, Luther eased the old Pontiac into the line for the Galveston Ferry. He counted the vehicles hoping to make the next boat. He wanted to keep the motor running and the A/C cooling the interior, but he was afraid the old heap would overheat. He shut the engine and unfolded his six-two body out of the seat careful not to hit his bandaged arm. A blast of hot mid-day air hit his face. He removed his cap, wiped moisture from his forehead and studied his reflection in the side window.

Even in the tinted window glass, his appearance seemed surreal. The redness in his scorched face had lightened some, but the color still contrasted greatly with the bleached skin on the top of his forehead and scalp. Like some damn albino, a ghost-like apparition stared back at him. Even the hairs in his nose were gone. He removed his wrap-a-round sunglasses for a closer look, and his eyes were instantly hit with the sun's glare. He reeled from the mistake and quickly replaced the glasses.

When the ferry began to load, Luther got into his car and eased forward with the line. The attendant guided the Pontiac onboard the ferry, motioning Luther to park and shut his engine.

Luther couldn't keep the engine on to run the air conditioning, and he sure couldn't open the windows. Not with all that pot smell in the car. Everyone on the ferry would be at his car looking for a toke. The fact that he almost giggled at his joke scared him. Best to slow down with the weed, he thought. The paranoia was bad enough; he couldn't afford the sillies too. He checked his stash, only one joint left.

He got out and walked to the stern. As the boat pulled away from the dock, he watched with awe the never diminishing line of vehicles moving into position for the next ferry—families returning home from the beach and cars crammed with lusty teenagers with too much money chasing the latest thrill. Luther smiled at the sight, a never-ending market for his goods.

Fifteen minutes later, Luther drove off the ferry and into the city of Galveston. He stopped at the first gas station and used the payphone to call Vinnie to let him know he'd arrived.

"Hello Luther," Vinnie said.

The menacing tone of Vinnie's voice sent a shiver across Luther's neck. "I'm in Galveston," he said.

"Just now getting there, Luther? You've wasted time somewhere. What you been doing?"

Luther had squandered valuable time at Waylon Fontenot's meth factory. Time he could have used searching for the bitch, Joy. But the effort hadn't been a total loss. He'd learned a valuable trade secret: how to make shake and bake meth.

"Needed some sleep that's all," Luther said.

"Clock is ticking, Luther. You found our goods yet?"

"Chill," Luther answered. "I'll be on time."

"You'd better be, Luther. And don't forget to call me again when you've got our package."

Luther hung up the phone visualizing Vinnie standing over him back at his house, threatening, ordering. He touched his cheek remembering the pain as Vinnie's hand smashed his seared face. He winched at the thought. Then be berated himself for being such a pussy. He'd had enough of the Calzone brothers pushing him around. He needed to steel himself, be a man. Who did those guineas think they were, coming down to his home turf, giving him orders? He was the lord of Lafourche Parish. It was decision time, and Luther went with opportunity. No way he was going to return the stolen meth. Screw those bastards.

Luther thought about Bolivar Peninsula, the vast beaches filled with tourists and the crowded ferry line. It was the perfect place to start fresh. He began to formulate a plan. Recovering the Royal Blue from Joy would give him enough supply to last until he could set up a shake and bake operation on the peninsula. He was through with cooking. Luther calculated he was 400 miles, six hours driving time from the Calzone brothers. They'd never find him hidden in some small shack on the Bolivar prairie.

And there was also Galveston. He wouldn't base his operation on the island, because the brothers' knew he was there. But it was an additional market if he needed it.

Luther had only been to the tourist mecca once before when, in a weak moment, he'd brought Joy home for her clothes. He was stoned the entire time and remembered little of the trip.

He decided to check out what the city had to offer a businessman of his prowess. He passed by the hospital and cut through a residential area filled with century-old Victorian homes nestled among spreading oaks and magnolia trees. He turned onto Broadway Boulevard passing grand churches and huge mansions. The esplanade was filled with tall palm trees, century-old oaks and lush-green oleander bushes alive with white-and-red flowers.

The scene reminded him of the Garden District in New Orleans, all pretty and nice. But like New Orleans, Luther knew there had to be a section where the down-and-out folks lived. He passed 25th Street and spotted a corner convenience store with bars on the windows and several black teenagers loitering in front. He turned at the corner and found what he was looking for, block- after-block of tenement buildings, shuttered businesses and battered houses.

Luther knew ghettos existed in every city. The poor had to live somewhere. Except they didn't live; they just existed. It was the land of the broken, where knots of unemployed men gathered on street corners or back alleys and working girls walked the streets eyeing passing cars. All living on the margin.

Where do-gooders saw the failure of society, Luther viewed opportunity. Where politicians counted the unemployed, Luther tallied prospects. Opportunity, after all, was in the eyes of the beholder.

Luther watched a middle-aged white man, dressed in a suit and tie, stop his Lexis at the corner. A black girl approached out of the shadows, got into the car and the man drove off. Two white teenagers in a pick-up stopped and exchanged folded bills for a brown-paper sack. Business was brisk, he observed.

Some of the two-story houses were shuttered at the top as though only the first floor was inhabited. The old houses seemed empty, but Luther knew better. Inside the lifeless relics, tired grandmothers watched over fatherless babies. They bought food at corner stores where proprietors ripped them off because they lacked transportation to supermarkets. Some of the mothers were out working minimum-pay jobs as care givers or housekeepers. Others were on the streets desperately trying to earn enough to satisfy their pimps and get another spoonful of heroin or crack.

Perfect, Luther thought. He felt his pulse quicken at the sights. Business unlimited. Entrepreneurship was the *American Way,* and Luther was an equal opportunity supplier.

Now, he wished he hadn't stopped and called Vinnie. If he planned to set up shop across Galveston Bay on Bolivar,

A. Hardy Roper

letting the Calzone brothers know he had arrived in Galveston was a mistake. Still, he thought, maybe the call would buy him time, smooth their feathers a bit. They would be pleased he was following instructions.

He crossed Broadway on 39st Street and followed the line of traffic to the beach. The neighborhoods improved appreciably as he neared the seawall, the older homes newly renovated, painted and patched.

He turned right on Seawall Boulevard toward West Beach. Out in the water, surfers plied the waves. Between the kids on the beach and the hopeless ones in the shadows, wonders never ceased. Luther smiled. It was definitely time to come out of the swamp. He continued along the boulevard to the down ramp heading west toward the end of the island. First things first, he thought. He needed to pay Joy a visit. She would be glad to see him—like how a mouse feels when a cat arrives.

Chapter Nineteen

Clementine opened her eyes realizing she'd slept through the wake-up call. She glanced at the clock on the table by the bed. Somewhere in the fuzziness of her mind, she remembered hearing a faint buzzing sound but had failed to react.

Her head felt as though someone was inside pounding with a sledgehammer attempting to break out. And she just knew the devil had sneaked into her room overnight and shoveled a pint of sand into her mouth. She struggled to the side of the bed, got her feet on the floor and hoisted herself to a sitting position. The room spun.

She was aggravated at herself for missing the little pre-hangover trick of an aspirin and glass of water at bedtime. Faint glimpses of last night crept into her aching head, a drink in the bar before dinner, a salesman dude with a red nose and loosened tie, a combo playing, a shove to a drunk at her door trying to get into her room. And the worst of it...no dinner, no stuffed shrimp or broiled red snapper. Nothing.

An hour later after a hot shower and extra-large breakfast, Clementine parked in the UTMB garage and rode the elevator to the fourth floor. She entered the Human Resources department and noted the same Hispanic woman she'd seen yesterday staffing the receptionist counter inside.

"May I help you?" the woman said in perfect English.
"Yes, I am hoping you can."
"I will certainly try, Miss...?"

"Garza," Clementine said, beginning her carefully orchestrated act. "That is my married name. My father's name is Henry Green. He was employed here some years ago."

Clementine trembled slightly. She blotted her moistened eye with her hand. "Sorry," she said. "It's just that... it's the stroke, you see...he is unable to care for himself."

"Oh, I am sorry," the woman said.

"Thank you," Clementine replied. "I am just so bewildered by all the responsibility. It's his social security. Something about the eligibility, the amount of time he worked..." Clementine manufactured a tear.

The receptionist handed her a box of tissues. Clementine removed a fresh one and dabbed her eye again. She turned her head to the side as though trying to regain her composure. "I am so embarrassed," she said.

"Please, don't be," the woman said.

"I just thought if you could check his records, I could get this straightened out. Social Security is his only income."

"I am so sorry," the woman said. "Personnel records are confidential. Do you have a power of attorney?"

"Father is in a coma," Clementine said. "I'll have to go through the courts. It could take weeks and...there is no money. The hospital bills, doctors...."

The woman remained silent.

"Well, never mind," Clementine said. She turned to go.

"Wait," the woman said. She rose, went into another room, and came back with a file. She opened it in front of Clementine. "Here we are," she said. "Henry Green. I have his employment records, probably everything you need."

Clementine glanced at Green's address in the folder.

"What if I gave you a letter attesting his employment?"

"Yes, thank you," Clementine said.

She left hoping Green's address hadn't changed.

Chapter Twenty

I arrived back at the bar with a slight buzz. Joe was inside listening to a portable radio he'd brought in from his mobile home. He saw me and turned the radio off.

"Five more minutes and I'd have gotten all the news," he said.

Joe knew how I felt about radio and television, good for nothing but numbing the mind. I owned a weather radio to keep up with storms, and reluctantly, a telephone—the telephone only so customers could call for fishing reports. I popped two beers out of the cooler and joined Joe at the table. He appeared a little forlorn.

"Surprised to see you back," I said.

Joe frowned. "Busted out during the shift change."

"Stupid thing to do."

"They wanted to put a bolt in my leg with threads on the end—all to screw a new leg onto. And if the bolt don't attach to the bone like it's supposed to, it's all for nothing. And you call getting out of there stupid?"

"You knew that before you went."

"Not about the procedure taking six months with a big chance of infection, maybe losing what's left of my legs. Screw it," he said.

Joe was almost screaming now. I got back into his face.

"Screw it is right," I said. "You screwed it with the VA. You bust out of the hospital like that, they'll never let you back in."

A. Hardy Roper

He waved his hand dismissing the thought. We were quiet for a moment, and then Joe said, "You had your share of grief, Parker. All those days in VA hospitals, doctors trying to figure out what was wrong with you. How'd you feel about that?"

"How do you think," I said.

I'd spent years battling the VA over my symptoms, a great deal of that time feeling angry and sorry for myself just like Joe was doing now.

I didn't want to fight with Joe anymore. He had too much anger bottled up from the war wrecking his dreams of a normal life. And for what—politics? Picking sides in a tribal war that had been going on for thousands of years. My team had interrogated hundreds of prisoners after the war. The most significant thing we learned was the individual's order of priority: family, tribe, religion. Country was never mentioned. It meant little or nothing. Most of them were unaware that the countries of the Middle East had been manufactured by European interests during the peace process following WWI. The Ottoman Empire, which had ruled the area for hundreds of years, was broken up. The French were given a mandate in Syria and Lebanon, while the British were given control over what would become Iraq, Jordan, Saudi Arabia and Palestine. It wasn't only the local inhabitants who were mystified. Our own soldiers didn't know the history, or care. They went because they were ordered there. And they returned battered.

Joe and I sat in silence, two lonely men at the end of the island, at the end of the world, each battling his own demons, struggling to make sense of the past. Maybe the reason I'd asked Joe to move to The Garhole was not for him, but for me.

I rose and moved to the opening I had cut in the wall. Past the parking lot and the field of fading summer flowers, I could see the distant image of the bridge over San Luis Pass.

Saving Jake

My grandfather had told me stories about West Beach before they built the bridge and before the road extended to the end of the island. Fishermen used to pack bait shrimp in wet sawdust to keep them alive. With no road, they'd drive the beach to the pass and camp in shacks with Coleman lanterns for light, fighting off mosquitoes as big as turkeys. But the air was fresh and clean and smelled of salt, the water clear to the grassy bottoms, teeming with redfish, trout and flounder.

I have fond memories of the old man, eyes alive with hope, his face crinkled and worn, leathered skin the color of copper. Many times, we stood on the berm by the bird pond gazing out across the marsh, his arm around my shoulder. When he died the good memories stopped, replaced by haunting feelings of desertion and loneliness, made worse by my mother leaving me for New York, never to see her again. An army psychiatrist once told me the only way I could achieve peace was to forgive my mother. Something easier said than done.

I thought about Jake and his memories—a mean old drunk for a grandfather and a mother strung out on meth. Not pretty images to recall about one's childhood. Thoughts like those made me want to mind my own business, made me wish I had ignored both of them. Maybe bought Jake and his mother a meal and left them in that Lake Charles café.

And then, as though he was reading my mind, Joe asked about Jake. I came back to the table and related the day's events—Joy's overdose and her trip to the hospital.

"Rotten way for a kid to live," Joe said. "What are you going to do about it?"

"About what?"

"Jake."

I hesitated a beat, exhaled a long breath. "I don't know. Nothing I can do, really."

A. Hardy Roper

Joe started up again, "You got yourself involved. You have no choice. You have to do something."

"His grandpa can take care of him."

"Not with a doping mother around."

I gave Joe a hard stare. "Look," I said. "My job is running this bar, making a living and minding my own business. And that's what I intend to do. If you're so fired up, do something yourself, but leave me alone about it."

"I don't know what your problem is," he said. "But this ain't the real you. You're not that cold. I know or you wouldn't have invited me here. So admit it."

I headed for the cooler and popped another beer. Jake rolled behind me continuing his rant.

"Didn't you give Jake a job checking the crab traps? What are you going to do about that...fire him? You can't let that boy live in that hellhole. It's not right."

I leaned against the sink and toasted the skeleton hanging over the bar, wondering if the gar had died on its own terms or if nature had stepped in. Maybe the poor creature had just reached the end of its time, witnessed all of life it wanted to and floated into that marsh with the tide.

"Call Harry?" Joe said. "He'll know what to do. Tell him Jake can live in my spare bedroom. He'll have a job, and we'll make sure he goes to school."

Joe's continual carping had hit my limit. "That's enough," I screamed.

I stepped out the back door trying to calm my emotions. But it was no use. I knew what I had to do. I stepped inside, grabbed the phone off the hook and dialed Harry's number. Harold Stein, lawyer extraordinaire, and my oldest friend. At seventy-seven, Harry enjoyed the semi-retired life, doing pro-bono divorces and wills for Galveston cops. Mr. Resource, I called him. Harry had more contacts than a Washington lobbyist.

Saving Jake

"Harry's still putting in fifty-hour weeks," I said as the phone buzzed in my ear. "Probably not even home."

He answered on the third ring. I pictured Harry perfectly coiffured as usual, pressed shirt and matching tie, goatee and mustache trimmed, and his head of full white hair combed straight back.

"Need your help," I said.

"Of course, you called didn't you?"

"And what does that mean?"

"Come on, Parker. You know you only call me when you need something. What trouble are you in now?"

Harry's tone was friendly, with a slight undercurrent of sarcasm. He was right, of course. It did seem I only called to ask his help. I tucked the thought away.

"It's not me," I said, and went on to explain about Jake and his mother.

"Remind you of anyone?" Harry asked.

"Why do you think I called you?"

"We'd have to get Child Protective Services involved. Are you willing to take the boy in?"

I hesitated knowing this was my last chance to beg off. What would I do with a 14-year-old kid? There were already two of us handicapped souls at The Garhole. I wasn't sure the gar head could handle another one.

Joe, hearing the conversation, mouthed, "Answer him. Tell him yes."

"How does it work?" I asked.

"First thing, CPS sends out an investigator. Probably take the child into custody."

"To where?"

"One of several emergency facilities in the county."

"How long?"

"Could be weeks, even months. The boy and his mother will each have an attorney assigned by the Court, all courtesy of your tax dollars. The mother will have to fight the drug charges, while at the same time trying to keep custody of her kid. Unless of course, she volunteers to relinquish her parental rights."

"She can do that?" I said

"Absolutely," Harry responded. "Happens all the time. But either way, CPS will complete a study and make a recommendation. And if the mother doesn't want to give the boy up, and CPS decides to go for termination, a judge will make the final call. If CPS wins, that's where you'll come in asking for custody as a foster parent. And with me representing you in court, there's a good chance you'll get it."

"Holy Mackerel," I mumbled. "Things have changed since you took me in at 16."

"More drugs on the street, more kids in trouble," he said. "CPS is totally overloaded. More screwed up parents than you can imagine."

Joe listened beside me, edging me on. The whole scheme was more than I'd bargained for.

"I don't know..."

"Decide, Parker. I have a board meeting of the Galveston Historical Society here tonight, and I'm making French onion soup."

"What's the first step?"

"Chopping the onions."

"No, I mean about Jake."

"I'll come out to The Garhole tomorrow. We'll make a plan."

"Jake is supposed to be here. It's his birthday. He may or may not show depending on what happens with his mom tonight."

"I'd like to meet him," Harry said. "The kid's carrying a load. What about his father? How does he play into the scenario?"

I thought about it and said, "Jake's mother never mentioned his father—and neither has Jake."

"It just gets sadder doesn't it?" Harry said. There was silence for a beat, and then he added, "I'll make some of my special cupcakes from scratch just in case he shows. But I have to warn you, Parker. My legal expertise doesn't come cheap. What's for lunch?"

"Gumbo"

"What kind?"

"Crab."

"Crab gumbo, huh? That'll do for a retainer."

A. Hardy Roper

Chapter Twenty-One

The Cadillac Deville crunched slowly over the gravel road. The last thing Tomas Calzone wanted was to flip a rock into his new car. He hadn't wanted to take the Deville at all but Vinnie's Lincoln was in the shop for a recall. Tomas had also wanted to return to New Orleans and change clothes instead of driving six hours in the same black pants and silk shirt. But time was short.

He sat hunched over the steering wheel, the seat pulled back to accommodate his bulging stomach, the fifty-peso coin dangled loosely outside his shirt, banging against the steering wheel each time he touched the brakes.

"This better be the right road," he said growling, not bothering to look at his brother.

Vinnie sat slouched in the passenger seat, eyes scrunched ahead. His muscled frame sank the leather seat to its springs. He ran his hand over his hair and moved his finger and thumb over his beard.

"We turned where he said, just past that big 'S' turn behind us," Vinnie answered. "Look for two large bushes on either side of the entrance."

The road wound past a stand of salt cedars and an old corral. A long retired windmill sat next to the corral, its blades rusting in the salt air. Around the next turn, a line of 10 foot high oleander bushes, thick and green and loaded with pink-and-white flowers, protected the property behind it from view.

"That's it," Vinnie yelled.

Tomas slammed the brakes, cutting the Cadillac's wheels toward the culvert. "Codger was right," he said. "Those bushes are so thick you can't see the driveway. Get out and push them back."

Vinnie, dressed in the same fine purple knit, matching pants, and mauve suede shoes he'd worn this morning, said, "No way. I ain't gonna mess up my clothes just to keep scratches off your new cock wagon."

Tomas frowned and drove through the opening. "You lazy dick," he said. "You gonna have my ride detailed when we get home, and you'd better hope them scratches come out."

Tomas inched along the sand lane across a weed-infested field to the top of a small knoll. The road dropped through a small depression filled with scrub oaks before rising again to another knoll. Tomas drove at idle speed, hoping to keep the sand off his car. At the top of the second knoll, a tall, pencil-thin, fifty-something man stood in front of an old doublewide waving the Cadillac on.

"Codger Moss," Tomas said. "Look at that old son of a bitch. How did you ever get a cousin like that?"

"He ain't old, and he ain't my cousin. He's your cousin," Vinnie said. "The Moss folks came from your old man's side of the family, not mine. Your daddy's sister got knocked up by a Moss."

"The whole family was a bunch of dopers," Tomas said. He grimaced and blew out a big breath. When he got to the top of the rise, he eased the Cadillac next to the doublewide and parked.

Codger stood by the wooden steps of the mobile home smoking a joint. He wore flip-flops, shorts and no shirt. Long strands of stringy hair the color of an old grandma's were pushed back and tied into a ponytail. The grey continued through his full beard and heavy mustache that curled down around the outside of his mouth.

"About time you a-holes showed," Codger said, grinning. There was a hole in Codger's mouth where his two central incisors should have been. His caramel-colored skin was like alligator hide, rough and wrinkled. At six five, his thin body towered over the Calzone brothers, but he always stood hunched over as if embarrassed about his height.

Vinnie got out and looked Codger up and down. "Jesus, Codger," he chided. "How can you even stand? Your ribs are sticking out."

"I can't gain no weight," Codger said. "Eat all I want."

"Yeah," Vinnie said. "Except there ain't no calories in muff burgers."

Codger chortled loudly, slapping his thigh.

Tomas remained in the car until the dust settled. He got out, immediately brushed something off his pants and pushed past Codger to the door. "Did you find her?" he said.

Codger trailed behind. "Checked this morning. Green still lives there. His car was in the driveway."

"Yeah, but was the bitch there?"

"Where else would she be?"

"You don't know for sure, do you?" Tomas asked, his patience growing thin.

"What'd you want me to do, go up and knock on the friggin' door? Scare her off for good."

Vinnie and Codger followed Tomas into the mobile home. The heat inside the trailer hit Tomas in the face like an iron-ore furnace. He sucked in a big breath fighting for air.

He whirled back to Codger. "Jesus H," he screamed. "Turn on the A/C. I can't breathe." He backtracked to the door and took in several gasps of air.

Codger brought a bottle of Jack Daniels and three glasses to the table. He set the glasses on the table and pulled up a chair.

"Broke two days ago," Codger said. "Dude's supposed to be out this afternoon to fix it."

A. Hardy Roper

"He'd better be," Thomas said. "It's a freaking oven in here."

Tomas slowed his breathing and joined Vinnie and Codger at the table. Codger poured the whisky. Tomas removed a cushion from the couch beside the table and used it to wipe the dust off his shoes. He tried to toss the cushion back on the couch, but it missed and fell on the floor. He let it lay there.

Codger pointed to Tomas' shoes. "Alligator, huh? Business must be good."

Tomas ignored Codger's remark. He studied the glasses and noticed a film of some kind around the edges. He glanced at a pile of dirty dishes on the counter and a plate of congealed beans beside the dishes.

"You got a go cup?" he said.

"Picky, picky," Codger said. He found three plastic cups and poured the whisky from the glasses to the cups.

"How'd you get a name like Codger anyway?" Vinnie asked. "Couldn't been born with it."

"Happened a long time ago. One of the girls in my stable said I reminded her of an old codger she used to trick. I kinda liked it, let it stay."

"What's your real name?"

"Albert."

"Albert?" Vinnie said, smirking. "No wonder you changed it."

Codger looked at Tomas. "Man I can't believe that dumb bitch stole your goods. Guess she ain't changed a bit. Stupid as always. But I'll tell you that Joy was one fine piece of ass. Shoulda never sent her to New Orleans."

"You got your cut," Tomas said. He finished the whisky and poured another glass.

"Off of one weekend in New Orleans? That was nothing. I was running her good here, making several bills a week. You guys owe me for my losses."

Tomas and Vinnie glanced at each other.

"We don't owe you shit," Vinnie said. "Figure she left you because of that nickel dick you carry in your pants. Maybe Luther was a real man."

Vinnie poured another drink.

"I get her back when this is over...right?" Codger said.

"Sure," Vinnie said, winking at Tomas. "You can have her."

Call that A/C man again, or I'm gonna have to go to a motel," Tomas squawked again.

"If we're here long enough to spend the night, we got more problems than the heat," Vinnie said.

"Not talking about spending the night," Tomas said, wiping sweat off his brow. "Just need a break."

Tomas got up and drank some water; something he rarely did.

"Getting a motel is a dumb-ass thing to do," Vinnie said. "Never know what's gonna happen. Be best if nobody knows we're in town. If you'd lost some of that fat off your ass like I told you to, you wouldn't be so miserable."

"Screw you," Tomas scowled.

The repair man won't be long," Codger said. "He's a customer of mine, girls and weed. I promised him a freebie if he hurried his ass."

A loud squawk shrieked across the room followed by static and a man's voice.

"Unit 69 to central."

Another voice. "Go ahead 69."

"In pursuit. Black ford convertible, two known occupants, now turning on 61st toward Broadway"

"You have a police scanner?" cried Vinnie.

A. Hardy Roper

Codger brought the radio to the table. "My new toy," he said. "Cops won't be sneaking up on my ass."

"Shut up and listen," Vinnie growled.

The radio blared again. "Central to Unit 69. Causeway is secure. Block a return on 61st."

"The numb nuts shoulda known better than head for the causeway," Codger shouted. "First thing that gets locked down. Everybody knows you can't out-run cops with a radio."

"Unit 69 to Central. That's affirmative...wait, the runner just hit the overpass support at 61st and Broadway. Oh, God, car's on fire. No one out."

"Turn that thing off," Tomas yelled. "I gotta think."

He glanced at the two-carat diamond solitaire on his finger, wishing he were standing on the balcony of his New Orleans penthouse watching the boats on the river. He was ready to leave before he got here. He shouldn't even have come. He was the brains of the outfit after all. Vinnie was the leg man. The sooner they recovered the meth, the sooner he could get back to his playground.

"Are we going in right away?" Codger asked, grinning.

"No sense takin' the risk," Tomas said. "Let Luther do the work. We're just here for insurance."

"Yeah, but what if he don't call," Codger said.

"He knows what will happen if he don't," Tomas said. "He'll wish that meth explosion woulda killed him."

Chapter Twenty-Two

Somewhere in the fog of several joints, Luther remembered the chain-link fence and the old boat in the yard. He pictured the upper deck connected to the front door and Green's station wagon parked by the gate. But he couldn't remember the name of the subdivision, nor its exact location. Joy said it was one of the older ones, but he just couldn't recall the name. He remembered the drive out to the house had taken 30 minutes from town. And he remembered the development was smaller than most of the ones they'd passed.

He drove past Pirates Beach and Jamaica Beach, each one containing hundreds of houses stretching across the island from the Gulf to West Bay, all built twenty feet off the ground on pilings. It was as though the residents expected a hurricane to arrive any minute and sweep everything into the Gulf of Mexico. Luther remembered Joy talking about how low the island was and how the last hurricane had devastated the area.

Just past Jamaica Beach, Luther stopped at a small grocery store to gas the Pontiac. The sign on the front said "Reds." He pulled in close to a pump and went inside to pay cash. A line of customers, dressed in shorts and flip-flops, waited at the register, holding beer and soft drinks. Luther slipped two twenties across the counter and pointed at his car outside.

Halfway through filling the tank, an old station wagon stopped at the pump ahead of him but on the other side of the aisle. Luther studied the rear window. The driver had white hair; the passenger wore a baseball cap. The passenger seemed smaller—like a woman or a child—or maybe he was just slumped in the seat. Baseball Cap stayed in the truck, but White Hair got out. He had a huge belly and a red face.

The man seemed distracted, frustrated. He never looked across the pump isle to where Luther stood. He fumbled some cash out of his pocket and went inside to pay.

Luther had only seen Slim Green once before, but there was no doubt it was him. It was good to know the old man was still alive and kicking. With Green still around, Luther was pretty sure Joy would have come home to papa. Luther wanted to ease past the car and check out the passenger but decided to wait. Better to follow.

He topped off the Pontiac's tank and drove to the front of the store and waited. He watched Green fill his tank and drive out onto the highway headed west toward the end of the island.

Good, Luther thought. Green wasn't driving back toward town. He's probably going home. Luther followed several vehicles behind but close enough to see the station wagon turn off the highway and then into a subdivision. The sign at the entrance read "Bay Harbor."

Luther drove parallel of Green, one street over. He caught glimpses of the station wagon between houses as Green rambled down the street. Luther turned at the end of the block and stopped at the corner. He watched the old man get out and open the gate. As soon as Ball Cap got out, Luther recognized him immediately. It was Jake.

A German shepherd bolted around the house and greeted Green, jumping and barking. Green took something from a paper bag and fed the dog. Then Green and Jake climbed the stairs to the deck and went inside the house.

Luther scanned a quick 360 view of the surroundings. Most of the houses in the area were shuttered. Probably weekenders, he thought. He hadn't seen another car driving anywhere in the subdivision. He decided to wait, see what happened next.

He leaned back in the seat and felt his head clearing from the marijuana, the pain returning, growing into those stinging needles again. "Damn it all," he cried and lit his last joint. He held the smoke in for a moment and blew it out, hoping the buzz would hit quickly.

He considered his options. The Calzone brothers had given him 24 hours to recover the goods and return to Louisiana. Except now, Luther had decided he wasn't going back. He was also supposed to call Vinnie again when he had the meth. But what could Vinnie do if he didn't call? The brothers were six hours away in Louisiana. He had plenty of time to grab the goods, take care of Joy and find a hide out. One, two, three—nothing to it, he thought.

Luther focused on the house. He could go in now and get it over with, but he wasn't sure Joy was there. And if she wasn't home, the meth probably wasn't there either.

He tried to put himself in Joy's mind, think like she would think. Or was she too wired to think? Maybe, he thought. But even wasted, she would need money. No doubt about that. But she also needed the meth. And with her habit, the meth would win out. She sure wasn't going to sell it all. There was enough in that duffel to last one person a long time. Still, she needed money. But she hadn't had time to find buyers yet. The duffel should be full except for what she'd used.

He wondered if Joy's mind was so totally cranked up that she thought she was safe in Galveston. She had to know he would come after her. And she had to know he'd figure out where the old man lived. So if Joy had any brain cells left, if they weren't all fried like crisp bacon, she knew she would have to run again, and soon. Maybe she already had. But the kid was still there, Luther mused. Maybe she'd left Jake as a decoy. Would she leave Jake? Maybe. Meth could do that to a person.

Luther smiled, thinking about the adrenalin rush he'd gotten each time he'd tormented Jake. A burn here, a burn there, the acrid scent of smoldering flesh. Jake's screams. Joy so desperate for a hit, she'd begged him to hurt Jake. Incredible power, Luther thought. A need so controlling, a woman would forsake her child.

Luther shuffled all the scenarios through his mind. In the end, he decided to wait, see what happened at the house. If Joy was in the house, he hoped she'd come out and show herself. He didn't want to approach the house and tip his hand, not yet. He wasn't afraid of the old man and the boy; the .38 would handle them. He checked the load again. Full. He positioned the extra box of ammo on the seat beside him.

Joy was the haggis bag of bitches, but the sex was incredible. She knew more things to do to him than the rest of the working girls put together. The bitch was a real pro. She used every orifice of his body, and hers. Holy crap, could the woman get him off.

Luther sucked in another lungful of smoke and held it. His throat stung. He blew the smoke out, and his throat hurt more. He continued to watch the house but nothing happened, no movement of any kind, not even the dog.

His mind drifted to the first time he'd met the Calzone brothers. They had appeared at his cabin wanting a special load of meth for a big computer convention in New Orleans. Luther was more than happy to oblige.

The brothers had a couple of local girls working the convention, but they needed more talent. One of the girls was from Galveston and knew Joy. So the brothers paid for Joy's bus ticket, and she came over for the convention. An afternoon with Joy was Luther's reward for his quick delivery with the meth. That's how it all started. Joy had smoked grass and snorted cocaine, but she'd never used meth. One hit from Luther's extra stash, and he owned her. She left the convention early with Luther and never looked back. A few days later, Jake arrived on a bus. Luther was incensed. Joy had never told him about the boy. He beat both of them. Joy threatened to leave, but she was hooked.

    Luther shook the thoughts away. He smoked the joint so close to the end, he couldn't hold it. He wished he'd brought a clip and more tokes. He tossed the butt out the window. He checked the house again. No change. He began to fidget, needed to get out and move around, stretch his legs. His fingers twitched; he couldn't still them.

    The pain in his throat was getting worse. He needed a beer, something to smooth the tingling. He remembered the store along the highway. Luther cranked the truck and did a U-turn in the street and drove back to the entrance.

    He stopped at the highway, looked both ways and turned toward the convenience store. As he accelerated, a hot-looking thirties something woman with short-blond hair and dark glasses, driving a Mustang convertible with the top down passed him going in the opposite direction. He watched in his rearview mirror as the Mustang slowed and turned into Bay Harbor.

A. Hardy Roper

Chapter Twenty-Three

Clementine checked the address she'd hustled from the woman at UTMB and matched it to the numbers on the mailbox. She parked the Mustang in the driveway next to an old station wagon. She toggled a switch on the dashboard and waited while the top rose out of the boot and closed down onto the front windshield. She pulled the roof tight and latched both sides.

Clementine had always wanted a convertible. There was something inherently sexy about the idea of dark glasses and windblown hair. But after checking her face in the mirror, she realized her makeup looked like butter melting in a microwave. She blotted her face with a tissue, fluffed her hair, applied fresh lip-gloss and forced a smile.

She scanned the rusted fence, the old boat and trailer, and the pile of driftwood in the yard. Then she focused on the upper deck, the closed front door and the shuttered windows. She listened for the hum of an air conditioner but heard nothing. Not even the sound of a blowing breeze disturbed the silence.

She stepped out of the car and eased to the gate. A large dog broke from around the house barking, teeth bared. The dog raced to the fence and jumped at the gate. Clementine reached for the baton tucked inside her jacket. She flicked her wrist and opened the baton to its full length. Buster leaped against the gate, growling. Clementine held the extended baton to the side and approached the fence. She began a monologue in a soft voice, telling the big German shepherd how she loved dogs and how good a friend she could be. This went on for several minutes until Buster raised his front legs to the fence and yawned. Clementine reached her hand over the fence and rubbed the top of the dog's head.

She collapsed the baton and considered putting it back in the car. She wanted a free flow of information and knew seeing a weapon might make her quarry nervous. Then she looked at the house and considered the shuttered windows. Something about the scene made her feel uncomfortable. She decided to be safe and holstered the baton inside her jacket, opened the gate and stepped inside the yard.

The front door of the house opened and an old white-haired man with a full beard appeared on the porch. Suspenders looped over his shoulders, down his protruding belly and connected to his ragged jeans. The man steadied himself on the railing and shouted.

"What do you want?"

Clementine rubbed Buster's head and pulled on his ears. She shouted back, "I'm here to talk to you."

"What about?"

This had to be Henry Green, Clementine thought. The address was correct and the age of the man worked. She walked toward the stairs. Buster followed, nudging her hand with his nose.

Green moved toward the top of the stairs and yelled again, "I said, what is this about?"

Clementine put a foot on the bottom step. She looked up and spoke in the same voice she'd used on the dog.

"It's about money, Mr. Green. Lots of money."

They sat at a table on the deck, a sun umbrella deflecting the afternoon rays. Slim held Clementine's business card at arm's length squinting at the type.

"I can't tell you my client's name," Clementine said. "It wouldn't be kosher. Certain amount of privacy in my business. Like lawyers."

Slim lay the card on the table in front of him. "Yeah," he said. "And I can't tell you nothing either. Cause I don't know nothing that could be any of your damn business."

Clementine continued pulling Buster's ears as he lay beside her. Green looked off toward the Gulf. She set her gaze on him and waited. After a moment, she said, "About 15 years ago, a man named Morgan Stanford attended UTMB Medical School and—"

Green's sudden movement stopped Clementine in mid-sentence. He grabbed the business card as he stood and sailed it back in front of Clementine.

"You mentioned money. What money?" Green said. "Where you going with this?"

Clementine noted the sudden rush of color in Green's face. She needed to say something before the old goat stroked out. She put her hands up, palms out.

"Please calm yourself, Mr. Green. I'll get to that."

Green turned back toward the Gulf. A southerly breeze appeared, sending momentary relief from the heat. Clementine moved a lock of hair back in place. She removed a tissue from her pocket and blotted moisture from her forehead.

"Do you recognize the name?" Clementine said to Green's back.

He turned and glared down at her. She searched Green's eyes looking for a flicker of acknowledgement. His poker stare revealed nothing.

"Why should I?" he said.

"You worked at UTMB during that time."

"Yeah, me and several thousand others. That's a long shot, don't you think?"

"Morgan had a girlfriend at the time. Her name was—"

The front door opened and Jake stood at the entrance looking out. "Hospital called, she's awake," he said.

Green rose. "You can go now," he said to Clementine. He strode across the deck, pushed Jake into the house and slammed the door behind him.

Clementine backed the Mustang out and drove toward the highway. She circled the block and picked a spot at the corner intersection with a good view to the house. She parked and popped a pink Vogue out of the cigarette pack and lit up.

She ran the scene through her mind. If the boy was 15, he was small for his age. Was it possible? The boy had said, "She's awake." Who was she? Green's wife? Or better yet...the boy's mother. Could be, she thought. Just could be.

Green came out of the house with a handful of clothes draped over his arm, the boy following behind. Green turned, yelling something, pointing to the door. The boy turned and went back inside. Green got into the old station wagon and drove away. Clementine decided not to follow. The boy was still in the house. If Green were going after the woman, he'd probably bring her back here.

Things were looking up, Clementine decided. She needed to check in with Stanford, bring him current, see how the old man's hammer was hanging. See if he'd reconsidered. She hadn't planned on spending the night in Galveston and the extra cost grated on her.

Best to leave here, she thought. A strange car parked for a long time might entice a concerned neighbor to call the police. She dropped the pink cigarette butt out the window but realized it was still lit. She opened the door and smashed the butt with her heel. Then she noticed the remains of a marijuana butt on the pavement. Clementine studied the joint. "Kids," she said softly.

Saving Jake

She studied the butt again trying to decide if there was enough left to smoke. She hadn't enjoyed a toke since her college days. She set the joint on the seat and drove across the highway to the beach. While the telephone buzzed, she picked up the joint, decided it was too far gone and tossed it out the window.

"Reginald J. Stanford, please."

The woman with the New England twang, curt and proper, replied, "Mr. Stanford is out, but I expect him shortly. May I ask who is calling?"

Clementine ended the call abruptly without comment, hoping the woman didn't remember her voice. She knew the old geezer wouldn't call back so there was no sense in leaving her name. She'd have to catch him in. She leaned back against the seat. There was nothing to do now but wait for Stanford to return and for Green to come back to his house with the mystery woman.

She decided she liked Galveston—the quaint Victorian homes, the hustle and bustle of the seawall area and the contrasting quiet of West Beach. She closed her eyes and allowed the sounds and smell of the surf to float through her consciousness. She took in the scent of salt air and the sounds of the shorebirds chirping and beeping as they worked their way along the sand.

She got out of the car to take a short stroll on the beach but noticed the rear tire seemed low. She put her ear to the tire and heard air escaping. Just great, she thought. A lonely beach and the sun sinking in the sky. What next? She opened the trunk and unhooked the tire jack from the side panel. She managed to pry off the hubcap, but when she fitted the wrench on a lug nut and heaved, nothing happened. The nut wouldn't budge.

"Damn it," she hollered and kicked the tire. She felt a twinge in her back and straightened.

A. Hardy Roper

A voice behind her said, "My goodness, such language."

A hunk of a man, maybe six foot, coal black hair a little long, day-old beard, good build—not all muscle bound but solid—early to late forties. Yum, she thought. The man wore tennis shoes, shorts and a navy blue T-shirt. As he approached, Clementine glimpsed a strange-looking fish imprinted on the front of his shirt and the words *Garhole Bar* printed in pink ink above the fish. He had come from the beach, dressed for a run. He didn't seem threatening.

In a perfect world, Clementine wished she'd had the opportunity to check her makeup, at least freshen her lip-gloss. She liked to make her lips, fuller even puffy. But with the man smiling only a few feet away, all she could do was lift the strands of hair out of her face and play the scene out, see what happened. She held the lug wrench to her side just in case.

Chapter Twenty-Four

I changed into shorts and my worn-out running shoes, rummaged through the dirty clothes pile and found my favorite shirt. When I first opened The Garhole, I'd had a couple dozen T-shirts made with the name of the bar and a hand-drawn picture of an alligator gar printed on the front. I'd kept one for myself and given the rest to customers. I slipped on the shirt and started the run.

I crossed the highway, jogged the sand trail to the beach, and turned toward Bay Harbor determined to make five miles. Out in the Gulf, puffs of dark clouds floated in toward the island. The only sounds were the folding of waves onto the beach and the low whistle of sandpipers and sanderlings scurrying ahead of me.

I'd hoped a late run on the beach would free my mind of everything I'd witnessed during the past few days. But my gut wouldn't let it go. Every stride brought disturbing images—Joy's pitiful plea at the café in Lake Charles and the gun battle with her ex-boyfriend. Jake's fighting back tears, manning-up as he fought for control after the trauma of his mother's overdose and near death. And then the most haunting picture of all, Jake's torture by that same madman. Life wasn't supposed to happen like that to a 14-year-old boy or to anyone.

The halfway point of the run was at the road that cut back across the highway to Bay Harbor. Normally, I'd reverse here and return the same way I'd come. But the thought jumped at me that I could easily turn inland and run past Slim Green's house.

The tug of war in my head about Jake continued. What would jogging by Green's house accomplish? Absolutely nothing, I told myself. Jake's problems weren't my business. They just were not. As I was about to turn back, I noticed someone bent over the side of a yellow Mustang convertible. I approached the vehicle to find a woman struggling with a lug wrench, her very attractive back end poised high in the air aimed directly at my face. Knowing any woman would be embarrassed to find a man staring at such a position, I backed off and waited until she had given up the struggle. She stood and arched her back, rubbing the spot just above her ample buttocks.

When I announced myself with a snide remark, she turned quickly. I noted the tire iron at her side and put my palms up in self-defense.

"Sorry," I said. "Didn't mean to startle you."

"Shouldn't sneak up on a girl like that."

I gave her my best smile. "You're right. But it'll be dark soon. Can I help with the tire?"

The energy in her eyes caught me unaware, just the tonic I needed coming from two days of total confusion. She was cute and perky and since I saw no rings, apparently single.

I extended my hand for the lug wrench. She hesitated for a moment, glanced at the sky and then back at me.

"You look like a native," she said. "Know what time it gets dark?"

I gazed toward the West and said, "In less than an hour. Better let me help you."

She pointed to my shirt. "So what is this Garhole Bar?"

"Best place to view the sunset this side of Hawaii," I said, gesturing toward the end of the island. "A mile that way, turn right at the first sandy road. You will see the bar at the end. Can't miss it."

She handed me the lug wrench. "Maybe I'll stop in," she said, an impish grin on her face. "Anything to eat at The Garhole Bar?"

"Always," I answered. I returned the smile and bent over to loosen the lug nuts. The thought flashed through my mind that I had intended to go by Green's house. But if Joy was still in the hospital, Jake and Slim Green were probably there with her. There was nothing to gain cruising Green's house now. I completed the tire change and dumped the flat tire and lug wrench into the trunk.

"My name's Parker," I said. "Hope to see you later."

She raised her eyebrows and smiled, but said nothing. She was definitely a tease, and a damned sexy one at that.

Back at the bar, I washed the grime from the tire off my hands, put a pot of water on to boil and jumped upstairs for a quick shower and shave. Thinking positively, I changed the sheets on the bed, fluffed the pillows and straightened the bedspread. I put fresh towels in the bathroom and turned the ceiling fan on to the cool the room. Now all I needed was a little luck.

A glance over the bay told me the sun was sinking fast. I dumped a bag of shrimp boil into the roiling water, then turned to the sink and ran water over a bag of frozen shrimp. I glanced at a table and spied Joe staring at me.

"What," I said, annoyed at Joe's intrusion.

"Just wondering what you're doing."

"Boiling shrimp. What does it look like?"

I knew what Joe meant. I rarely cooked anything after dark. By the time night fell, most of the fishermen were halfway to Houston cursing traffic and dreading the next day at work. The few customers dropping in this time of day were locals looking for an evening libation and a little conversation.

Joe rolled his wheelchair to the bar and heaved himself onto a stool.

"Something else is happening," he said with a pie-eating smirk on his face. "You never shave at night."

"Okay, okay," I mumbled. "A woman I met on the beach may pop in to watch the sunset."

"Whoa," cried Joe. "Want me to disappear?" He turned and made a feint as if he was about to get back into his wheelchair.

"Nothing like that," I said. "It's just that it's been a while."

And it had been. Two years to be exact. I hadn't been with a woman since I'd gotten involved in the Cuban spy caper. The most beautiful woman I've ever known walked into The Garhole Bar. She was early thirties, five six or seven, slim and well-proportioned, dark features and hair past her shoulders. She had classic high cheekbones, pouting lips and eyes darker than midnight in the desert.

Alejandra Contreras, a reporter for a Miami-based Cuban newspaper, was on the trail of the Cuban spy. We joined forces and in the heat of the chase became more than friends. I can't think of Alex without visualizing her body over mine, hair in my face and the sweet smell of sex in the air.

But then my thoughts invariably turned to Alex lying unconscious in the UTMB intensive care unit, near death from a bullet too close to her heart. After a year-long recuperation, Alex was now back in Miami living with the editor of the newspaper where she'd worked. We kept in touch for a while, but things happen. Life moves on, but the memories linger. I turned and gazed out the window studying the shadows enveloping the dock.

"What is it?" Joe asked.

"Oh, it's just that I made a big deal about the sunset. She seemed interested. But the sun's gone and I thought she'd be here by now. What could she be doing on the beach after dark?"

"Maybe she was jiving you," Joe said.

I shrugged and thought about his comment wondering if I had read too much into the chance meeting. A pang of disappointment crossed my gut. But her smile, the sparkle in her eyes, the inflection of her speech—all seemed so genuine.

"She a local?" Joe continued.

"Definitely not."

"Maybe she got lost," Joe said. "I'll hold the fort here. Go back and check on her."

The chances of her having another flat were slim, and the Mustang was new enough not to have had mechanical trouble. She was probably on her drive home or to some motel in Galveston. I sure wasn't going to chase that far.

But after another prod from Joe, I decided to make a precautionary run, just in case she was in trouble. If nothing else, I'd cruise by Green's house to see if he and Jake had brought Joy back from the hospital. Maybe I'd take Jake out for dinner, get him away from his drug-crazed mother. She still had the bag of meth she'd stolen from Luther. No doubt she'd be taking another hit as soon as she was home.

A. Hardy Roper

Chapter Twenty-Five

Luther decided it would be better to approach Green's house after dark. He lounged in his car in the parking lot of Red's Grocery, smoking cigarettes and sipping beer. His recent purchases, a T-bone steak wrapped in butcher paper, a carton of smokes and a twelve pack of beer sat beside him. Half the beer was gone, the empties tossed onto the back floorboard.

For the past hour, an endless line of bikini clad, almost nude, teenage girls had moved in and out of the store with their macho boyfriends. The guys with fake IDs carried beers and cigarettes. What Luther had heard about Texas girls being beauties was true. The view from his car wasn't as titillating as loitering closer where he could smell their heady mix of sweat and perfume. But the explosion had left him looking like a circus freak, and he knew it. For now, he would stay hidden in his car, away from the constant stares and giggles from the girls. But the time for these nymphs would come. One hit off his shake-and-bake special and their lives would change forever. He'd suddenly look real good to them.

He smiled thinking about Bolivar. If the beaches there were loaded with little beauties like these, how hard would it be to develop a stable of meth-dependent little friends? The bitch Joy was getting old, too old for his taste. He lowered the window and sniffed the air imagining the scent of teenage bodies filling his nostrils.

Luther didn't know exactly what the Calzone boys got for his batches on the street, but he knew it was a ton more than they paid him. Probably four or five times more. Then he remembered the sight of Waylon mixing chemicals in a plastic bottle. Hell, Luther thought. He could do that. Probably make all the *ice* he needed that way. If he kept the operation small and sold direct, there would be less chance the Calzone brothers would find him. They wouldn't be looking for a small-time operator.

Plus, he wouldn't have to worry about another explosion. Unless, what was it that Waylon had said? Oh yeah, you have to shake the bottle just the right amount, then quickly release the pressure, or boom! Luther flinched at the thought. He touched his cheek still hurting from the explosion.

He checked his watch. It was time to go. It had gotten too dark to enjoy the parade anyway. Luther cranked the engine and backed out to the highway. If Joy was at the house, the meth wasn't far away. He would grab the stash, give Joy her due and head for Bolivar. Find some cheap crib to hide in until the Calzone brothers quit the search. Luther smiled as he turned into Bay Harbor. Good plan, he thought. A good, good plan.

Chapter Twenty-Six

Considering the time difference between Galveston and Boston, Clementine figured Reginald J. Stanford had probably left the office, and she didn't have his home number. She knew she should have called again earlier, but she just couldn't stand talking to the arrogant prick. Still, she had to try.

She had a hunch she was on to something with the kid she'd seen at Green's house. Could be a bonanza, the big case that would put her name on the investigator's map. But she needed to get old-man Stanford on board.

Clementine dialed Stanford's number. She heard one buzz and then nothing. Her phone showed low battery. She opened the glove compartment then slammed it shut remembering she'd forgotten to bring the car charger.

She tried the call again and the phone went totally dead. She cursed and slammed the steering wheel in disgust. She pivoted in her seat and studied the scene behind her. The sun appeared low in the sky hidden behind a wall of haze. She had no way to judge the time remaining before the sun completely disappeared.

The image of the dark-haired hunk on the beach replaced the haze. Darkest eyes she'd ever seen, boring right into hers. Sexy son of a bitch. She felt her crotch and realized she'd gotten wet just thinking about him. And it was clear he was interested. He'd invited her to drop by. So she'd miss the sunset. So what? He was wearing a T-shirt with the bar's name printed on its front. If he were the owner, he'd still be there.

A. Hardy Roper

Bars don't close until late and the proprietor is the last one to leave.

She had time to call Stanford and still get to The Garhole early. She remembered a phone booth at the small store a few miles toward town. She turned the Mustang around and spun out on the highway toward Reds. The dark-haired stud muffin would have to wait.

Halfway to the store, Clementine's turned on her headlights. Coming toward her in the opposite lane, an old Pontiac was cruising fast, headlights off. Clementine wanted to blink her lights to alert the driver, but he whizzed past before she could.

She parked at Reds and entered the phone booth. She gave the operator her credit card number and dialed Stanford's Boston office. The same haughty woman answered on the first ring.

"Mr. Stanford's office. May I help you?"

The woman's New England nasal twang made Clementine momentarily pull the phone back from her ear. She couldn't decide whether to answer in an exaggerated Texas drawl or just imitate the same bitchy tone as the woman on the other end. She decided to hold back with the snappy retort. Sarcasm wasn't going to get her anywhere. She answered in her most professional crisp voice.

"Yes, this is Clementine Garza. I am the private investigator Mr. Sanford engaged for a confidential project. Is he in?"

"No, Mr. Sanford has left for the day."

"It is most important that I speak with him," Clementine continued. "May I have his cell or home number please?"

"I am afraid that is not possible, Ms. Garza. I am quite sure Mr. Stanford would have given you his private number if he intended for you to contact him after hours."

Clementine had reached her limit in nicey-do. She wanted to jump through the line and put the New England bitch in a chokehold.

"Yea, well...if you value your job, Ms.—whatever your name is—I suggest you get ahold of old Reggie boy and tell him to give me a buzz. That is, if he gives a shit about having a heir to the family jewels."

Clementine slammed the phone back on the hook and huffed out to her car, thinking if that didn't get the old man's blood boiling, nothing would.

At the last minute, Clementine remembered her dead cell phone. She bought a car charger in the store and plugged in the phone. The image of the hunk on the beach came back to her. But first things, first. She'd already missed the sunset. The Garhole Bar would have to wait. She needed to stop by Green's and see if the old man had returned with the woman.

A. Hardy Roper

Chapter Twenty-Seven

Luther parked at the same corner as before, a block past and across the street from Green's house. The view was perfect. Green's station wagon was not there. The house appeared shuttered and empty. Nothing to do now but wait. He flipped open the glove box, searching for a joint but knew better. He slammed the lid shut, then remembered the toke he'd dropped on the street. He opened the car door and looked down.

"What the—?" The joint was gone, but the remains of a pink cigarette lay in its place. "Kids," he murmured.

He was about to slam the car door shut in disgust when Green's station wagon pulled in and parked. Luther eased the door closed and watched.

Jake got out of the passenger side and opened the fence gate. The dog raced to Jake. He rubbed Buster's head and then quickly returned to the car. He held the door open and helped Joy out. Slim Green followed Jake and Joy across the yard. He scooted around them and hurried up the stairs.

Luther straightened in the seat and leaned over the steering wheel. Joy appeared edgy. She twitched her head side to side and seemed to be mumbling something. Luther smiled. The bitch needed a hit. If the stash was inside, he knew Joy would be into it soon.

Jake held his mother's arm while she climbed the steps. Slim was already inside. Jake and Joy went in and closed the door.

It was getting darker by the minute. Luther decided to wait, let them get settled, relaxed. He smoked a cigarette, opened another beer. He glanced at his watch. According to the Calzone brothers' timetable, he had just enough time to grab the goods and drive back to Louisiana. But, of course, he had no intention of returning. That decision was firm. Luther was no one's fool. He would ditch the Pontiac and sell enough *ice* to buy a vehicle for cash. Maybe one of those big hogs like Waylon had. Money wouldn't be a problem. Then he'd hide out until the bro's quit looking. Life was good.

Time to go, he thought. He sucked down the rest of the beer and tossed the empty can into the roadside ditch. He cranked the engine and idled toward the house. He parked on the street and studied the covered windows. He didn't think anyone could see out.

He eased to the fence gate with the steak package in hand. When the dog came in a rush, growling but not yet barking, Luther unwrapped the butcher paper and tossed the steak over the fence. The dog braked to a stop and sniffed the meat. He grabbed the steak in his teeth, trotted to the edge of the house and settled in.

When Luther opened the gate and started toward the steps, Buster emitted a low growl.

"Good dog," Luther whispered. "Good dog."

Luther approached the dog slowly, continuing to whisper. He thought he saw confusion in the dog's eyes. Buster alternated between growling and chewing the meat. Luther squatted and gently patted Buster's head. Then, in a quick movement, he grabbed the dog's collar and at the same time reached behind his back for his pistol. He slammed the butt of the gun into Buster's head. Bone cracked. The dog seemed stunned. Luther hit again and again. Blood oozed from the dog's ears and nose. Luther waited until Buster's soft whimpers finally faded out.

Luther smiled—one down. He crept up the stairs, pistol in hand. There was no porch light. He put his ear to the door and heard nothing. He put his hand out and slowly turned the doorknob. He felt no resistance. A large-screen television blared from across the room, masking the noise from the door. When the clacking of the Wheel of Fortune finally settled, the program host asked the guest a question.

Luther scanned the room methodically taking in every fixture with a quick glance. There was an empty couch in front of the TV. Next to the couch, Slim Green's white head poked above a large easy chair.

Along the wall to Luther's left were two doors, both closed. Probably bedrooms, he thought. The old man was alone in the den, and Joy and the kid were in one of the bedrooms. Luther smiled. This would be easier than he'd figured. He envisioned Joy in the bedroom dipping into the bag and pulling out a rock for the pipe. First, he'd take care of the old man, then Jake, then Joy. Leave no witnesses.

A. Hardy Roper

Chapter Twenty-Eight

I didn't think that Joe was right about the Mustang chic being lost. I had given her good directions: drive toward the pass and turn right at the first sand road. Shouldn't have been a problem You could see the bar from the highway. How hard was that? No, the odds were good the sexy blond with the big brown eyes and nice rack was just a flirt. And now she was back in her nest somewhere laughing her ass off. Or maybe she'd just been dumped and needed to salvage her ego by testing her skills with me. But then again, maybe she was legitimate. If she'd had another flat, she wouldn't have another spare. A woman alone on the beach at night is not a good idea. I smiled at my creative imagination. A red-blooded male can rationalize any scenario to his favor.

I turned onto the beach crossroad at Bay Harbor and pulled to a stop where she'd parked the Mustang. Nothing. I drove farther toward the surf and turned in a big circle, my headlights covering the area on either side of the beach entrance. No sign of the yellow Mustang. The chic had flown the coop.

When I stopped at the highway, my headlights hit the sign to Bay Harbor. I checked the road in both directions. Turn left and I am back at The Garhole for another night of drinking beer with Joe Stubbs. Turn right and I could end up chasing my tail hoping to run into the Mustang. But I knew finding the blond was a long shot. Then I thought about Jake and Slim Green wondering if they'd returned from the hospital.

A. Hardy Roper

I crossed the road and turned onto the street where Green lived. His station wagon sat in the driveway. But if Green and Jake were inside tucked in for the night, who's old Pontiac was parked on the street beside the house? I eased beside the Pontiac and spotted the bullet hole in the door from my .45 automatic. The thought of Joy's boyfriend in the house sent shivers across my neck. Jake was right, Luther had returned. And he sure as hell wasn't here on a social call.

I parked and grabbed my .45 out of the glove box. I checked the magazine, chambered a round and slipped an extra box of cartridges into my front pocket. If war was coming, I wanted to be ready.

The front gate was open something Green would never have allowed. I expected Buster to come full bore at me, but he didn't show. I stepped inside the gate. The upstairs shutters were closed as usual, but on the far end, light flickered from the edge of a window. Probably a television, I thought. I considered the TV to be a good sign, until I eased farther into the yard and found Buster lying on his side in a pool of blood. He had a big cut on his head, but he appeared to be breathing. I was ready to rush the house and start blasting.

Luther crept across the room, shifting his vision between the bedroom doors and the back of Green's head. Two steps more and he reached the chair. He placed the barrel of the .38 directly behind Slim Green's head and pulled the trigger. The report reverberated throughout the house, drowning out the laughter from Pat Sajak's one-liner. Blood and matter and bone splattered sideways and forward into Green's lap and across the floor. Green's head fell forward. His body remained slumped in the chair. The door at the back bedroom flew open. Joy stood with a hand over her mouth, her face contorted, eyes flashing from Luther to her father's blown-out head. She screamed.

Saving Jake

The boom from a shot echoed out the walls. There was no time now for stealth. I swallowed hard, took the stairs two at a time and surged across the deck, gun in hand, ready for mortal combat. Almost 20 years in the Army, and I'd never fired my weapon in anger. In fact, never killed a man in combat. I had killed once, smashed a man's throat with the jaws of the gar head that hung over my bar. It had been a moment of desperation, a struggle for life. Was I ready for that again? I couldn't think about that now.

I crashed through the door and found Joy and Luther wrestling on the floor with Joy on top scratching and clawing. Luther's face flowed red from her fingernails, a stark contrast against his bleached skull. Luther held the gun in his right hand trying to fend Joy off with his left, laughing, toying with her. He needed her alive to find the meth, but I doubted he was planning to take them back. Not after his little stunt at the Intracoastal Bridge.

I rushed at Luther. He brought his gun across Joy's body to shoot me, but she hit his arm. The gun exploded. Joy collapsed into Luther's chest. I kicked the gun from Luther's hand and aimed the .45 at his head, inches away, my hand tightening on the trigger—less than a second to decide—kill or be killed. He grabbed my foot and twisted. I hit the floor hard. The impact ripped the .45 from my hand. Luther jumped on top of me before I could react. He pinned my lower body with his massive weight and throttled my throat with his hands. I tried to punch at his face but he kept his head back from the blows. I tried to break his wrists from my throat, but he leaned forward adding the weight of his upper body to the strength in his hands. I twisted upward to break his hold, but his hands grew tighter. I was out of air, all consciousness leaving. Strange shards of fire and lightening flew through my head like electrical currents—a mass of colors and designs and zigzag streaks. I felt my hands give way and fall to my sides and then...nothing.

I regained consciousness with someone's lips on my mouth, but it wasn't a caress. Forced air streamed into my throat. My eyes opened to blond hair across my cheeks. I smelled perfume and powder. I tried to focus, to realize where I was and what was happening.

The lips came off and the face pulled back. I gasped and took in a deep breath and blew it out. I did it again. I felt the weight of a body straddling me.

A woman's voice said, "Oh, man. You had to go and shave didn't you? Ruin that sexy stubble."

My mind was just starting to work. I concentrated on the liquid brown pools over me.

"Did you clean up just for me?" the voice continued. "Sorry I missed the sunset."

I coughed and breathed in again, then blinked a couple of times, trying to focus. The blond from the Mustang straddled me. My throat screamed raw from Luther's hands. It hurt to talk. I managed a faint whisper, "Who are you?"

She bent lower, her eyes boring into mine. "Clementine Garza, Private Investigator Extraordinaire," she said.

I remembered her lips on mine and managed a weak smile. "Guess you saved my life."

"No need to thank me, you've already French kissed me twice."

Then I remembered Joy. As Clementine rolled off, I stretched out and felt Joy's body beside me.

"She's breathing, has a pulse," Clementine said. "But she's in bad shape. Shot through the chest. Someone called 911. I hear sirens."

Joy breathed with shallow, labored breaths. There was no external bleeding. Nothing we could do but wait for the ambulance. Green's body lay sprawled in the chair, blood and gore all around. Luther lay face down.

I rubbed my mangled throat and winced from the soreness. "What happened?" I asked.

"When I got to the party, Green was dead and the big animal on the floor was choking you blue. I whacked him a few times with my baton, and he collapsed. My last strike accidently got him across the throat. I think he's dead. Didn't bother to check."

I rolled Luther over and studied the gash. "Broke his windpipe. He's dead all right."

I turned and met Clementine's eyes. "There was a boy... Jake?"

Clementine took the front bedroom, and I rushed toward Joy's room. A double bed and a cot against the wall furnished the space. I searched the closet and under the bed. The duffel I had seen Jake stash under the bed when Joy overdosed was gone. But who took it, and where was Jake?

Clementine came in. "The front bedroom was Green's," she said.

I moved closer to the cot next to the wall and spied Jake's LSU ball cap on the floor.

"Jake and Joy slept in here. So where is...?"

It was then I noticed the open window. I stuck my head out and saw nothing but a torn window screen on the ground below.

"He must have dropped out of the window when he heard the gunshot."

I checked Joy again. Her pulse was weak but steady. The sirens were getting closer, sounding like a pack of coyotes, police, EMS, maybe even a fire truck.

While Clementine stayed with Joy, I raced down the stairs to the rear of the house. The ground below the window was as hard as asphalt. There were no tracks, no way to tell in which direction Jake had gone. I retrieved a flashlight from my truck and hustled to the back boundary of Green's yard searching along the fence. I found a shard of clothing stuck to the top of the wire.

I flashed the beam out into the marsh that bordered the rear of Green's lot and saw nothing but tangled grass and clumps of salt cedars. I was about to jump over the fence when a voice blared behind me.

"Police! Show your hands."

I was reluctant to raise my hands fearful the cop might mistake the flashlight for a weapon. Then I remembered in a panic, I'd left my gun on the floor upstairs.

"I don't have a weapon, officer. I have a flashlight in my right hand. Don't shoot."

Chapter Twenty-Nine

I turned slowly and raised my hands over my head. Two police officers approached weapons out, flashlights trained on my face.

"On the ground, now!" shouted the younger of the two, his eyes wide, jaw ridged. His index finger lay inside the guard, tense on the trigger.

I dared not move a muscle. One nervous twitch and I was dead. His nametag said, Todd. The other officer's tag read, Welch. Officer Welch was older with a heavy paunch around his mid-section and a more relaxed face. His finger lay alongside the trigger guard.

"Easy, officer," I said, focusing on Todd. "I am unarmed. The perp is dead, upstairs. I'm looking for the kid who lived in the house. I think he—"

"Drop that light and get your ass on the ground," Todd broke in. He went into a slight crouch, gun extended. "I won't ask you again."

I thought if I dropped the flashlight to the ground it might startle the rookie into firing.

"I'm going," I said, my voice calm.

I eased to my knees, the light still in my hands. I gingerly laid the light on the grass and then folded forward to the ground, my arms extended to the sides.

Officer Welch holstered his weapon. He bent over me, twisted my arms behind my back and fastened the cuffs. He ran his hands over my body, then helped me up.

Another cop led Clementine down the stairs, her hands cuffed behind her.

"Two dead upstairs," the cop said. "And two handguns, a .38 and a .45." He held up two plastic bags each containing a weapon. "And I found this on the woman." He handed Todd Clementine's baton also enclosed in a bag.

Todd stepped closer to Clementine. "Who the hell are you?" he asked, his face puffed and red.

"Private Investigator," she said. "My license is in my back pocket."

The cop beside her removed her wallet and handed it to Todd. He flipped it open. "Clementine Garza, P.I., San Antonio, Texas. Long way from home, *Sug*."

Clementine shrugged.

Todd said to Welch, "We'll wait for the Lieutenant. Put them in the back of my unit."

I glanced up to see paramedics bringing Joy down on a stretcher. She had an oxygen mask on her face and a tube attached to a saline bottle stuck in her arm. At least she was alive...for now anyway.

Minutes later, Life Flight whirled in out of the night sky, its powerful light searching for a place to land. The bird maneuvered to a vacant lot several houses away, kicking up sand and loose grass as it landed. The paramedics loaded Joy and the helicopter lifted off.

An unmarked cruiser arrived, lights flashing, siren off. The investigating officer got out of the car, glancing about, taking in the scene. I'd seen pictures of Galveston's top homicide cop in the local paper. Lieutenant Daniel Oliver was so impeccably dressed, I wondered if he ironed his boxers. He wore a snappy button-down shirt with a club tie, a light windbreaker, pressed slacks and highly polished cordovan wingtips. Oliver looked early thirties, with a carefully parted, ivy-league haircut and a well-trimmed mustache.

Saving Jake

He pulled Todd aside and immediately dressed him down. With the windows up I couldn't understand what the Lieutenant said, but I knew proper procedure would have been to keep witnesses separated. Putting us in the same patrol car gave us a chance to synchronize our stories.

Oliver opened the car door, told me to get out and ordered Clementine to stay in the back seat. We stepped out of hearing range from Clementine.

I went through everything with Oliver step-by-step—giving Joy and Jake a ride from Lake Charles, Luther tracking us, killing Green and wounding Joy, and finally, Clementine saving my life and Joy's. I left out any reference to the gunfight by the bridge and the meth.

"Then you didn't actually see the confrontation between Garza and this Luther Bourdain character," Lieutenant Oliver said to me. He stared, waiting for an answer.

"No," I said. "As I told the other officers, I didn't see what happened. I was too busy dying."

Oliver got in my face. "Show some respect, McLeod. You're gonna get tired of that smart-assed lip. I've got all night. Every time you wise off, you'll tell the story again."

I was tired of the rigmarole. Slim Green and Luther Bourdain were dead. Joy Green was on the way to the hospital, and I had no idea what had happened to Jake.

"Hey, I'm the victim here, remember?" I blurted out. "Take my cuffs off and for God sakes, take the cuffs off Ms. Garza. She's been through enough."

Oliver ordered Clementine out of the patrol car, her hands still cuffed behind her. He led her to the center of the yard, questioned her and a few minutes later brought her back. Oliver said to Todd, "Get anything back yet?"

"They're both clean," Todd said. "No warrants, no sheet."

A. Hardy Roper

Oliver nodded. "Un-cuff both of them," he said. Then he looked at Clementine. "You may be here working a case, Garza. But that P.I. confidentially crap don't cut it with me. You're going downtown for more questioning. You don't kill somebody in Galveston County, Texas and think you're ready for a day on the beach. Get in the car."

"How about my baton?" she asked.

Oliver shook his head. "You gotta be shittin' me. The baton is evidence. So is the .38 and .45. We'll test them both." Then he formed a nasty smirk on his face, and said, "For all we know, McLeod's .45 killed Green."

I wanted to punch him out on the spot but held back. Todd opened the back door of Oliver's unit and guided Clementine into the seat.

Oliver turned to me. "McLeod, you don't have a concealed gun permit. Lucky I don't run your ass in for carrying. But you are going downtown for questioning. Get in my car."

"Like hell I will. A 14-year-old boy is missing. That was his mother in the helicopter. The kid's out there somewhere probably scared beyond belief. I've told you everything I know. I'm going to look for the boy."

"We'll have patrols out looking for him," Oliver said.

"Have your officers patrol the roads in case he makes it to the highway. I'm going to search the marsh. I know every inch of this end of the island. I don't know what the kid saw. He may have seen his mother shot. He may think Bourdain is still out there somewhere looking for him. If you want more from me, I will be in first thing in the morning. But not tonight."

"Oh, yeah," Oliver said, sneering. "I recognize you now, McLeod. You own that old fish camp. Weren't you some kind of spook in the Army?"

"Spook equates to CIA. I was Army Intelligence."

"Stationed where?"

"Germany."

"Messing with *frauleins*?"

"Messing with the East German Stasi," I said.

"Well whatever you were," Oliver continued. "It doesn't mean shit to me, McLeod, got it? I expect you in my office at 10 a.m., rain or shine."

I stood stone faced.

Oliver turned to Officer Todd. "Wrap the whole house with tape and stay here until you're relieved."

A. Hardy Roper

Chapter Thirty

What I knew about Clementine Garza was that she was damned good-looking, had a tight body, and she wielded a mean baton. I also knew she was a P.I. from San Antonio; she was in Galveston working a case, and the case obviously had something to do with Slim, Joy, Jake or possibly Luther Bourdain. But I had no idea, which members of the group she was hired to investigate or for whom. I eliminated Bourdain because Clementine had referred to him as "the big guy," possibly meaning she didn't know his identity. But that still left the Green family.

She told Lieutenant Oliver she was here on assignment and couldn't disclose confidentialities. Oliver hadn't liked her answer, and I wondered if she would disclose more during her interrogation downtown.

Regardless of Clementine's reason for being at Green's, if she hadn't shown, my remains would be en route to the coroner's office along with Slim Green's. And Luther Bourdain's broad ass would be on its way back to Louisiana. When the images of the burns on Jake's arms flashed through my mind, I felt even more grateful for Clementine's appearance.

I leaned into the back window of the patrol car and told Clementine if she would call The Garhole when Oliver finished the interrogation, I would drive in and take her back to her car. Meanwhile, a couple of neighbors offered to shuttle her Mustang to The Garhole, and one of the officers volunteered to take Buster to a 24-hour vet clinic in town.

A. Hardy Roper

While Officer Todd wrapped the house in bright yellow crime tape, I scurried to the field behind Green's back fence. With dark clouds covering the moon, I knew finding a trail would be difficult. Just before the batteries in my flashlight died, I happened across a small path threading through the brambles. It was an old cattle trail now grown over, the remnant used by coyotes and varmints. At a bend in the path, I noticed a slight indentation from a tennis shoe. The track had to be Jake's, but the path was too overgrown to follow in the dark.

The trail headed west. And there was nothing between Green's house and my place but clumps of salt cedar trees, tangles of cord grass, prickly pear cactus and rattlesnakes. I remembered when Jake first showed at The Garhole, he said he'd walked two miles. I retraced my path back to Green's house and drove to The Garhole hoping Jake was there.

The light over the front door of the bar was off and the inside was dark. Strange. I eased around to the back dock and had just turned the corner when a voice rang out.

"Jesus, Parker. I almost shot you."

Joe Stubbs sat in his wheelchair beside the mobile home pointing a shotgun at my head.

"Is Jake—?"

"In the trailer," Joe said. "A ball of nerves, worried about his mama, wondering what happened to her after he escaped. He wanted me to take him back to Green's house, but I said we'd wait for you."

I flipped on the inside bar lights, and we moved to a table. Joe asked about Joy.

"Don't know for sure," I said. "She was still alive when the bird took off."

"And his Grandpa's dead...what a mess."

I nodded.

Saving Jake

Jake came out of the mobile home, and we climbed into my truck for the trip to UTMB. On the way to the hospital, I explained what had happened after he escaped through the bedroom window—grandfather and Luther dead and his mother wounded.

"I heard a helicopter," he said. "Was that the police?"

"Lifeflight," I said. "Your mother is getting good care. The helicopter took her directly to the hospital in Galveston, one of the best trauma units in the area."

We arrived at the hospital and waited for word. After an hour, a doctor came out. He told us Joy was stable for now, and there was nothing more to be done tonight. After a lot of protesting, the doc finally convinced Jake that his mother was in good hands in intensive care, and it would be best if he went home, got some rest and came back in the morning.

Jake glanced at me, a bewildered expression on his face. "Home?" he said.

I knew what he meant. What home? I dropped my arm over his shoulder and guided him out to the truck.

Joe had called the hospital to tell me Lieutenant Oliver was finished with Clementine. I swung by the police station. Clementine stood on the steps, smoking a cigarette. She smashed the cigarette into the butt can at the entrance and hustled to the truck. Jake was asleep with his head on his chest. I scooted him to the center, and Clementine climbed in.

"This is Jake," I said, "Joy's son."

Clementine studied Jake's sleeping form as we drove toward the seawall. Then she laid her head back against the seat. Even with no sleep, no lipstick, and mascara smeared on the bags forming under her eyes, she looked damn sexy. Never mind the fact that she'd just slashed a man's throat with a baton.

"How'd it go with hotshot Oliver?" I asked.

Clementine spoke in a soft voice trying not to wake Jake. "Standard bad cop, good cop bullshit," she said. "Grilled me for an hour trying to trip me. Then another Dick, Mr. Nice Guy blows in. Like I don't know that routine. He told me not to leave town for a few days, at least until he could interview Joy Green. Get her side of the story."

"That may not happen for a while," I said. "She's in bad shape."

Jake stirred at the mention of his mother's name. He mumbled something then crashed again. For the rest of the trip, we sat like zombies, three abreast in my old truck.

The Garhole glowed like a football stadium on Friday night, every light inside and out turned on. Inside the bar, Joe was in his wheelchair at the stove stirring a pot of chili.

He turned when he saw us and tried his best to smile. "Thought you'd you be hungry," he said.

I introduced Clementine to Joe, and we moved to a table. We polished off the chili without conversation, too exhausted to talk. After I promised Jake we'd return to the hospital in the morning, Joe took him out to the mobile home.

Clementine rummaged through the cooler. "The sign says this is a bar. Where's the wine?"

"We don't get many women out here," I said.

"So men don't drink wine? What cave you been hiding in, Neanderthal Man?"

I moved my hands around indicating the inside of the bar.

Clementine frowned. "Okay, the hard stuff, then. Vodka?"

"Don't have a license for the hard stuff."

Clementine moved behind the counter and lifted my half-full bottle of Famous Grouse. "What's this?" she asked. "Private stock?"

She poured a full glass, took a big gulp and moved to a table taking the scotch with her.

I grabbed a Shiner and sat across from her. I'd seen photographs of firefighters sitting exhausted after a big fire, staring into space, too drained to speak. Put a suit on us and we'd look like that now.

Clementine finished the glass of scotch and poured another. She focused on the gar head.

"So you named the bar after that skeleton hanging from the ceiling? I can't tell if the monster is smiling or measuring me for lunch."

I nodded, following her gaze to the rows of razor sharp teeth glowering through vacant eye sockets.

"Know what you mean," I said. "But the truth is, whether its smiling or frowning depends on you."

Clementine scrunched her forehead. "What does that mean?"

I gestured at the Famous Grouse. "Used to drink two or three bottles of that a week."

Her eyes showed surprise.

"I came back from Desert Storm with a lot of pain and problems the doctors couldn't treat. Only whisky worked. The gar kept staring me down, watching me kill myself with booze. It wouldn't turn me loose, finally shamed me into going to the VA. That's when I found out my liver was shot. Doc Kennon got me into a program, and the program worked. I quit the hard stuff when the bottle you're drinking from was half full. I kept it on the shelf as a reminder. Long as it was there and still had whisky in it, I passed the test.

"Lucky you," Clementine said, topping off her glass.

"So you see...at first the gar head did nothing but snarl at me. But now, it's smiling. That is, until I screw up."

"Sounds more like your personal god to me," she said.

"More like a good friend. I've spent many a night in here, some drunk, some sober, talking to my god as you call him."

We sat in silence, each to our own thoughts. It had been a tough night. Maybe we were just too tired to move or maybe something else kept us there, across from each other, not wanting the scene to end.

"Clementine," I said. "Interesting name. Your mother liked sweet fruit? How do you say Clementine in Spanish?"

"I have no idea," she said. "Only Spanish I know is what I've picked up around San Antonio."

"But your last name is Garza."

"My father came from Mexico, but he was old school. Believed since I was born in the U.S., I should be proud to be an American. He never spoke his native language around me. My mother's maiden name was Smith. Don't get more WASP than that."

"And Clementine?"

"My mother was a huge Henry Fonda fan, watched all his movies a thousand times. Did you ever see *My Darling Clementine*? Henry Fonda played Wyatt Earp. They had a big shootout at the OK Corral."

"May I call you Clem?"

She refilled the glass and steadied her gaze on me. "No," she said. "You may not."

I shrugged and sipped beer.

After a beat, Clementine said, "Lieutenant Oliver wanted to know your connection with Joy Green."

"What did you tell him?"

"The truth. I have no friggin' idea why you were there."

"For Jake," I said.

"Not Joy?"

Saving Jake

The way she asked stirred something inside me. Her eyes seemed more penetrating, searching. I wanted to blink, to look away, but I held her gaze.

"No, not Joy," I said. And then I told her the parts of the story I'd left out with Oliver, the shootout beneath the Intracoastal Bridge and Luther Bourdain torturing Jake. When I finished, she reached across the table and put her hand on mine.

"You're a good man, Parker McLeod," she said. She lifted her hand and sat back.

"Thank you for saving my life," I said.

She shrugged. "Okay, that's enough of the gooey stuff."

"You started it. Told me I was a good man and—"

She raised her palm signaling it was time to stop. She sipped some scotch, and I drank some beer.

I waited a beat and said, "So after hearing what Bourdain did to Jake do you feel better about—"

"Killing a snake?"

I nodded.

"Out in West Texas you see a lot of chaparral, roadrunners some people call them. They kill rattlesnakes. Did you know that?"

"No."

"Well, I asked one of them one time why they killed rattlesnakes. Know what he said?"

"I have no idea," I answered.

"He said it needed to be done."

And then, as though some deeply hidden source of righteousness had just recharged Clementine's soul, she sat up and leaned toward me.

"Luther Bourdain was a piece of dung," she said. "Needed to be stepped on and wiped off the shoes of the world."

"Remind me not to piss you off," I said.

Clementine waved me off and sat back in her chair. She sucked out the last drop of booze and poured more scotch.

"Oliver also wanted to know *my* interest in the Green crowd."

"I would like to know that myself," I said.

She furrowed her brow. "You know I can't tell you."

"Okay," I said. "Just tell me what you told Oliver."

"I didn't tell Oliver much," she said, looking down. She moved her finger around the rim of the glass, hesitating. Then she stopped and looked at me. "But on second thought, maybe I can tell you. I don't even know if I still have a client."

For the next few minutes Clementine brought me up to date about the call from Reginald J. Stanford, Morgan Stanford's death and her visits with Dr. Dussair and Detective Scruggs in Del Rio. Then she added the strange phone call she'd received from LuAnn Dussair, the doctor's wife.

"LuAnn is also Scruggs' sister," Clementine said. "Scruggs had told LuAnn that Morgan and Kurt were both banging Morgan's girlfriend at the same time. LuAnn told me about a woman in Galveston named Barnes who knew Kurt and Morgan. Barnes turned out to be Sloan, and Sloan put me on the trail of Slim Green and his daughter Joy." Clementine finished the story indicating that she suspected Morgan Stanford was Jake's father.

Right now, it's just a hunch," she admitted. "Still have some work to do, but if I'm right...?

"What about this Kurt Dussair character?"

Clementine scrunched her forehead. "What about him?" she said.

"Well, if both Dussair and Morgan Stanford were dipping their pens in the same inkwell at the same time..."

"Thanks a bunch, Parker!" Clementine exclaimed. "Why did you have to go there?"

Saving Jake

"You're a smart lady," I said. "Don't tell me you didn't consider Dussair could be the daddy."

"Of course, I've considered it. I just didn't want to think about the possibility."

"That's it, Ms. Ostrich, keep your head in the sand."

Clementine shot me the bird and drank more scotch.

"Dussair's wife must be thinking the same thing," I said. "That's why she called you. She wants to find out if her hubby's got a bastard kid somewhere and has been living a lie all these years. Wouldn't come off too cool at the couple's weekly bridge games. Not to mention his status at the hospital and all those Del Rio charity balls."

"I hate to admit it," Clementine grumbled, "but you may be right. Dussair completely changed his attitude when I told him I was a P.I. He either knows something or is concerned about what he doesn't know."

"All's not lost," I said, trying not to sound teasing. "It's still 50-50 that Morgan's the father. That is…unless the local postman was also dropping mail in the slot."

"That's enough," Clementine screeched.

She was clearly upset, her face flushed from the combination of booze and frustration. She wadded a napkin and threw it at me.

"Calm down," I said. "It's not over. Take it one step at a time."

She blew out a big stream of air trying to relax.

"You're right," she said. "First thing I need to do is get in touch with Stanford. Get the green light. I can't afford to keep dogging this thing without his go ahead. And so far, he doesn't seem interested. He already thinks I'm trying to scam him with the lost relative thing. And I'm sure not going to muddy the water by bringing up the roommate complication."

"I'm with you," I said.

She gave me a quizzical look.

"Tell you what," I said. "I'm as interested in finding the truth as you are. Stay in Galveston and we'll work it together."

Her eyes searched mine as they'd done before, as if wanting to trust. Color returned to her face as she calmed.

"The truth is..." she said. "I'm about out of funds. And old man Stanford, he's—"

"Okay, then," I jumped in. "I'll be your client. You work for me."

Clementine cocked her head to the side. "Well...maybe," she said. "But you'd have to give me an advance. I need to eat."

"Food's good here at The Garhole."

"And I need sleep."

"There's a bed upstairs."

"One bed?"

Chapter Thirty-One

Tomas Calzone came into the kitchen naked, except for a pair of white boxer shorts large enough to use for a bed sheet, his two-caret diamond ring on his finger and the Mexican coin dangling from his neck. He wiped sweat from his forehead with a towel.

Codger Moss stood at the sink with a can of bug spray in his hand aimed at the counter. Just then a roach scurried across the drain board. Codger gave it a shot spraying the entire counter.

"Got you, you son of a bitch."

Vinnie Calzone looked up from his plate of scrambled eggs at the table thinking this was the last time he'd eat anything in this shithole.

"Damn it, Codger," Tomas said. "What happened to the air conditioning guy?"

"Busted," Codger said. "Heard it on the scanner. Some bitch cop working a sting nailed his ass for trying to get a load off on Post Office Street."

"That's just great," Tomas said, wiping his forehead again. "What time is it?"

"After midnight," Vinnie answered, shoving the plate of half-eaten eggs away.

"Midnight!" Tomas scowled. "I told you I was taking a short nap. Why didn't you wake me? Luther is probably halfway to Louisiana."

"Luther Bourdain is on his way to hell," Vinnie broke in.

Tomas changed his focus to Vinnie. "What?" he said.

"He's dead," Vinnie said. "You should have stayed up and listened to the scanner. Cops all over the place at Green's house. Green's dead too."

"So what happened?"

"Cops are calling it a domestic dispute, like Luther was just there to get his woman back."

"So who killed Luther?" Tomas asked.

"It wasn't the bitch, Joy," Vinnie said. "The way I got it, they think Luther killed old man Green and then some twat came in and killed Luther."

"A woman? Who?"

Vinnie shrugged. "Didn't give her name. Don't know who she was."

Tomas sighed and shook his head in disbelief.

"The good news is," Vinnie added, "nobody's said nothing about any dope."

Tomas began to pace the floor, his huge gut hanging over the elastic band of his underwear. He turned back to Vinnie, "You think, Joy hid the stuff?"

"She probably did hide it," Vinnie said, lighting a cigarette. "She couldn't be a complete dumb ass, else how could she have stolen it in the first place?"

Tomas continued to pace. "If the cops are thinking it was a domestic problem, they would have had no reason to search the house. And if Joy's in the hospital and the old man's dead...maybe whoever killed Luther did us a favor."

"Favor?" Vinnie said, blowing out smoke. "What you talking about?"

Tomas stopped walking to explain. He looked at Vinnie. "With Luther out of the way, the house empty, and the cops wrapping it like a crime scene—"

"Nobody will be nosing around," Vinnie said.

Tomas nodded.

Codger broke in. "What about Joy's kid—Jake?"

"What about him?" Tomas said.

"I mean, he lived there too. What if he's in the house?"

"How old is he?" Tomas asked.

"Joy talked about him once," Codger said. "I think he's about 15."

"He's a juvenile," Vinnie said to Codger. "He'll be in custody or whatever they call it. Besides, everyone the kid knows is dead except Joy, and she's in the hospital. They sure ain't gonna let that kid stay in that house alone."

"What we gonna do?" said Codger.

Tomas glanced at Vinnie and then back to Codger. "We're going in," he said.

A. Hardy Roper

Chapter Thirty-Two

We went at it like a couple of Whirling Dervishes' on speed. I mean holy mackerel, the woman was insatiable, my clothes stripped off before the door shut. She pounded from the top like a pile driving machine on steroids, and then in a frantic move, she rolled over and pushed herself up to me like a baby bird with its beak open waiting for a worm. Except by now the worm had turned...or was dead anyway.

Thirty minutes later we went at it again, slower this time, partly out of necessity to pace my 46 year old body, but also—at least on my part—wanting to explore, to learn, to please. But Clementine was a machine, moving, working, pushing those big boobs against my cheeks—store-bought or not, who cared—moving as though this was forever and ever the last time, as though at the inevitable end of our session sex would be illegal, punishable by guillotine. After the finish, I closed my eyes and rolled over.

"You wuss," Clementine said. She slapped my butt and went after me again. I raised my hands in self-defense, pleading for rest. But there was no rest, no break. And after the third time, we both passed out, exhausted.

Morning sunlight peeked past the shade. My eyes opened at the sound of an outboard motor cruising into my dock. Who would be coming at this time of the morning?

I gingerly lifted Clementine's leg off mine and eased out the other side of the bed, stealing a glance at her naked body only have covered by a sheet. I paused, relishing the moment, admiring the form of Clementine's natural beauty. It had been a while.

I grabbed my shorts and a T-shirt off the floor and slipped down the stairs. Jake stood shirtless in the boat with his back to me. The muscles in his small shoulders flexed as he lifted a tub full of crabs and sat it on the dock. Even from several feet away I could see the burn scars on his arms.

"Good catch," I said, looking down at two-dozen big blues.

He turned, surprised. "Didn't want to wake you."

"Let me grab a quick shower," I said. "And we'll head to the hospital."

He turned back. "Gotta clean these crabs first."

I sensed the emotion in his voice but couldn't see his face. I stepped closer. He turned, eyes red and swollen.

"I need this job," he said. "Gotta help my mama."

We cleaned the crabs, iced them in the cooler, and left a note for Joe to boil the batch for the lunch crowd. I climbed the stairs and met Clementine at the bedroom door dressed and ready to go. I showered quickly, and the three of us piled into my truck.

We arrived on Seawall Boulevard to find the parking spaces along the street packed with cars. Out on the beach, kids with shovels played in the sand while mothers covered with oil and pot-bellied daddies roasted in the sun. It all seemed normal, an ordinary hot August day in Galveston.

Except for us, it was anything but ordinary. Beside me was a boy whose mother, a meth addict, lay in intensive care fighting for her life with a bullet wound in her chest. And looking out the window in the passenger seat was a female P.I. who, fresh from killing a man a few hours earlier, had also just given me six months' worth of sex in about six hours. Normal? I don't think so.

Saving Jake

As much as I had looked forward to leaving the Army and returning to Galveston to fish and run the bar, life hadn't worked out that way. In the four years since I'd returned to my little West Beach paradise, I had killed a neo-Nazi from Germany, who was trying to kill me, and two years later tracked down a Cuban spy. Now this. Stuff just seemed to happen at The Garhole Bar. I must have a sign on my back that says, "Parker McLeod, Ass Saver."

At the next red light, sombrero-clad Mom and Pop and their three squabbling little angels, crossed in front of us on their way to the beach. Mom held a string with several balloons floating overhead that said, "Happy Birthday."

The balloons triggered a thought and I said, "Jake, it's your birthday."

He didn't respond.

"Really, Jake?" Clementine said. She turned to look at him, a big smile on her face. "How old?" she asked.

When Jake didn't answer, I said, "15. We're having a party at The Garhole this afternoon."

I remembered Harry was bringing cupcakes out today, but I couldn't remember if we'd set a time. I asked Clementine to call Harry on her cell. She punched in the numbers and handed me the phone.

Harry's normally tranquil voice screamed through the speaker.

"Parker, where are you?"

"On our way to see Jake's mother at the hospital."

"The Police Chief gave me a heads up this morning. Lieutenant Oliver is looking for you. He knows you have Jake. He wants to interview the boy."

"Did you make the cupcakes?"

"What?"

"You said you were bringing cupcakes for Jake's party."

"This is serious, Parker."

"Okay, I'll swing by the station after the hospital. But we're still having the party."

"I don't know what you're thinking, Parker. You can't keep Jake. He's a minor."

"The juvenile judge is a friend of yours, right, Harry?'

"Up to now, anyway," he said. "But I don't like where this is going."

"See if you can arrange a meeting. I want to meet with the judge before Oliver interviews Jake."

"That's what I was afraid you'd say," Harry quipped.

Clementine and I sat in the ICU waiting room while Jake went in for a five-minute visit with his mother. He came out, head down, wiping his eyes with his hand.

"She don't look good," he said. "Bunch of wires and tubes hooked to machines."

"That means they're taking good care of her," Clementine said. She motioned Jake to sit between us.

"She can't talk," Jake continued. "Looks awful."

"Was she awake?" I asked.

"I said her name and she opened her eyes. I'm pretty sure she knew who I was. She raised her arm, had a tube coming out of it. It was cold, but she squeezed my hand. I guess that's good."

"Very good," Clementine said.

I left Jake with Clementine and stepped inside ICU to see if Joy could talk. A nurse hurried over.

"Are you a relative?" she asked, her voice low but firm.

"I'm here with Jake Green," I said. "He was just in here visiting his mother, Joy Green."

I pointed to her bed several feet away. As bad as Joy looked, I had seen worse at Walter Reed in Maryland and Brook Army Medical Center in San Antonio. Men so badly shot up or burned their own mother wouldn't recognize them.

"I'm sorry. You'll have to leave," the nurse said. She touched my arm.

"I know," I said. "I'm taking care of Jake right now. He's scared to death. Can you tell me anything?"

The nurse hesitated. I gave her my most soulful, pleading expression.

"I can't tell you much," she said. "Joy Green is critical. If she lives, she'll have a difficult recovery. It's not just the wound," she paused and gave a furtive glance around the room. "She—"

The nurse stopped in midsentence as though she was about to divulge something she shouldn't.

"Yeah, she's a meth addict." I said.

"We're dealing with a complicated situation. Withdrawal will be difficult. We'll probably have to restrain her. And then there's the possibility of shock and even pneumonia."

"I understand. I'll try to explain her condition to Jake. Have the police interviewed her?"

"Her physician wouldn't allow it. She can't talk now anyway."

Back in the waiting area, Jake stood by the vending machine sipping a Coke.

"We'll check on your mom again," I said. "Right now, we have a meeting with a judge."

We left the hospital and drove along the harbor. At the docks, shrimp boats and snapper fishermen waited to unload their catches for the seafood houses. One of the big cruise ships was loading passengers. As we turned toward the courthouse, Clementine dialed Harry's number on her cell and handed me the phone.

"Any news?"

"About time you called," Harry said. "Judge Abrams is waiting for us. Where are you?"

"Two minutes," I said.

We drove on a few blocks toward the municipal courts complex.

"Drop me off at the county clerk's office," Clementine said. "I want to check on something."

In the middle of the next block, Clementine got out and started across the concrete apron. I watched her move, my mind already dancing ahead to tonight, after Jake's birthday party.

Chapter Thirty-Three

Clementine felt Parker's eyes on her back. She pivoted on the top step and glanced back at the street, but he'd driven away. Then she smiled, thinking about the sex. Not bad for a forty-something stud, she thought. Old Parker had been ready all right. Or, maybe it wasn't Parker at all. Clementine figured she could have strummed that big a play out of any half-virile man. She knew the tricks of the trade. But no matter who brought the party, Clementine couldn't help thinking how tonight would go.

She removed a pink Vogue from her purse and lit up. She inhaled, held the smoke in for a beat and blew it out. She immediately sucked in another lungful of smoke and exhaled again. She snuffed out the remaining butt and pushed it into the metal container outside the door.

Clementine entered the courthouse lobby and proceeded toward the building's security checkpoint where two uniformed officers manned the metal detector. She reached to her side for her baton knowing if it activated the machine, she'd have a lot of explaining to do. She brushed her hip with her hand and then remembered the police had confiscated the baton for evidence. She felt strangely naked, her security blanket missing. And she knew from her experience as a cop, it might be weeks, even months before it would be returned. It might even go accidently missing from the evidence room. She had so much confidence in her baton she'd often left her 9mm Beretta at home. This time it had been a stupid mistake. She passed through security, rode the elevator to the third floor and stepped out. The sign over the glass doors read, "Vital Statistics."

She found a vacant computer and scrolled to the section for birth certificates. She typed in today's date, Jake's birthday, but fifteen years earlier. She scrolled through the records nine month earlier until she found what she was looking for: Jacob Henry Green, white male, born at 2:50 p.m., seven pounds two ounces. Mother: Joy Green, Father: unknown.

Clementine checked her watch. She had no idea how long Parker and Jake's meeting with the judge would last. She located Parker's truck and left a note on the windshield telling him to meet her at Deborah's, a boutique she'd spotted on the Strand. As she walked toward the boutique, she couldn't help but think about Jake's birth certificate. Why hadn't Joy named a father? Was it because she didn't want to name him or because she didn't know who the father was?

"Damn it," Clementine's mumbled aloud, her hopes sagging. This wasn't going to be as easy as she'd hoped. She had a lot more work to do.

Chapter Thirty-Four

We met Harry inside the municipal courts building dressed extra sharp as usual, decked out in a poplin suit, lightly starched yellow shirt and blue tie. His white hair was expertly combed, not a stand out of place, and his snow-white mustache and goatee were perfectly trimmed. I got hungry for fried chicken just looking at him.

Seeing Harry made me realize I was going before a judge asking to be Jake's guardian, and I hadn't even gotten the boy clean clothes. I wasn't dressed so spiffy myself, wearing jeans and a wrinkled polo. But to be fair, I had no idea this was going down today. We'd left The Garhole only a few hours before, too concerned about Jake's mom to worry about our dress.

The judge's office contained photos of her with certain dignitaries, none of whom I recognized, and a framed certificate from University of Texas law school at Austin.

Judge Janet Abrams was a looker, maybe 35, with medium brown hair that rested on her shoulders, and a line-free face pure as an alabaster vase. She appeared casually dressed wearing dark blue pants and a white-cotton shirt that protruded magnificently in the right places. She approached Harry with her hand extended, a small smile on her lips.

"Good afternoon, Counselor," she said to Harry. "Photo shoot for Esquire today?"

Harry took her hand, smiling. "Always the best for you judge. Thank you for seeing us on short notice."

"This better be as urgent as you indicated. I have a tennis date in an hour."

When Harry introduced us, Abrams gave me an all business appraisal, then turned to Jake and smiled. She chatted briefly with Jake, asking innocuous questions to set him at ease—what he liked to do, what sports he played if any, and about his favorite subject in school. When Jake replied he didn't have a favorite subject, Abrams smiled again. She then asked Harry to seat Jake outside in the waiting room.

With Jake absent, Judge Abrams retreated behind her desk and the friendly smile disappeared. "Proceed, Counselor," she advised.

Harry launched into the details about Jake Green, his mother Joy, his grandfather Slim Green, and the now deceased Luther Bourdain. He explained that Jake's mother was currently hospitalized in intensive care and that Jake had no other relatives. He was alone in Galveston and the house in which he lived was now a crime scene.

Abrams lowered her head. Then she looked up and said, "Does it never end, Harry?"

No one spoke, but we all knew what she meant. I could only imagine how many of these stories Judge Abrams had heard during her time on the bench.

After a moment, Abrams said, "What do you want?"

Harry nodded. "I am asking that you appoint me to represent the boy as his *attorney ad litem*. And I would further ask that you appoint Parker McLeod as his temporary guardian."

"I see," Abrams said. She looked at me. "Are you an approved Foster Parent, Mr. McLeod."

"No your, honor."

"What is your occupation and where do you live?"

"I own The Garhole Bar on west beach and live over the bar."

Abrams frowned and looked at Harry, "Really, Counselor," she said, the sarcasm obvious.

Harry stepped closer, "Mr. McLeod is a retired army Major with a sterling record of service, your honor. He is a Galveston native. I have known Parker for 30 years and vouch for him completely."

Abrams sighed and looked down at her desk.

I spoke up and said, "The boy trusts me, your honor."

Harry then explained how Jake's first instinct the night his mother was shot was to rush to Parker's house for protection. He also told Abrams about Parker almost getting killed when he went to check on Jake.

"I noticed the bruises on your neck, Mr. McLeod," the judge said. "Appears you were fortunate."

"Yes, your honor, I was."

Harry continued, "We are only asking for temporary guardianship, your honor. A matter of a few days until Jake's mother recovers."

"And if she doesn't," Abrams said.

"We will rely on the court for a more permanent solution."

"Harry," she said. "You're putting me in a bind on this. If I didn't know you so well..." Abrams paused, contemplating. She checked her watch. "Bring the boy in."

Abrams spent another five minutes questioning Jake. She asked about relatives in Louisiana. She explained that she could send him to a foster home, a nice couple, who were also looking after another boy his age.

"I want to stay with, Parker," Jake blurted out. "Until my mama is better."

The judge's forehead wrinkled and her eyes narrowed. She sat back in her chair. She put her palms together and laid her chin on her index fingers. Then she relaxed her fingers and gazed out the window. No one spoke. She turned back.

"Okay, Harry," Abrams said. "I will grant a temporary guardianship. But only until I can convene a formal hearing next week." And then she paused again. "And Harry," she said. "I am holding you personally responsible. I hope you know what you are doing."

After we left, Harry said in a low voice, "I'm way out on a limb here, Parker."

"Don't worry," I said.

"Oh, I'll worry," he said. "I just called in all my chits with the judge. And if I hadn't represented her in a nasty divorce last year, we'd still be out in the cold on this."

Out in the parking lot, Harry motioned for me to put Jake in the truck, and we stepped to his Cadillac. He opened the trunk and handed me a heavy paper sack.

"My Model 911...how did you—?"

Harry put his finger to his lips to silence me. "The police chief and I go back a long way. Your weapon wasn't fired so..."

I took the sack not surprised at Harry's connections. Over the years, he'd represented dozens of Galveston police officers, most of it *pro bono*, involving everything from wills to divorce and even wrongful arrest charges.

I had to ask. "Does hard-ass Oliver know about this?"

Harry shrugged. "We'll find out," he said. "We have a meeting in 10 minutes."

Chapter Thirty-Five

Clementine wished she'd brought a change of clothes from San Antonio. The problem was since old tight-ass Stanford hadn't approved the trip, she'd planned to return the same day. But finding Jake's birth certificate had changed everything. She knew she was on to something good, and she was determined to see it through, old man Stanford be damned.

The prices at Deborah's Boutique reminded her of the money she'd just spent for clothes in San Antonio. Clothes now hanging in her closet 200 miles away. She had no choice but to stand in line and hope her VISA card wasn't maxed out. When the customer in front of her moved on, Clementine lifted her purchases to the countertop. She'd selected a pair of beige shorts with two matching T-shirts, sandals with rhinestones on the straps, several pair of bikini panties in different colors and two bras. She'd also picked out a pair of jeans and a summer-weight dark-blue pantsuit.

Two customers lined up behind her. Clementine tensed. She crossed her fingers as the clerk swiped the card. "Please, please, please," she mumbled, her lips barely moving. The clerk stared at the machine waiting for approval. The woman behind Clementine shifted impatiently from one foot to another. And then the clerk tore the charge slip off the machine and pushed it across the counter. Clementine felt the color in her cheeks returning and her pulse slow.

She stepped out into the broiling August sun. Perspiration gathered on her face and underneath her blouse. Her cell phone buzzed. She moved into the shade from the building and set the packages on the sidewalk. She dug her phone out of her purse and answered the call.

A woman's voice said, "Ms. Garza, my name is Jennifer Hillbro. I have been retained by the law firm Higginbotham and Perry in Houston. The firm represents Reginald J. Stanford the third."

Clementine didn't respond. If foggy-bottom was the third Stanford to share the name. She wondered why Morgan wasn't the fourth.

"Hello...Ms. Garza?"

"How can I help you?" Clementine asked.

"It's about your employment with Mr. Stanford. Can we meet this afternoon at your convenience? I am here in Galveston."

Clementine spotted a bar across the street and agreed to meet Jennifer there in 20 minutes. She crossed the street and entered the bar. She stopped just inside to allow her eyes to refocus to the dark interior. The place was empty except for two thirty-something barflies wearing shorts and Hawaiian shirts, looking as if they'd just stepped in off Waikiki Beach. One was large and dark like a real Hawaiian. The other was smaller and blond. Clementine figured their wives were somewhere on the Strand buying T-shirts for the kids while these two dickheads slopped brew and watched baseball on TV.

Clementine ignored the tropical wannabes and headed for a computer she'd spotted at the far end of the bar. She set the clothes packages on the floor, ordered a vodka and tonic from a twenty-something bartender with tattoos covering his arms and powered up the computer. Just as she'd entered a search for Higginbotham and Perry, a voice came from beside her.

"Hey hon, whatcha doing? Checking your hot dating site?"

Saving Jake

The dark-haired barfly stood to her side, sipping beer, a big grin on his face. Clementine turned and checked him out. The dude wasn't bad looking, but the ring on his finger marked him as a typical horny toad, testing his charm after bolstering his courage with alcohol. Clementine finished her drink and signaled for another.

"Buzz off, Don Ho," she said. "Before your wife catches you and cuts you off for the weekend. Go sing "Tiny Bubbles" to the bartender."

The man's mouth gaped open. He turned and retreated to his barstool.

An attractive brunette, about 30, stood at the entrance scanning the room. Clementine waved, sizing up Jennifer Hillbro as she approached.

She had attorney written all over her, Clementine thought. Hair pulled back and twisted into a knot. Large-rimmed glasses and makeup so austere only a woman would notice she was wearing any. She even dressed the part—dark skirt, white silk blouse, matching jacket and mid-heeled pumps.

Jennifer Hillbro introduced herself. Clementine picked up her new drink, the lawyer ordered a Coke, and they moved to a table. Clementine waited for Hillbro to speak.

"Thank you for meeting me on short notice," the lawyer said.

Clementine nodded, thinking Hillbro's smile seemed genuine.

"It appears you have piqued Mr. Stanford's interest."

"Is that good or bad?"

"That's what Higginbotham and Perry want me to find out."

"The bastard can go screw himself," Clementine snorted. "I don't work well with stuffy old goats."

"Ah ha," Jennifer said. "I see you've experienced Mr. Stanford. I hear he's typical old money. Boston rich and boring

A. Hardy Roper

as grape jelly. Type of person who puts a quarter in a gumball machine and hopes a white one comes out."

Clementine laughed. There was something about this Jennifer Hillbro she liked. She finished her second vodka tonic and signaled for another. Then she said, "Not a nice way to speak about a client, Jennifer."

"Please, call me Jenny. And I don't actually work for Higginbotham and Perry. I have my own practice here in Galveston."

"And your connection is...?"

"My father is a partner in the firm at the Houston office. "He asked me to arrange an eye-to-eye with you while they check you out."

"What's there to check?" Clementine said.

"From what I hear, Old Reggie boy counts his money more often than Scrooge McDuck. He's worried you have conjured up some kind of scheme, inventing a grandchild."

"Hey, he called me, or didn't you know that?"

Jennifer didn't respond.

"Looks like I made a mistake tipping him so early. Got him all in a snit."

Clementine waved her hand as though she was through with the whole idea. But she knew she wasn't. If she could prove Jake had royal blood, the case would make national news and the Garza star would rise in the East. It was the break she needed.

Jennifer said, "Let's talk about this grandson. Tell me what you have."

"Can't do that," Clementine said. "Last time I actually spoke to old tight-ass Stanford, he accused me of double dealing and hung up on me. I don't see how he's still my client."

Jennifer opened her briefcase and removed several sheets of paper and a check.

"Actually, we've already investigated you," she said. "And you passed. Good report from your former employer, the San Antonio Police Department. And then there was your successful rescue of those little girls."

Clementine nodded and sipped her drink.

Jennifer passed the check and papers across the table. "This check is a retainer for $10,000. And the contract, stipulates Stanford will pay all your expenses and a reasonable fee going forward. You will report your progress to me. Of course, the contract also states you will maintain confidentiality on anything you discover. All we need is your signature."

Clementine glanced at the contract, then studied the check thinking about her Visa bill and car payments. This was the real McCoy, a chance for the big time. Of course, that assumed Jake was the product of Morgan's time in the saddle and not Dussair's or worse, some street druggie. If she accepted Mary Ann Sloan's version, the possibilities were endless.

Then she thought about the deal she'd made with Parker. Was it serious? Were they really partners? Parker had held to his end of the bargain—furnishing room and board. And there was also the promise of tonight after the party. She pushed the check and contract aside.

"I'll have to let you know," she said.

Clementine caught the questioning look on Jennifer's face and told herself this was not the time to create suspicion. She needed to keep Stanford's offer on the table until she'd squared it with Parker.

"It's not a problem. I just need to talk to someone," Clementine said.

Jennifer started to rise just as Don Ho's buddy arrived at the table.

"Don't know what you told my friend," he said to Clementine. "But now that there's two of you. We could have a few drinks and..."

Clementine stood, moving closer. "Really," she said, grinning.

The man rested his hand on Clementine's shoulder and squeezed it just a little too much. She reacted so quickly it even surprised her. Her peripheral vision was excellent. She knew exactly where to aim. She faked a turn and then drove her elbow deep into the man's abdomen. A great whooshing sound exploded from his mouth. He backed away holding his gut, stumbled, and crashed into a table.

Clementine pivoted quickly to her right, ready for Don Ho. The big kahuna sat motionless on the barstool with his mouth opened in silence. The bartender reached for the phone.

"Wouldn't do that," Clementine said to the bartender. "Cops take forever. Cost you the rest of the day's business. We're all done here."

The bartender replaced the receiver.

"You shit birds need to pay and get out," Clementine said to the Shirts.

Don Ho eased off the stool never taking his eyes off Clementine. He helped his buddy to his feet, and they turned toward the door.

"Don't forget the tip," Clementine said.

Ho took some bills out of his pocket and laid them on the bar.

Jennifer Hillbro sat through the entire episode without moving a muscle. After the two men exited, she stood and waved to the bartender for the check.

"The tab's on me," she said to Clementine. She raised her eyebrows and blew out a big breath, indicating she was impressed.

Clementine shrugged, as though it was all in a day's work.

As they exited the bar, Jennifer said, "Higginbotham and Perry have their own P.I.s they like to work with, but I think Stanford made the right choice. I was instructed to make you the offer, but Stanford has little patience. You have until tomorrow to decide."

A. Hardy Roper

Saving Jake

Chapter Thirty-Six

The three of us sat outside Oliver's office watching the Lieutenant scream at someone on the phone. He saw us through the glass partition and frowned.

A moment later, Oliver came out, walked straight to me and put his face close to mine. "What are you doing here, McLeod?"

"It is not necessary to be rude, Daniel," I answered. "We are brothers in a way. Both of us involved in apprehending bad guys so to speak. Be nice."

"Screw you, McLeod," he said. "You and your girlfriend aren't off the hook yet, so watch your tone. And it's Lieutenant Oliver to you."

"Well if that's the best you can do," I said. "This is Jake's attorney of record, Harry Stein. Harry, meet Lieutenant Daniel Oliver, one of Galveston's finest."

Harry extended his hand and Oliver took it.

"I've heard of you, Counselor," Oliver said. "How did you get mixed up with McLeod?"

Harry answered stone-faced. "I'm not 'mixed up' as you put it. I am Jake Green's *attorney ad litem*, and Parker is his legal guardian."

"His what?" Oliver shouted.

"His legal guardian. And as such he is entitled to be present during any questioning of the boy."

"Bullshit," Oliver said. "As of when?"

"As of 30 minutes ago," Harry answered. "In Judge Abram's office."

All this time, Jake had been standing next to me, eyes averted to the floor. We moved inside Oliver's office. For the next hour, the Lieutenant repeated the same questions to Jake several different ways—what did he see? Where did he go when he jumped out the window? How did he feel about Luther Bourdain? What was his relationship to Bourdain? What was his mother's relationship to Bourdain? Why did Jake and his mother come to Galveston?

Jake answered as directly and honesty as he could while leaving out any reference to drugs. He simply stated his mother was fleeing an abusive boyfriend.

When Oliver finished questioning Jake, he stood. "The interview is over for now."

"You mean interrogation," I quipped.

Oliver shot daggers at me and then turned to Jake. "Boy," he said, "you and the Green woman's story better match."

I stood and stepped between Jake and Oliver. "She is not the *Green woman* as you put it. Her name is Joy, and she is Jake's mother."

I rose and guided Jake out the door. Harry followed.

Oliver hollered at our backside, "We're not through with you or the boy, McLeod. Do not leave town. Either of you."

Chapter Thirty-Seven

We said goodbye to Harry, and by the time we arrived at the Strand to pick up Clementine, Jake was asleep in the cab. Clementine arranged her packages in the pickup bed and slipped into the passenger side.

"What store did you buy out?" I asked, noting the haul.

"A girl needs clothes," she said.

Clementine asked about the meeting with the judge. I told her everything went well with Abrams and explained her ruling. On the way back to The Garhole, I attempted a few light-hearted barbs trying to keep the upbeat mood going, but Clementine seemed distracted, absorbed in her own world.

My thoughts went back to Jake. We hadn't discussed his feelings about the death of his grandfather Slim Green, but it appeared to me Jake was either in denial about the loss, or he hadn't known him well enough to have deep anguish. Or maybe he was so upset about his mother, the old man's passing hadn't registered yet. Green's body was still in the morgue awaiting final disposition, a decision Joy would make whenever she was capable.

The most significant event was Luther Bourdain's death, ending the threat to Jake and his mother. Assuming Joy continued to improve, things should go uphill from here. It was only the challenge of overcoming the meth habit that brought doubts. Sergeant Martinez with the Galveston Police Department had told me a high percentage of meth users fail to kick the habit during treatment. The real test would be Joy's fear of losing parental rights for Jake versus the pull of the poison. I hoped she could handle rehab.

The birthday party began in the late afternoon. A *Happy Birthday Jake* sign and colored ribbons all arranged by Joe Stubbs hung from the ceiling. Clementine assembled a green salad, and I fried trout and mounds of french-fries. Harry's chocolate and strawberry cupcakes complete with icing and sprinkles disappeared quicker than a magician's sleight-of-hand. Even the gar head, smiling throughout, seemed to enjoy the festivities. By the time we all joined in for a rousing chorus of *Happy Birthday,* the sun had dropped below the horizon.

When the sky darkened and the bay waters began to cool, I turned on two large stadium lights mounted at the top of the dock. The beams of light spreading across the water attracted baitfish, which brought in the trout. Jake and I went out to the dock to fish. Out in the lights, we could hear the popping sounds of trout feeding on top of the water. Within minutes, Jake hooked a decent sized fish.

"Reel in when the fish is swimming toward you," I said, standing beside him. "Keep the line tight. When he turns away, let him go, don't reel, just hold on and let out the line if you have to. Play the fish, that's the fun of it."

Jake learned quickly and within moments brought the trout into the dock.

"This one's a keeper," I said, scooping the fish into the net.

Jake looked at me with sorrowful eyes, "Do we have to?" he asked.

And in that moment, I understood. With his grandfather murdered and his mother fighting for life, Jake had reached his fill of death. I unhooked the trout and released it back into the bay.

"Enjoy your party?" I asked.

"I wish my mama could have been here," he said.

I looked out over the water. "Me too," I said.

"What's going to happen to me, Mr. Parker?"

"You heard what the Judge said today. You will be with me."

Jake sighed heavily. He laid his head back on the bench and gazed at the stars. "I mean afterwards."

"After what?" I said.

"After my mama dies."

My heart dropped. I couldn't begin to put myself inside the kid's head. He'd been dragged though more rat holes in his short existence than most people see in a lifetime.

"Your mother is in good hands, Jake. They are doing everything they can. We have to take this one day at a time."

"But the days are so long," he said.

"Joe and I will take care of you. You know that don't you?"

"I guess," he said. And then he bent over with his head in his hands.

I gave him a hug and said, "You're just going to have to trust me, Jake."

He straightened and said, "Can I go see mama tonight?"

It had been a long day, but I knew I couldn't refuse. I went inside the bar to tell the group. When I came back outside, Jake stepped out from Joe's trailer wearing one of the short-sleeved shirts I had given him.

I smiled letting him know I understood. By exposing the burn scars inflicted by Luther Bourdain, Jake had signified he was through with secrets. He wasn't going to let past tragedies dominate his life. A feeling of pride surged in my gut. Jake had turned a corner. By a small act of internal heroism, he had taken his first step on the road to recovery.

Harry stepped beside me. "I'm going that way," he said. "I'll take Jake to the hospital. You can pick him up. I'll stay with him until you get there."

Before I could answer, Joe cut in, "No offense, Harry. But I'd like to take Jake. When Parker got custody, it made me sort of a godfather."

Jake stepped behind the bar and took a cupcake out of the refrigerator. "Saved this one for mama," he said.

No one spoke.

After everyone left, Clementine and I stacked the empty bottles in the trash and wiped the tables clean. I shut the big opening in the front, officially closing the bar. Clementine hadn't said much. I felt she'd more or less avoided me the entire evening. When we finished working, I realized Joe and Jake wouldn't return for a couple of hours. I caught Clementine's eye and nodded toward the bedroom upstairs. Instead of the return smile I anticipated, she said, "Get a beer and have a seat, Parker. We need to talk."

We moved to a table and Clementine related her meeting with Jennifer Hillbro. She told me about the check and the contract. She spoke in a rapid, nervous cadence, getting it all out without taking a breath. Then she sat with her mouth open and eyes wide, waiting for me to respond.

"Don't ever play poker for big money," I said.

"What?"

"You're breathing quick, shallow breaths, which in turn have caused your ample bosoms to heave. An attractive sight, I admit. Stirs my imagination. But I don't like to see you in such distress. Your guilt has popped out on your face like a set of hives."

She nodded, "That obvious, huh?"

"Afraid so," I said. "You want to work for Stanford, even though I was the one who stepped in during your time of need. Tsk, tsk, such gratitude.

"You don't want to cheat me, so you used this phony act to make me feel sorry for you, hoping I would let you out of our deal, enabling you to assuage your guilt at the same time. Bottom line...if your plan worked, it would save face and still allow you to get what you want."

Her face lightened, the lines dissipating.

"Thank you, Dr. Freud," she said. "Now tell me it's all just a result of my repressed sexual desires."

"Well, probably," I answered. "But fortunately, there is a recognized treatment for that condition."

"Parker, you shit," she said. "How can we work this out?"

"Well, I do all my business in my private office upstairs."

Clementine reached for my hand. "You're sick, Parker. You know that? Really sick."

A. Hardy Roper

Chapter Thirty-Eight

I'd had wild women before but nothing like Clementine Garza. If she had an inhibition, I never discovered it. We rolled, humped, panted and rocked. Our hearts pounded, slowed and raced again. We sweated, finished, took a shower and started over. We stretched muscles, ligaments, and tendons until our backs hurt and our legs were too weak to walk. If we'd had a trapeze, we would have broken it.

The first session ended rather quickly because she wouldn't stop moving. We took a five-minute power nap and went at it again. It was as though we were both trying to get in as much sex as possible in case the Rapture was coming, and we wouldn't qualify.

When the moon reached high in the sky, we were laid out in Adirondack chairs on my top deck too exhausted to move. After a while, I shuffled to the railing and gazed out on West Bay. The moon sent slivers of light across the water illuminating the surface turned slick as glass from the dying wind. A yellow-crowned night heron sat perched like a statute on the dock below, waiting silently for the telltale swirl in the water indicating feeding fish. A popping sound came from a swirl and before the sound cleared my ears, the heron swooped off the deck, low and quick. The bird hit the water without slowing, grabbed the trout in its beak, and lifted off to some safe haven where it could relax and enjoy its evening meal.

It reminded me that regardless of our personal chaos, the world continued to turn; life at its most basic level threaded on. In truth, it was only the never-satisfied humans who disrupted the scheme of things, absorbed in their own narcissistic worlds, always battling the future, grubbing and competing.

And tonight I was guilty as charged, the top mercenary at the head of the line—a self-centered, self-seeking, son of a bitch. It had been a long time since I'd been with a woman like Clementine Garza. I felt no remorse, only greed. I wanted all of her I could get.

Clementine moved behind me and put her arms around my chest, her head on my shoulder. We stayed that way for a moment, content to enjoy the quiet of the night.

I looked at Clementine's watch. "It's later than I thought. I'm worried about Joe and Jake. They should be back by now."

"Jake probably wanted to stay longer," Clementine said.

"Maybe," I said.

We went down into the bar to wait for their return. I wanted an update on Joy and find out how Jake was handling his mother's condition. Clementine made a pot of coffee. We sat in silence at a table. I tried to relax. But something nagged at my consciousness. Something I couldn't understand. I retraced the scene at Green's house, Slim dead, Joy wounded, Jake missing. And then it hit me, something I hadn't thought about since the shooting at Green's. Where was the bag of meth Joy had stolen from Luther?

Chapter Thirty-Nine

Joe Stubbs sat alone in the ICU while Jake was in with Joy. It was long past normal visiting hours, but the nurse had made an exception and let Jake stay. Joe had tried several tricks to stay awake—slapping himself in the cheek, pinching and even humming '80s rock songs.

And then his mind flashed to a girl in high school he used to dream about during his dark days in the hospital after the Gulf War. She was short and cute, legs firm and brown. When all seemed lost, the memory of her smile had kept him going.

Joe had always wondered if she liked him, but he never had the courage to ask her out. What if she'd refused or even worse, laughed at him? Then his best friend pounced and took her off the market. Joe drooled when he saw them together. His friend told him she had the strictest dad on the island. She used to sneak a pair of short-shorts out of the house in her purse and put them on later. Joe remembered those shorts, solid red and tight. He often wondered what had happened to her. But that was 10 years ago. Before his Humvee got hit by an RPG, before his legs were blown off, before his world ended, at least the world as he had known it.

The door to ICU opened and a tall, fortyish woman came out wearing a flowered nurse's uniform. She had high cheekbones and smooth skin. Joe thought how nice she'd look fixed up on a Saturday night. But now, in the middle of her shift, her eyes were weary. It seemed an effort to manage a smile.

"You must be Joe Stubbs, Jake's friend," she said. "I am Kathy Landry." She held out her hand, and Joe took it.

"How is Joy?"

"Stable from the gunshot," Landry replied. "She's started withdrawal, and it's going to get nasty. I let Jake stay past visiting hours to get as much time with her as he could. After tonight, I don't think he should see her until she's past the worst of it."

"That bad, huh?"

"Methamphetamine use is epidemic. Between what the Mexican drug cartels smuggle in and what the locals produce, the streets are out of control."

The door to ICU banged open and Jake burst out, his face contorted in pain. "Something's happened. She's, she's..."

Landry rushed into ICU. Jake followed. Blood seeped through the bandage on Joy's chest. Landry struggled over her, trying to control her flailing arms and thrashing legs.

"Hold her legs," Landry shouted. "We'll have to strap her."

When Jake reached over to hold his mother's legs, Joy broke Landry's grip on her arms and slapped wildly, hitting the nurse in the chest. Then she dropped back, beating her head against the mattress. More stitches ripped open, more blood seeped out. Landry strapped one arm at a time to the bed railing and did the same with her legs and feet. She fastened another strap across her forehead. Joy's eyes flared as red as a rabid wolf. Her tongue danced at the edge of her mouth while she babbled constant, unintelligible sounds.

A doctor appeared and shoved a needle into Joy's arm. She calmed within seconds and went unconscious. The doctor held Joy's wrist, timing her heartbeat.

Landry turned to Jake, "Thanks for your help," she said. "We'll take it from here."

Saving Jake

Jake went out to the waiting room and sat as though in a trance, staring at the wall. A few minutes later, Nurse Landry came out. She sat beside Jake and spoke slowly, methodically.

"Jake...look at me."

Jake raised his head, fear radiating from his face, lips twitching, eyes like saucers.

"We need to talk about your mother's condition," she said.

Jake straightened in the chair.

"Your mother is a methamphetamine addict. It's one of the most devastating and ruinous drugs around. But she can recover from it with help. It will aid with the treatment if we know how long she has been addicted."

Jake nodded. "We used to live in Galveston," he said. "She smoked pot here, but she didn't smoke *ice* until we got to Louisiana. Maybe two years ago. I can't remember for sure."

"That helps," Landry said, her voice soft. "The shorter the time she's been using, the better the recovery chances. The first few days of withdrawal are the worst. But we'll watch her closely."

"What can I do to help," Jake asked.

"Give her support," Landry said. "Let her know you love her and that she can get through this."

Landry paused. She put her hand on Jake's shoulder. "I watched you in there, Jake. Helping with your mom. If I had a son as brave as you, I'd want to be around to see him grow up."

Jake sighed, a slight nod.

Landry hugged him and whispered, "And I'll bet your mom is going to feel the same way."

Landry pulled back. "The doctor is with her now," she said. "You can go in for a few minutes."

Jake looked at Joe. "It's okay Jake. We'll stay a little longer."

When Jake went into ICU, Landry turned to Joe. "This is not going to be easy," she said. "Methamphetamine withdrawal is the worst of all the drugs. Cocaine, heroin, you name it. You saw the blotches on her face and the rotted teeth. She's aged 30 years in two."

Joe nodded.

"Affects every part of the body," Landry continued. "She could have a stroke, a heart attack. Probably has liver and kidney damage from all the heavy metals used in cooking the stuff. Her immune system is certainly out of whack. We'll have to run tests and watch for all of that. Her body will have to completely detox. For the first few days, she'll be very aggressive. She won't sleep much. She'll be fatigued and yet anxious at the same time. She'll hallucinate, may become paranoid, even suicidal. She'll have incessant conversations with herself or an imaginary companion. "

"So sad," Joe said.

"If she gets through those stages, deep depression may set in. She'll be flat, unemotional. She'll speak quietly, make poor eye contact. After she's completely dried out, we'll move her to a treatment facility."

"What happens there?" Joe asked.

"Sleep medication for a couple of weeks. Lots of therapy, including her family if she has any. They'll assess her for suicidal thoughts. Antidepressants and tranquilizers if she needs them. Educational seminars and, of course, the 12-step program."

"How long will that take?'

"Depends on Joy," Landry continued. "If she makes it through all that successfully, she'll have outpatient visits for another six months."

"Sounds like it'll never end."

"May not," Landry said. "Meth is the worst scourge since the Black Death."

"I understand," Joe said. He reached his hand out and Landry took it.

When the nurse went back into ICU, Joe rolled his chair to the wall phone. Just as he reached for the receiver, the phone rang.

A. Hardy Roper

Chapter Forty

I screamed through the phone line, "What is going on? Something happened to Joy? Where's Jake?"

"Calm down," Joe said.

"Thought you'd be back by now."

"Haven't left the hospital. Joy had some problems, and Jake wanted to stay."

"What kind of problems?"

"She's started withdrawal."

"How long you gonna stay?"

"Not sure."

"I'm on my way."

"No need," Joe said. "Everything is under control. Jake wants to stop at Green's house on the way back and get some clothes. Go on to bed, we'll see you in the morning."

"It's a crime scene. Taped off."

"It's also the middle of the night. Come on, Parker. Get real. I'll go in for him."

"How are you going to do that with no wheelchair ramp? I'll go over in the morning and get what he needs."

Joe didn't respond for a moment, and then he said, "Well, okay, Parker, but Jake's not going to like it."

I hung up, frustrated that I had let Joe take Jake to the hospital in the first place. I should have been with him.

Clementine took my hand. "Your pulse is racing, Parker. Take it easy. It's not that big of a deal. Joe can handle it. There's a good moon tonight. How about a walk on the beach?"

A. Hardy Roper

We drove to San Luis Pass in my pickup, cut off the highway just before the bridge, and parked by the surf. The beach was deserted except for a lone fisherman who'd backed his truck to the water and put out poles and lines.

The windless night had calmed the surf and the moon lighted the shore. We strolled hand in hand.

"Tell me about you," she said.

"Not much to tell," I said.

"All that time in the Army?"

"Not by choice. Drafted at 18. I decided I liked Army life and stayed."

"Marriage?"

I turned and pushed Clementine back to arm's length. "My High School sweetheart."

"Kids?"

"Janie got pregnant on prom night. Her mother was Galveston's society queen. Old money. She wanted to send Janie off to have the baby. But Harry Stein talked her mother into letting us get married. Then...Janie miscarried."

"Oh...I'm sorry," Clementine said.

"Me too," I added. My mind flashed back to those terrible, lonely days. We were just kids. When I needed someone the most, my mother was dead and my wife Janie was never really there. I realized later she'd had her own demons to fight. Through the years, the thought of the baby girl I'd lost was never far from my mind.

"What happened then?" Clementine asked.

"During the first few years in the service, the Army sent me all over the U.S., intelligence schools, language schools, you name it. Janie stayed home with her mother. Then, because I was in Intelligence, the Army sent me to Germany, the epicenter of the Cold War. Janie never visited, much less lived with me. Wasn't much of a marriage. We split after I came back from the Gulf War. She's happy now, I guess. Married to some insurance mogul in Houston."

"That when you opened The Garhole Bar?"

I nodded and gazed out over the silent water.

"Good place to hide out," she said.

"Better than most," I said.

Then I told Clementine how I inherited the land when my mother was killed in New York.

"How much land do you own?"

"Three-hundred acres. Stretches from the edge of the bay, where we're standing, across the highway to the edge of the beach. My grandfather bought the land back in the 1930s during the Depression."

"Why don't you sell it? Move to the big city?"

"Never happen," I said. "Traffic, pollution. People scurrying like ants, working, watching television, sleeping, working. Not my kind of life. West Beach is bad enough. Every year more housing developments. More canals cutting through the marsh. Estuaries disappearing. I figure the least I can do is keep a little piece of the island as pure as possible."

"It is peaceful here," Clementine said.

"Most of the time anyway," I said.

"What do you mean by that?"

"I don't know. Bad feeling, I guess."

A. Hardy Roper

Saving Jake

Chapter Forty-One

Jake came out of ICU and awakened Joe, napping in his wheelchair.

"She's asleep now" he said. "We can go if you want. I left the cupcake by her bed. She likes sweets."

They left the hospital at two in the morning. As Joe backed out of the lot, Jake said, "Don't forget to stop at Grandpa's."

Joe didn't answer. He'd left the impression with Parker that he'd bring Jake straight home without stopping at Green's. But Jake had been through so much tonight, he hated to disappoint him. Maybe it wouldn't hurt to stop, he thought. Save a trip tomorrow. Then he thought about Jake going in alone, facing the scene where his grandfather had been killed and his mother wounded. He wondered about the blood splatters and the possibility of seeing Luther's form outlined in chalk on the floor. He passed Bay Harbor without slowing.

Jake straightened in the seat. He turned to Joe, a confused look on his face. "You missed the turnoff," he said.

"It's late, Jake. You need some rest. Parker is waiting up for you. He said he'd go over in the morning and get what you needed."

"It's my house," Jake said, a defiant tone to his voice.

Joe didn't respond. He drove down the road to The Garhole noticing Clementine's Mustang was in the front but Parker's truck wasn't.

Jake noticed it too and said, "Parker's not even here. Let's go back to grandpa's house."

"No," Joe said, adamant now and tired himself. "I don't know where Parker is, but you're not going to wait up for him. You're going to eat something and go to bed."

Inside the bar, Joe scrambled eggs while Jake sat at the counter. When they finished eating, Joe ordered Jake into the mobile home.

"Take a shower and hit the hay," he said. "We'll talk in the morning."

Jake frowned, but followed orders and left out the back door.

Joe popped a beer out of the cooler and cleaned the dishes, waiting for Parker to return. A few minutes later, disgusted at Parker for not being there after all the fuss he'd caused, Joe decided to go to bed. He rolled up the ramp to the mobile home and, hearing nothing, checked Jake's bedroom. Empty.

He rolled out to his truck, lifted himself into the driver's seat and engaged the crane to take the wheelchair back to the pickup bed.

He backed out and floored the truck up the lane to the highway. "Parker," he cried out. "Where the hell are you?"

Chapter Forty-Two

"You bring a flashlight?" Tomasso Calzone asked Codger as he turned out of the drive headed for Green's house.

"I got one," Codger said. "Don't know how long the batteries are gonna last. Wanna stop and get some more?"

Vinnie Calzone piped up from the back seat, a sarcastic smirk on his face, "It's two in the morning, dumbass. Anybody seeing you this time of night would remember you. We don't need that."

"You sure you know the way?" Tomas said to Codger.

"Turn right on Stewart Road," Codger said. He shifted the shotgun he'd brought to the left to give himself more room in the seat. "Bay Harbor is the last development on FM3005 before you get to the toll bridge over San Luis Pass. Green's house is on the last street. Nothing behind his place but marsh. Sometimes big old bull alligators slip in there during the rut. Horny sons of bitches."

Tomas squinted at his alligator shoes and swore under his breath, wishing he'd brought a change of clothes. If the trip to Galveston had been as quick as he'd figured, the drive back to New Orleans for more clothes wouldn't have been worth the time. But things had changed. Luther had to go and get himself shot.

"Think there's any mud in the yard?" Vinnie asked, checking the shine on his expensive Italian loafers.

Codger turned to face Vinnie in the back seat. "Ain't rained much. Nothing but sand out there anyway. Be dry as granny's muff."

Tomas glimpsed at Codger sitting next to him. The sight of Vinnie's scraggly beard, ragged shorts and dirty T-shirt sent bile edging up in his esophagus. He wondered how the old derelict could run a stable of girls.

He turned back to the road and noticed the moonlight flooding through the front windshield had caused a momentary sparkle in his two-caret diamond ring. He smiled, pleased at his success in life. From a barber's son to a big house in the Garden District. Not bad, he thought.

"Keep going straight," Codger said.

A few minutes later they approached a sharp curve in the road. As Tomas took the turn, the shotgun tilted, the barrel pointing just below Tomas' shoulder.

"Get that damn gun away from me," Tomas yelled. He slammed the brakes. The Cadillac screeched to a stop. He slid out of the car and stood in the road. He rubbed the gold coin hanging around his neck, thanking his good luck piece that the shotgun hadn't gone off.

"You dumb son of a bitch," he yelled to Codger. "Put that thing in the trunk."

Vinnie, in the backseat, chuckled at the scene. He lifted a 9mm Smith & Wesson automatic out of his waistband. The gun only held nine rounds, but because it was smaller and fit easier into his pants, he liked it better than the automatics holding 15. He yanked the receiver back, slammed a bullet into the chamber and laid the weapon on the seat beside him.

Tomas turned right on 3005. As they passed through Jamaica Beach, Codger cautioned him to slow below the 30mph speed limit. Tomas spotted a local cop backing into a slot in front of the hardware store. He braked to 25 and stared straight ahead.

"Lucky I saw him," Tomas said.

Vinnie twirled the automatic on his finger. "Maybe it was the cop that was lucky."

"Christ sake," Tomas muttered to himself, amazed at everyone's stupidity but his own.

"Used to have a girl that lived in Jamaica Beach," Codger said. "Her old man worked the night shift at the refinery in Texas City and Gloria worked nights for me. She knew the trade. Great lay."

"How much farther?" Tomas asked, impatience growing.

"Sea Isle is next. No cops there. And then a couple of miles."

Minutes later, Codger directed Tomas into Bay Harbor. They drove to the last street and turned toward Green's house. The street was dark, no street lamps and no lights on at any of the houses.

"Cut your headlights," Vinnie said.

"Not till I get to Green's house," Tomas answered. "If there's a cop out front, we'd look pretty stupid driving by with no lights."

"That's it on the left," Codger said. "I remember the fence and that old boat in the yard."

And then they saw the bright yellow crime scene tape wrapped over the front fence and around the entrance to the house.

"Nice present," Vinnie said. "Tied up in a pretty yellow bow just waiting for us to open it."

Tomas cruised by at idle speed. They watched for movement in the yard and the house and saw none.

"I think we're good," Tomas said. "No cops. No cars at any of the houses."

"Mostly weekenders out here," Codger said. "Folks from Houston trying to escape. Been trying to figure a way to get some of my girls out here, but there's no place for them to work."

"They could walk the street," Vinnie said.

"3005 is 20 miles long," Codger answered.

"Get more girls," Vinnie said.

Tomas idled past the house. He drove around the block again with the headlights off. At the corner, a block from Green's house, he turned the car around and parked back from the intersection.

"Codger, you're our lookout. Stay in the car," Tomas said, taking the flashlight from Moss. "Me and Vinnie will walk in from here. No sense in some nosy neighbor seeing a car parked in front and calling the cops. I hope Green don't have a dog."

"Didn't see one when we passed," Vinnie said.

Tomas reached under the seat and removed his .380 semi-automatic Ruger. He jammed back the slide to chamber a round.

"What you want me to do if I see a cop?" Codger asked.

"Don't do nothing. If he comes up the stairs, we'll handle him."

Codger frowned. "Why don't I just shoot the prick?"

Tomas turned around and gave Codger a look as if not believing what he'd just heard. "You shoot a cop. We'll never get off the island."

Tomas and Vinnie crossed the culvert and stopped at the gate in front of Green's house. Vinnie ran his comb along the chain-link fence attempting to flush out a dog. Nothing. They opened the gate, ducked under the crime tape, re-latched the gate, and crept up the stairs surprised to find the front door unlocked. Just as they entered the flashlight went out.

He shook the flashlight and it came back on. "We'll have to hurry," he said. "Can't risk turning on the lights."

They entered Green's room and completely ripped it apart, dumped all his clothes from the dresser and closet on the floor. They jerked the mattress and box springs off the bed. They searched the closets looking for secret compartments but found none. They ripped the meds and toiletries out of the medicine cabinet and threw them to the floor.

They moved to Joy's bedroom. Vinnie checked the drawers in her nightstand and found a glass pipe. He held it up for Tomas to see.

"My, my," he said. "Looky, what I found."

Tomas took it from Vinnie and sniffed the bowl of the pipe.

"Where there's smoke there's fire," he said.

Finding the pipe spurred them on. They tore everything out of the closet and ripped the bed to shreds. They missed nothing, leaving the room in tatters.

They moved to the kitchen, searched every pot, every drawer and cabinet. They dumped the contents out of the freezer and rifled through the refrigerator. They tore the cushions off the sofa and flipped it over.

Standing in the middle of the room, Tomas yelled, "Damn it! Where did that bitch hide the stuff?"

Vinnie said, "You think the cops found it and left it out of the story on purpose? Trying to trap us?"

"They don't even know we exist," Tomas said. "And Luther is dead. Be more likely the bastards found it and kept it. Sell it themselves. Happens all the time."

"Let's check the bitch's bedroom again."

They were in Joy's room for one last search when the front door opened.

"What's that?" Vinnie said.

Tomas peaked out the bedroom door and saw Jake backlit in the doorway.

From his vantage point a block away, Codger had watched Jake approach Green's house, climb over the back fence, and run across the yard. When Jake reached the stairs, Codger thought about honking the horn to alert the brothers but decided they could handle a kid.

Then he spied a pickup coming down the street toward Green's house. He slid low in the seat, his eyes just above the bottom of the window, hoping the people in the truck hadn't seen him. When the truck turned into Green's driveway, Codger felt his heart race. He didn't know what to do. If a cop arrived, he wasn't supposed to do anything. But this was no cop.

The truck's headlights beamed through the fence and across the yard. The driver honked the horn. What was that all about? He wondered.

Codger took the keys out of the ignition and slipped out the passenger door. He eased the door closed, kept his profile low and edged around to the trunk. He slid the key into the lock and held his hand on the top of the trunk, keeping it from popping open. He removed the shotgun and eased the trunk closed. He looked back at the truck. The lights were still flashing across the yard, but no one got out.

Codger hoped Tomas and Vinnie had seen the truck lights but there was no way to know for sure. He studied the distance to the truck, contemplating the best way to approach. The ditch alongside the road wasn't deep enough to completely conceal his body, but it would help.

He moved rapidly along the ditch hunched over hoping to conceal his tall frame. He stopped directly behind the truck but across the road. He hoped the driver was focused on the house and not on the truck mirrors. He crossed the road and moved quickly to the rear of the truck. He noticed the crane and the wheelchair in the bed. He smelled exhaust from the tail pipe and realized the truck's motor was running. Good, he thought, hoping the noise would mask his approach.

He ducked low and ran to the side of the truck. Codger grabbed the barrel of the shotgun with his left hand and the stock with his right. Just as the figure turned toward him, He drove the gun butt hard into the man's head. Bone crunched.

Saving Jake

The man slumped to his side in the seat. Codger jerked the door open. The body lay across the seat, his head almost at the passenger door. Codger leaned in to hit him again, but something held him back. The stump of the man's cutoff leg pushed into Codger's thigh. And then he saw the other stump. Codger hesitated, swallowed hard. Blood seeped from a large cut on the man's cheek, running into his nose and mouth. The man coughed and spit. Then he closed his mouth and started a low moan.

Codger eased out of the truck. He turned the lights and engine off and threw the keys into the ditch. He paused and studied the house. No sound or movement. He surveyed the neighborhood. Nothing had changed. No lights on or people outside. He wiped the stock of the shotgun across the grass to remove the blood and gristle and hustled back to the Cadillac.

When Jake came into the bedroom, Vinnie grabbed him around the neck and dragged him into the living area. "You see what we did to this place. You got one minute or the same thing's gonna happen to you. Where is it?"

Vinnie's powerful hand closed tighter. Jake coughed and sputtered, trying hard to breath.

"Let loose," Tomas said. "He can't talk the way you got him."

Vinnie released his hand from Jake's neck and slammed him to the floor. He stepped forward. Jake scooted across the floor and cowered against the wall.

"Who...who are you?"

Vinnie kicked Jake's leg. "Shut up. We do the asking? Where is it?"

"What? Where is what?"

Vinnie kicked Jake's leg again. "Don't play the dumbass. It's not in the house. Where did that slut mother of yours hide the stash she stole from Luther?" Vinnie raised his hand to slap Jake's face.

Jake raised his arms to protect himself and screeched, "I don't know where she hid it."

"Bullshit," Tomas said. "You ever want to see that bitch old lady of yours again, you better talk. And you're outta time."

Chapter Forty-Three

We arrived back at The Garhole to find the parking lot empty except for Clementine's Mustang.

"Not back," I said.

"Hasn't been an hour yet," Clementine quipped.

"Long enough," I said.

I called UTMB and the receptionist transferred the call to the ICU waiting room. The phone rang at least 20 times. I didn't want to get paranoid about Joe and Jake not being home yet, but I couldn't help the feeling building in my gut. I leaned against the stove and looked up at the gar head.

Clementine slipped onto a barstool. "You're studying that thing like it's the West Beach version of a crystal ball."

"If only," I said.

"You think something happened to Joy? She got worse or...?

"Joe would have called."

I put a second call through to the ICU waiting area. No one answered. I called the Galveston police dispatcher. No accidents reported past midnight.

"Let's go," I said.

I cranked my old pickup and sped toward the deserted highway. Dark clouds had moved in over the moon. There were no stars. The night was as black as tar. Daybreak was three hours away. In the dog hours of the morning, the only noise on the highway was the gentle knock of my truck engine. I slowed at the entrance to Bay Harbor.

"Let's check Green's house first," I said. "Maybe Jake conned Joe into stopping for his clothes."

Clementine nodded and hunched forward in the passenger seat, studying the road ahead. We turned onto Green's street and rolled toward his house. Joe's truck was parked in front, but the cab appeared empty. I glanced at the upstairs of Green's house and saw total darkness. Why were there no lights in the house? Where were Joe and Jake? Neither of us said anything, but the tension in the truck was palpable. I gripped the wheel harder and felt Clementine stiffen beside me. She braced a hand against the dashboard and narrowed her eyes.

I braked to a stop behind Joe's truck and jumped out. I found Joe sprawled across the seat, blood matted on his face, his pulse weak. I cursed Joe and cried for him at the same time. Why had he stopped?

Clementine yanked open the passenger door, cell phone to her ear, hollering at the 911 operator.

I bent to his ear, "Joe, it's Parker. Help is on the way. Stay with us." I squeezed his hand and asked him to squeeze mine if he could hear me. He responded with a slight moan.

Joe's breaths came quick and shallow, his face pale, skin clammy. I feared his body had already gone into shock, organs shutting down from lack of blood and oxygen. The dark circles around his eyes indicated a severe concussion or even worse, internal hemorrhaging that we couldn't see and could do nothing about. With the side of his head severely crushed, I feared he'd injured vertebrae in his neck. Army training had taught me any sudden movement of his body could produce permanent paralysis.

Clementine met me at the back of the truck holding my .45 automatic. I glimpsed the tense lines in her forehead and tightened jaw and knew my face mirrored hers. My heart banged against my chest.

Saving Jake

"Stay with Joe," I said, reaching for my weapon.

It appeared Joe had not attempted to get his wheelchair out of the truck. Maybe he'd seen the stairs and decided against going up. Or maybe the crime tape had deterred him. Either way, it was possible that when someone attacked Joe, Jake had escaped. But it was also possible that if someone had attacked Joe while Jake was upstairs, Jake and the attacker were still there.

The Army had taught me how to bug a telephone and shadow a suspect without being observed but nothing about the proper technique for storming a house. I crept across the deck and put my ear to the door. If the attacker was in the living area, my first shot would have to be quick and accurate. But how could I do that in total darkness? The last time I had tried this, it hadn't worked out so well. I had busted through the same door the day before to find Luther Bourdain, with a gun in his hand, struggling with Joy Green. I hesitated. Maybe lightning did strike twice. I could wait for the cops. But with Joe hurt and Jake missing, I decided to go full bore and hope for the best.

I hit the door with my shoulder full on, gun out, ready to blast away, hoping Jake wasn't being used as a shield. I rolled to the floor and scurried behind a chair. Nothing happened. I waited for my eyes to adjust to the darkness and scanned the area, then braced for an attack from one of the bedrooms. I heard no movement, not even a footfall or a hammer going back. I waited a few beats, decided no one was there, and got up and turned on the lights. Someone had wrecked the place, leaving nothing untouched—seat cushions shredded, pots and pans dumped to the floor, even the refrigerator contents emptied. The bedrooms were worse, mattresses ripped open, clothes thrown about.

Then I saw Jake's purple and gold LSU cap on the floor. I remembered he was wearing the cap when he left with Joe for the hospital.

I hustled back to the deck in time to see the EMT's loading Joe on a backboard. I caught up with the paramedic just after he closed the back door of the ambulance.

"How is he?" I said.

"Breathing okay," the medic responded. "Blood pressure's not good. Need to get some fluids in him."

As soon as the ambulance departed, my mind flashed back to Jake. I turned to Clementine. "Where are the cops?"

She put her hand on my arm. "Calm yourself. Stroking out won't help Joe or Jake. The paramedics said they got here quick because they'd just finished another call close by. Cops probably had to come from town. Even with sirens wailing, it's 20 minutes."

I took a deep breath and blew it out. "You're right," I said. I pressed my hand over my eyes trying to focus. I told Clementine about finding Jake's hat in the back bedroom indicating he had made it to the house.

"Someone took him," she said, her tone final.

"Maybe," I said. "But when Luther shot Green, Jake jumped out the window and took a back trail to The Garhole..."

"Yes, but the bedroom window is not open now."

"Maybe he got out the door. I'm going to The Garhole."

"I'm going with you," Clementine said.

"No, stay here. If Jake's hiding close by, he may see you and come out. I'm going to check The Garhole. If he's not there, I'll come up the trail from that end. I hope to God he's out there."

The ambulance pulled away leaving the scene eerily quiet. There wasn't a sound on the street. I handed Clementine my .45 in case the attacker was still around. I climbed into my truck and said, "Call Harry Stein and tell him about Joe. He's close to the hospital."

I raced to The Garhole, jammed the truck to a stop in the parking lot and ran inside. I checked the bar, Joe's mobile home and my bedroom upstairs. No sign of Jake.

The trail to Green's house came by the pond where Jake and I had gone bird-watching. I drove to the berm overlooking the pond and hustled around the water toward the motte of oak trees. I found the entrance to the trail and cursed myself for not bringing a flashlight. I shouted Jake's name several times, but got no response. In the darkness, it was all I could do to stay on the trail. Find Jake, I kept telling myself. Find Jake. I followed the trail to the halfway point, thinking if Jake were on the trail, he should have made it this far. Things weren't looking good.

It was then I heard a rustle of bushes behind me. I turned. Something hit my face hard and everything went black.

A. Hardy Roper

Chapter Forty-Four

I came to my senses with my face in the mud, my mouth full of nauseous muck from the marsh, and my arms shackled behind me. A burly cop grabbed my arm and hoisted me upright. I spit several times, tried to blink. My left eye was almost shut.

"Get moving," the big cop barked. He jabbed my back with the huge flashlight he'd slammed into my face.

The behemoth towered several inches over me and weighed a hundred pounds more. His nametag read Kay.

I glared at him with one closed eye. "Hope you broke your friggin' flashlight."

Kay jabbed me in the back again, sending pain through my shoulder blades.

"Still seems to work," he said, a nasty smirk on his face. "Wise off again and I'll close your other eye."

We trudged up the trail toward the patrol cars in front of Green's house. Headlights and blue and red strobes lit the area. Clementine rushed over.

"Parker, are you okay? What happened?"

"Stay back," Officer Kay said.

And then Lieutenant Dan Oliver, my favorite do-gooder stepped up.

"You again, McLeod? Don't you ever learn? Officer Kay says you assaulted him."

I glanced at Kay slapping the flashlight into his open palm, a sneer on his face.

"Yeah," I said, returning Kay's smirk. "I assaulted his flashlight with my face."

Clementine touched my cheek. "He needs medical attention," she said.

"He'll get it downtown," Oliver said. He motioned for Officer Kay to put me in the patrol car. Kay jabbed my back.

I spun around with a heavy glare. "Listen Bozo."

The cop raised the flashlight, then thought better and lowered it.

I said to Oliver, "You know I was out there looking for Jake. Take these cuffs off."

"Can't," Oliver said. "You just threatened an officer of the law."

"Oliver, you son of a bitch. What about Jake? He's a 15-year-old kid."

"Do you have any idea who attacked Joe Stubbs?"

"Of course not."

"The house was ransacked. What were they looking for?"

I shrugged.

"Hospital says the woman is a heavy meth user. Officer Kay thinks you may have been hiding something out in the marsh."

"Bullshit," I said. "Take these cuffs off, and I'll tell you what I know."

Oliver nodded. Kay removed the cuffs. We moved up the front steps to the house. Clementine cleaned the cut over my eye, put ice in a towel and held it gently to my wound. My head throbbed, like someone pounding it into concrete.

Oliver waited impatiently for me to speak. I wanted to get the interview over as quickly as possible and resume the hunt for Jake. I explained about the duffel bag full of crystal meth that Joy had stolen from Luther.

Oliver wasn't happy. He stood and paced the floor. Then he stopped and turned toward me, scowling, "Why didn't you tell me about this the first time?"

Saving Jake

I waited a moment to compose myself. My temper had flared enough, and I didn't want to get hooked further by the Lieutenant's wrath.

"I didn't know about the meth until Jake told me after Luther was killed," I said, calmer now. "By then I was so worried about Jake and his mother, I completely forgot about the dope."

Oliver shook his head. "You screwed up big time, McLeod. If you'd told us about the meth, we would have searched the house when we were here the last time. Probably found it and put it on the news. Nobody would have come looking for the stash. Joe and Jake would be at that shitty little bar of yours eating crab."

"Great," Clementine said. "So now you're a psychic. Think about it, Lieutenant. It's obvious someone else knew about the meth. They tossed the house, couldn't find it and took Jake thinking he knows where it is."

"Or maybe they found the meth and took Jake because he could identify them," I added.

Oliver said, "If that's the case, there would have killed him here. No need to take him anywhere."

My heart fell. Total exhaustion set in, I needed sleep, but knew I had to keep going. I gritted my teeth wanting adrenalin to kick in.

I looked at Oliver. "Jake didn't have the bag when he arrived at The Garhole after escaping from Luther. Either Joe's assailant found it in the house, or Joy hid it somewhere else."

"We'll take it from here," Oliver said. He turned to Officer Kay. "Get the others and search downstairs, the yard, everything. Check out the boat. I'm going to the hospital and interview Joe Stubbs."

Kay left and Oliver said to me, "All we know for sure right now is there was an assault, and a kid may or may not be missing. Maybe the kid fled, could be hiding around one of these houses or out in the field. We'll send officers to patrol the area."

"That's all?" I said. "How about shutting the causeway, closing the island?"

Oliver gave me a look like he thought my suggestion was insane. His expression was so smug I wanted to kick him in the gonads. See if that would get him off his cloud.

"Real cool, McLeod" he said. "Do you have any idea how many tourists come to Galveston on the weekends? Not going to create panic over this."

"It's only a boy's life," I said, the sarcasm obvious.

Oliver hesitated. "I'll send out a BOLO (Be on Lookout). Best I can do. Now get the hell out of here, and let my men do their job."

As soon as Oliver left, Clementine conned one of the cops into driving us to The Garhole. For the next hour, we circled the streets of Bay Harbor. At daybreak, we repeated the routine and added searching the adjoining fields with binoculars. We scoured the beach from Bay Harbor to The Garhole. We drove to the tollbooth on the San Luis Bridge and checked with the attendant. Between midnight and dawn, not one vehicle had passed over the bridge headed off the island.

On the way back, my head slumped. Clementine poked my chest.

"No time for that, Parker. What now?"

"The hospital," I said. Our only hope was to see if Joe could tell us what happened. Maybe the bastard who took Jake dropped a name or said something that would give us a clue to follow.

"Hurry," I said, and closed my eyes.

Saving Jake

Chapter Forty-Five

Harry Stein stood at Joe's bedside. He put his finger to his lips indicating quiet and came toward us.

"Parker you look terrible," he said, whispering. "Ought to be sharing a room with Joe."

Joe was either asleep or knocked out with drugs. They had strapped his head to the bed along with his arms and legs. Harry motioned us outside to the corridor.

"He's lost several teeth and his jaw is broken, wired shut. They're keeping him sedated. Doctor is concerned about bruised vertebrae in his neck."

The machines registered a slightly elevated temperature, but his heart rate seemed steady. I stood over Joe's bed hoping for eye movement, hoping he'd come to. But it didn't happen. I waited a few more minutes and then squeezed his hand.

"I'm here for you, Joe," I said. "Hang in there, buddy. I'm going to find the bastard who did this to you."

Harry suggested we move to the cafeteria. The eggs looked tired and old, the same way I was feeling. But I devoured a plateful anyway along with the usual sides. I refilled my coffee cup several times hoping the caffeine would kick in soon. Clementine duplicated my order dumping a bottle of hot sauce into the mix of eggs. Harry toyed with a cup of yogurt.

None of us said much. I was exhausted and Harry and Clementine didn't seem any better. The food and coffee had warmed my body, but my head still ached from the smash of the big cop's flashlight. I needed sleep.

"Has Oliver been by?" I said to Harry.

"Yes, but Joe was asleep. He hasn't been awake since I've been here. The Lieutenant said he'd return later."

"Great," I said. "One person dead, one missing, and two in the hospital unable to talk. All because I felt sorry for a woman and her kid. Damn it all...everything's my fault."

Clementine moved her coffee cup from her lips to the table. She screwed up her face. "What do you want us to do, Parker? Patronize your self-loathing ass with some bullshit about 'how it's okay,' and 'you did everything you could' and a load of crap like that?"

She'd fired both barrels. I couldn't do anything but listen.

She ragged on. "Well, it ain't gonna happen. You got a lot of nerve feeling sorry for yourself now. This isn't about you. It's about Jake and your friend Joe." She bounced her napkin off the table and strode off toward the restroom.

The shock on Harry's face continued during Clementine's entire rant. But as soon as Clementine left, his expression changed to: *So what are you going to do about it?*

Clementine was right, of course. I was wallowing in self-pity. Fortunately, I had lack of sleep and a bruised eye to blame for my fall from grace. Out of nowhere, the taste of scotch suddenly crossed my tongue for the second time in the past few hours. I thought about the neighborhood bar where I'd recently spent the afternoon, wondering if they stocked Famous Grouse. Hard booze had helped me through the pain I'd suffered after the Gulf War. Maybe it was time for another crutch.

Harry stood. "It's been a long night, and I'm too tired to mediate a lover's quarrel." He turned and paraded toward the exit sign.

Saving Jake

Clementine returned sans smile. She stood beside my chair with her arms folded across her ample chest, a practiced frown on her face.

"Apologize and let's get on with it. We've got a job to do."

I rose to my full six-foot height and looked down at her five four frame..

"Look Clementine, I'm carrying a boatload of guilt right now. I should have taken Jake to the hospital last night instead of Joe. But I let my little head control the big one and spent the night with you. I'm tired, and my head is killing me. I need rest, but I don't have time for it. I'm not apologizing for a goddamn thing. You want to help find Jake, good. Otherwise, stay out of my way."

She held my gaze for a few beats, then she unfolded her arms and dropped them to her sides. She nodded slightly and said, "That's what I wanted hear, big boy. Let's check on Joe and then go find Jake."

I eased the door open to Joe's room to find an attractive brunette leaning over Joe's bed. She turned to meet us.

Clementine stepped beside me and said, "Jenny?"

Jenny Hillbro was plain yet somehow alluring at the same time. A nice look for a lady lawyer, probably something she'd developed over time. The white cotton pants and low-cut blouse appeared rather casual for her profession; but this was Galveston—city by the beach.

Jenny removed her large-rimmed glasses and wiped her reddened eyes with a tissue. "I heard about Joe from friends on the police force. Couldn't believe it."

"You know him?" Clementine asked.

Jenny nodded. "I haven't seen Joe since we were in high school. I dated his best friend, but we all hung out together. I thought he was still in the Army. Didn't know he'd been wounded in Iraq. And now this..."

Clementine put her arm around Jenny while I stepped forward to check on Joe. His breathing seemed normal. I hoped he wasn't in any pain. I knew Joe was tough. He had to be to have suffered through so much at his young age. I squeezed his hand again.

I glanced back and noticed Clementine and Jenny leaving the room. I could have related to Jenny all I knew about Joe's injuries from the war—about Joe coming home a hero only to be attacked by a worthless thug. Where was the justice in that? Thinking about it made my blood steam. Whoever had mugged Joe didn't know it, but he'd doubled me up...two reasons to find the bastard—Jake and Joe. The man was going to pay... I could have told her all that, but there wasn't time.

With Joe in an induced coma, my only hope left was that Joy Green was lucid enough to interview. Maybe she had an idea who had taken Jake and where. Joy had grown up in Galveston. Was it possible Joy had tried to sell some of the meth to a local and the plan backfired? Maybe the buyer kidnapped Jake to make Joy give it up. It was a long shot, but still...

I told Clementine I was going to check on Joy and to meet me in the lobby in 10 minutes.

Chapter Forty-Six

Clementine guided Jenny to a small waiting room at the end of the hallway. She waited while Jenny took a moment to compose herself.

Then Jenny looked up and said, "I used to dream about Joe calling me. But his best friend kept asking me out. What could I do?"

Clementine shrugged, remembering the rage of hormones during her teen years. "It was high school," she said. "We didn't know any better."

She figured Jenny was still a virgin at the time, unaware of her power. Too bad, she thought. The girl missed out on a lot of fun.

Jenny continued, "And then Joe joined the army. We lost touch. I finished law school and here I am. I never knew he was back, living on Bolivar."

"You never married?"

Jenny shook her head.

Clementine averted her eyes. This poor woman was a regular goody two-shoes, she thought. She owns the best tool ever invented, and she keeps it locked in a cold-storage bin. She dresses like an old-maid schoolmarm, hair tied in a knot. And those glasses... And then Clementine remembered her own tool had healed over until Parker McLeod busted through. She smiled at the thought.

"What?" Jenny asked, noticing the grin.

"Sorry," Clementine said. "My mind drifted."

Jenny laughed. "Wish mine would," she said.

After a few moments, Jenny spoke again. "You think any more about Stanford's offer?"

"Yes," Clementine replied. "I think I'm on the right track but..."

"Oh, my God!" Jenny exclaimed. "You think Jake is the boy who—"

"Yes," Clementine said. "But..."

"But what?"

Clementine exhaled a breath and bit her lip. "With Jake missing, I feel guilty even talking about it."

"I understand," Jenny said. "But no matter what happens—Stanford will still want to know."

Clementine nodded. "I guess that's true," she said.

Jenny removed the contract and a pen from her purse and said, "I like you Clementine Garza. But before we go any further, I want you to sign the contract."

Clementine took the pen. Everything flashed through her mind at once—a 15 year-old boy robbed of his innocence, his grandfather dead, his meth-addicted mother shot, and Joe Stubbs, a good man, almost killed. Life sucks, she thought. No way to know if Jake was dead or alive, but if by some twist of fate, he was alive, then he deserved all he could get. And Clementine knew it was up to her to get it for him.

She signed the agreement and handed it back to Jenny. Jenny put the contract in her purse, took out the check and gave it to Clementine. Clementine smiled, thinking about bringing her VISA bill current and a payment on the Mustang. She slipped the check into her purse and focused on Jenny.

"What do you know about DNA?" she said.

"Probably more than you want to hear," Jenny answered. "When I was an assistant DA here, we used DNA samples to convict a baby killer. I did a lot of research for the trial. Deoxyribonucleic acid was discovered in 1869 by a Swiss Scientist. It was first used in forensics in England during a 1988 murder trial. The concept is known as profiling which is the process of stringing lengths of DNA together. I got to know the head of Galveston's crime lab pretty well." Jenny hesitated, and then with a wry grin said, "Really well."

So, Clementine thought. Some lucky dude had plucked Miss Jenny's cherry after all. Good for her. Clementine pulled a toothbrush wrapped in tissue out of her purse and laid it on the table.

"Jake's?" Jenny asked.

Clementine nodded.

"I'll run this over to the lab right away," Jenny said, picking up the package. "Get my uh...my *friend* to do a sequencing. You think you can get old-man Stanford to forward a sample for comparison?"

"We can do better than that," Clementine said. She took her cell phone out and called information for a number in Del Rio. She dialed the number, spoke quickly, listened, and then terminated the call. She replaced the phone in her purse and said, "We got lucky. Morgan Stanford's body is still on ice in the morgue. But not for long. Daddy Warbucks is going to have him cremated."

Jenny Hillbro put her palm up. "Let me handle that," she said. "Probably need a court order. I'll get one for Joy Green while I'm at it." Jenny pulled out her cell phone and started to punch in numbers. She looked up at Clementine, "Anyone else?" she asked.

Clementine shook her head no. She thanked Jenny and turned to leave. On the way to the lobby, she couldn't help thinking about what Jenny had meant when she'd said, "Anyone else?" Clementine didn't think Jenny suspected anything. How could she know that Kurt Dussair and Morgan Stanford were sleeping with Joy Green at the same time? Clementine decided it was just an off-hand remark.

But what if Morgan Stanford and Jake Green's DNA didn't match proving Morgan wasn't the father? Was it her responsibility to carry it further? Get a DNA sample from Kurt Dussair and rule him in or out at the same time? What did she owe LuAnn Dussair? Nothing. Nothing at all.

But, no matter what, Jake deserved to know who his father was. And if Morgan Stanford wasn't the father, and her agreement with Reginald J. Stanford terminated, maybe she could engage LuAnn Dussair as a client. Old Lou baby had seemed desperate to know the truth. But Jenny Hillbro didn't have to be involved in that. Clementine would get her own court order for Kurt Dussair. Nothing wrong with a backup plan.

Saving Jake

Chapter Forty-Seven

I rode the elevator to Joy's floor and peeked into ICU. The nurse came over.

"Looking for Joy Green," I said.

She smiled. "Are you a relative?"

"Friend," I said. More or less anyway.

The nurse checked the computer and told me Joy Green was now in a special rehab area one floor up from Joe. Then she hinted about Joy's withdrawal symptoms and added, "Visiting is probably not a good idea right now."

I had reached a dead end. I needed information from Joe Stubbs and Joy Green, but Joe was unconscious and Joy had started withdrawal. According to the nurse, Joy was hallucinating so badly they still had her strapped to the bed. The only source of information left was Lieutenant Oliver. We weren't on the best of terms, but it didn't matter. I needed an update on the search for Jake, and Oliver was the only source. Whether he was willing to help or not, I wasn't the type to circle the wagons. I had to stay on offense.

I met Clementine in the lobby, and we drove to the police station. We parked in the back and caught Oliver coming out the door. I screamed his name from several parking spaces away. He ignored my outburst and got into his car.

"Hold up," I said, approaching the car window.

"I'm late for a meeting, McLeod. Your eye's not looking too good. What a shame."

I swallowed hard, ignoring his dig. "Anything new on Jake?"

Oliver shook his head. "We got a man at the bus station."

"The bus station?"

"Yeah, in case the kid runs."

"What are you talking about?"

"Think about it McLeod. Who else could have known about that bag of crystal meth except the kid? We think he assaulted Stubbs and took off with the dope."

Oliver started to back out. I grabbed the handle, jerked open the door and screamed in his face. "You're a goddamn idiot, Oliver. You know that?"

Oliver reached for his weapon.

Clementine grabbed me around the waist and jerked me back. "Stop it, Parker. This isn't the way." She spun me around and shoved me to the side.

Then before Oliver could un-holster his gun, Clementine slammed the car door shut. Oliver backed out, jerked the car into drive and burned rubber as he peeled out of the lot.

I broke Clementine's grip and ran after Oliver's car screaming, "And an ass too, Oliver. Got that? A donkey-sized ass."

Clementine stood behind me, hands on her hips. She didn't look happy. "Way to go, McLeod," she said. "Really cool. If you thought Oliver was a shit before, you can forget about him helping us now for sure. What are you going to do if he files charges on you for assault?"

"I never touched the bastard."

"Attempted assault is a felony."

"He's got an ego the size of a four-star general. If he filed, he'd have to admit he couldn't handle a simple bar owner."

Saving Jake

I didn't have a clue what to do next. And then I thought about Oliver's theory that Jake had attacked Joe and escaped with the meth.

Most of my work as an Army Intelligence officer involved keeping tabs on the military intentions of the Soviet Union. I spent the 80s tracking Russian Army field exercises and tank movements. I also recruited East German soldiers to spy on their countrymen. Of course, we never trusted any of them. The objective was not so much to gain information, but rather to use the recruits to unknowingly circulate disinformation.

And it was the thought of disinformation that was giving me problems now. If Lieutenant Oliver actually believed Jake was complicit in his own disappearance, the view could infect the entire department changing the impetus from that of a kidnapped child to a druggie runaway. The case could be shuffled lower in the deck, no different from a hundred others. The more I thought about the possibility of fading police interest, the more I realized just how alone in the fight Clementine and I were. And there was no doubt my little *tête-à-tête* with Oliver hadn't helped.

Clementine and I left the police station and turned onto Broadway Boulevard headed toward 61st Street. My head hurt and the coffee was barely keeping me awake. I had no idea where she was going. I wondered if she did. Things seemed hopeless

On the inbound side of Broadway Boulevard, a huge banner stretched across the top of the street announced a weekend Beach Party with live bands. Summer was fading fast and the Chamber of Commerce wanted all the action they could gather in the next few weeks. Traffic slowed precipitously after Labor Day.

I had just closed my eyes, hoping for a few precious moments of rest, when Clementine punched my leg.

"Don't you dare doze off on me. I need sleep as badly as you. We have to talk."

"About what?"

"A plan, Parker! We have to have a plan."

I shook my head and blew out a breath.

Clementine gave me a disgusted look. Her cell rang. She grabbed the phone out of her purse, listened quietly and terminated the call.

"Harry wants us at his house right away. Said it's urgent."

Chapter Forty-Eight

The summer breeze off the Gulf quit as suddenly as the blades of a fan stop. The ambient temperature edged upward outpacing the sun moving across the sky. Ultraviolet and infrared rays zeroed onto the aluminum roof of the mobile home, penetrating the thin insulation like gas burning through an outdoor grill.

It was late morning. Codger Moss glanced at the clock on the wall and wondered how Tomas and Vinnie could sleep through the stifling heat. He sat in his shorts, batting away flies that had spent the night twitching on the dirty dishes in the sink but were now summoned by the scent of carbon dioxide fleeing from his noxious skin. He had untied his ponytail during the night and a great mass of stringy gray strands flopped over his ears.

Codger had scratched his diseased scalp raw and was hoping the joint in his lips would ease the pain. He sucked in one last lungful of smoke, held it as long as he could and blew it out. He dropped the spent joint on the floor and smashed it with his flip-flop.

The police scanner spewed out continual rhythms of assault, robbery, rape and mayhem. He listened contently all the while shoveling in slices of lukewarm pizza he'd thawed in the microwave. Bits of cheese and pepperoni hung in his mustache. He sneezed suddenly, causing the crumbs to dislodge and fall atop the last piece of the pie. He shoved the slice into his mouth, extra morsels and all, and let out a burp that sent the flies scurrying across the room. He reached for a nearby beer can, sucked out the last few drops and threw the can across the room. The can missed the trash bag, bounced off the wall and rolled to a stop. Codger yawned and rubbed his bloodshot eyes, fighting to stay awake.

Codger loved the scanner. He spent hours every day, hovering over the magic box, listening to police communications on the island. One of Codger's police contacts used to tell him that once every few months, when public outcry about working girls became loud enough, the police chief would authorize a general roundup. The chief would often coordinate a sting along with the bust. But when the rousts netted some of Galveston's more prominent citizens, the police chief was known to paraphrase Shakespeare saying, "Discretion is the better part of valor."

The scanner had made Codger's life a lot easier. When a call came over the radio that the police had arrested one of his girls, Codger simply called the sleaze-bag attorney he used and had him post bail. Codger hoped his low profile meant the cops didn't know he was still in business. But there was always the chance one of the girls would squeal.

If that ever happened, Codger had a backup plan. As soon as he heard on the scanner the cops were on their way, he would simply scurry out the back and hide in the brush before the patrol car made it up the long entrance.

Codger heard a moan and glanced back at the table. Jake was slumped in a chair, his chin on his chest and his arms tied behind the chair back. A heavy, wool blanket was wrapped around Jake's body from his feet to under his chin. A dark bruise appeared on Jake's cheek and blood hung from his lower lip.

Codger had opened the windows, but with no breeze, he knew the temperature inside had to be as bad as outside, maybe worse. And in mid-August, that could mean the high 90s by noon. Codger had sent his lawyer to bail the A/C guy out of jail, but there was no way he could have the man out with Jake here. They'd just have to tough it out.

"Water," Jake mumbled his voice barely audible.

Codger looked away. Running girls and even breaking the cripple dude's head with a shotgun was one thing, but watching the kid suffer was getting to him. Eight hours had ticked by since Tomas had wrapped Jake in the blanket. During the first four hours Jake had endured nonstop badgering by Tomas with no food or water and no respite. Finally exhausted, Tomas and Vinnie had gone in for a rest and left Codger to guard Jake with strict orders not to offer any relief.

Once, around dawn, when he knew Tomas and Vinnie were still passed out from the night of booze, Codger had defied Tomas and risked giving the kid a drink. He wanted to give Jake more water, but it was almost midday; the brother's would be up soon. Codger didn't want to chance getting caught.

And then Jake's swollen tongue dropped outside his lips. His breaths came quick and shallow. The sounds he emitted were more pronounced, as if each breath brought pain.

Codger moved closer. Jake's face was pale and dry. There was no perspiration on his brow or under his nose or anywhere on his face. Codger didn't know what the signs meant, but he knew it wasn't good.

It was then that the familiar tinge crossed Codger's spine invoking images of his childhood. As he had done a thousand times before, Codger winced from the thought of the pain and tried hard to push the reflections away.

He only remembered bits and pieces of his youth, a few special days like, when on his eighth birthday, Child Protective Services dropped little Albert Moss off in the living room of his third foster home. He also remembered his ninth birthday, when a CPS social worker left his open file on the kitchen table while she stepped out of the room. It was then that Codger learned his mother had died with a broken needle stuck in her arm in a Beaumont flophouse, and his father was doing life in Huntsville for selling tainted heroin.

But it's what happened on his tenth birthday that left the deepest scar on his psyche. It's the memory that kept him awake most nights listening to the scanner because sleeping might bring dreams he didn't want to endure. It was the day little Albert slipped out a window and pleaded with the clerk at the corner store to call the CPS hotline. It was the same day his foster father was hauled away in handcuffs cursing and ranting. It was the same day he saw the anguish on the doctor's face, during his physical examination at the hospital. He remembers all of that and many of the days leading to his cry for help. But he doesn't remember anything about the subsequent surgery to repair the damage to his bottom.

"Water, please," Jake cried.

Jake's pleas broke Codger's spell. He glanced at Jake's face, and for the first time, understood the sorrow in Jake's eyes.

Codger crept to the bedroom door. Tomas lay sprawled across the sheets, his huge belly making a cow-sized indentation in the mattress. Sweat from his chest ran down to his navel and dropped into the hole on the bed. Vinnie lay curled in the fetal position on a couch, wearing only a speedo.

Codger tiptoed to the sink and filled a glass with water. He gently raised Jake's head and held the glass to his lips. Jake's lips quivered, and his mouth opened. Codger tilted the glass. Jake's eyes opened. The more Jake drank, the more Codger tilted the glass. And then it was empty.

"More," Jake pleaded. "Please..."

And then Tomas screamed from the bedroom door. "What the hell are you doing?"

Codger turned, "Trying to keep the kid awake, so we can talk to him some more."

Tomas came into the room naked except for the gold coin hanging from his neck. His huge belly bounced as he walked. His pompadour had fallen during the night and now stood out from the sides as though his head had wings attached. He stood before Jake studying his face.

"Wake up you shit," Tomas yelled. He grabbed Jake's hair and yanked his head back. Jake's eyes fluttered but didn't open.

Codger said, "I told you. He don't know nothing."

Tomas turned and slammed the table with his palm. "Well, goddamnit," he screamed.

Vinnie appeared at the bedroom door still in his speedo, his package puffed out as though he'd stuffed in a rolled sock. His muscles appeared pumped like after he'd finished a workout. But he hadn't done anything. They were just big.

"Listen to me," Codger shrieked. "I been listening to the scanner all night. The dude I busted is in the hospital unconscious. He never gave the cops a description. They ain't looking for me."

"So what?" Vinnie said. He opened the refrigerator and removed a beer.

"But they got an APB out for the kid."

"Of course, they know somebody took him," Tomas said.

"No they don't," Codger answered back. "That's what I'm trying to tell you. I been listening like I said, real close. They think the kid hit the dude and ran. Took the meth with him."

"Perfect," Tomas said. "The cops don't even know we exist."

"Right," Codger said. "Gives us time and a free hand."

"Time we don't have," Vinnie added. "If we don't get back to New Orleans, the Bastone gang is gonna move in on our customers. We'll be out of business. We can't let that happen."

Codger had eased closer to Jake during the conversation. He let him sip more water and started untying the blanket.

"Stop it!" Tomas barked.

Codger ignored Tomas' outburst. He removed the blanket and dropped it on the floor. "It's a hundred degrees in here," he said. "How we gonna find the goods if the kid dies?"

"Well, he's seen us," Tomas said. "Knows who we are."

The way Tomas cocked his head when he said that made Codger realize he wasn't planning on letting Jake go. Codger felt close to panic. The tingle along his spine returned.

"If the kid knew anything, he would have told us by now," Codger said.

"Well then, who does know?" Tomas said.

"Joy," Codger said. "She knows."

Vinnie had sat quietly during the exchange between Codger and Tomas. He pressed his forefinger and thumb down over his mustache and beard. Then he rose and started toward the bedroom. He turned at the door and said, "Which hospital is the bitch in?"

Saving Jake

Chapter Forty-Nine

Harry lived in a quiet neighborhood not far from UTMB. We arrived and parked in front of a large oak tree. Harry greeted us from a front porch that stretched the entire width of the house. I pictured the old days, before television and air-conditioning, when folks spent their evenings on these grand galleries sipping tea in rocking chairs and chatting with neighbors. It was the simple life I'd hoped for at The Garhole.

"Nice home," Clementine said.

"Greek Revival," Harry said. "Original slate roof and hand-blown windows."

"He could bore you for another hour if you want?" I said to Clementine.

Clementine gave me the evil eye. "It's your wise cracks that bore me," she said.

Harry beamed at Clementine's retort and waved her ahead of him. He chauffeured us through the large, high-ceiling living area into the kitchen.

Special Agent Maurice Matthews sat at a table next to a fiftyish, balding man with alert eyes that missed nothing. Both men stood as Clementine entered the room. Matthews introduced the new man as Special Agent Bernard Hebinck. Harry directed everyone to sit and took drink orders. I asked for a beer and Tylenol.

Matthews spoke. "Agent Hebinck is a kidnap specialist out of D.C. He happened to be in Houston for a seminar, so I dragged him to Galveston."

"Matthews filled me in on the basics," Hebinck said. "But please tell me everything. Try not to leave out any details, no matter how trivial they may seem."

I spewed out everything that had happened from meeting Joy and Jake at Captain Billy's Oyster House in Lake Charles to the altercation with Lieutenant Oliver today. Hebinck listened intently, only occasionally interrupting for a point of clarity. When I finished, he nodded and formed his hands like a church steeple in front of his face, concentrating.

He turned to Harry, "What can you tell me about Lieutenant Oliver?"

Harry shook his head. "Nothing really," he said. "I didn't meet him until yesterday."

Hebinck continued with Matthews, "How would you feel about an official FBI intervention."

"We could try," Matthews said. "But as you know we are usually invited in. We don't know for sure Jake has been taken. Oliver doesn't think so. And remember when Luther Bourdain busted into the house and shot Jake's mother, Jake scooted out a window and ran. He may have done the same thing again."

I jumped in. "And that's what Oliver is basing his theory on now...that Jake saw an opportunity with his grandpa dead and his mother in the hospital, to grab the meth and run."

Hebinck faced me. "So how does Oliver's theory sit with you?"

"Asinine. Just like Oliver. Jake wouldn't leave his mother. And Joe and Jake are friends. No way he would hurt Joe. Oliver's theory doesn't compute."

"So what do you think happened?" he said.

"There is someone else involved," I said. "Someone that knew Joy Green stole the meth."

"But who?"

Saving Jake

"Someone local or from Louisiana," I added. "Either way, when the kidnapper learned old-man Green was dead and Joy was in the hospital, he went to Green's home looking for the stash. He saw Joe, assaulted him and took Jake."

"Why take the boy?"

"Because he ransacked the house and didn't find the meth. He figured Jake knew where the stuff was hidden."

"If Jake knew where it was, why wouldn't he just tell him?"

"I can't answer that."

"That might be the hole in your theory that Oliver thought through and made him decide that Jake ran off with the dope," Hebinck said.

"Bullshit," I said. "That idiot can't process that many levels of thinking."

Clementine broke in. "Maybe Jake didn't tell because he thought he was somehow protecting his mother." Clementine paused and looked at me. "Would Jake have done that?"

"He's a tough kid," I said. "Had to be to survive in that snake pit with Luther Bourdain."

The room went silent, everyone thinking, sipping their drinks.

"There are other reasons to take the boy," Clementine continued. "Jake may have witnessed the assault on Joe. Or maybe the kidnapper plans to use Jake as leverage against his mom thinking she hid the meth, and she will give it up to save Jake."

"How long before we can interview her?" Matthews asked.

"Hard to say," I said. "She's detoxing from the meth."

Matthews continued, "If Jake doesn't know where the dope is, the kidnapper will probably wait until Joy finds out Jake has been taken. He'll put the squeeze on her to give it up.

Either way, it means Jake is still alive and probably still on the island."

Harry said, "If he were taken because he witnessed what happened to Joe, he could already be...."

Harry graciously refrained from saying the word no one wanted to hear. Then Agent Hebinck noticed the gloom and tried to ease the tension.

He straightened in his chair and said, "Kidnappers keep hostages alive as long as they are useful."

No one spoke. I studied Hebinck looking for reassurance and found none.

When he noticed me looking at him, he said, "Did you know about the meth, Parker?"

I couldn't tell if Hebinck's tone was suspicious or just inquiring. I nodded and said, "It was obvious Joy Green was on something, but I didn't put it together for sure until later when Jake told me she'd stolen the meth from Luther."

More silence. I got up for another beer and came back to the table.

"It's my fault," I said. "Jake warned me Luther was coming back, but...it all happened so fast. I thought Jake was safe with me and then his mother overdosed and..."

I glanced around the room. Everyone had averted their eyes except Hebinck. We glared at each other for a long beat.

I said, "You're the specialist, Agent Hebinck. Got any ideas?"

Hebinck looked at Matthews.

Matthews said, "Burney, let's run by the Galveston Police Department. See what we can find out."

Chapter Fifty

We left Harry's home and drove to the intersection at Ferry Road. Clementine stopped and looked toward the terminal.

I followed her gaze and said, "I came in from Louisiana with Joy and Jake on the ferry from Bolivar Peninsula. Joy knew the route, and she seemed to know Galveston well."

"She grew up here," Clementine said. "Went astray somewhere along the line. By the time she met Morgan Stanford, she was already doping. Probably got Morgan hooked."

"She had drug connections?"

"It doesn't take *connections* to buy drugs. Just about any street corner will do."

A horn blared behind us. I glanced back at a bunch of kids in a jeep heading for the beach. Clementine raised a finger high over the seat. The driver honked again. Clementine peeled out, burning rubber, her finger still in the air.

We drove to Seawall Boulevard. Vehicles of all descriptions including hotrod pickups, convertibles, dragsters, and all manner of motorcycles inched along the boulevard. The traffic lights seemed deliberately out of sync, probably timed to keep distracted teenagers and drunks from running over the pedestrians attempting to reach the beach.

We were not only jammed in traffic, we were stuck in general. I glanced at Clementine. She seemed in a daze, eyes glazed over. We both looked like zombies on the prowl. The pain pills Harry gave me had kicked in, and even with all the noise, I was fighting to stay awake. I laid my head back on the seat desperate for rest. An instant later, a booming sound from the Mustang's front speakers rattled my eardrums.

"What is that?" I shouted, covering my ears with my hands.

Clementine had come alive, jiving and bouncing in her seat as though a piece of prickly pear was trapped beneath her. When I reached for the volume control, she slapped my hand away.

"I need this to stay awake," she said. "This one's my favorite, listen."

'Cause the boy with the cold hard cash
Is always Mister Right, 'cause we are
Living in a material world
And I am a material girl
You know that we are living in a material world
And I am material girl

Kids in the vehicle next to us jumped and screamed to the music from our car. When the song ended, I hit the off button and said, "Please."

"You don't like Madonna?"

"Who?"

"Madonna, the Queen of Pop."

"Pop what? Soda pop. Pop Goes the Weasel?"

"Cute, Parker."

"Well, whoever she is, borrowing the name is a little irreverent don't you think? I doubt if the choir down at the Sisters of Holy Moses Convent sings her tunes."

The word *material* from the song kept running through my mind. Material...relevant...basic. There was something I'd left out.

The possibility that someone local was involved kept coming back to me, but I couldn't figure where to go with it. I considered calling Sergeant Martinez head of Galveston's Drug Enforcement division but knew there were hundreds if not thousands of users in Galveston County. I tucked the thought away as a last resort and decided finding the meth was my best shot. If Jake knew where it was, he would probably tell sooner or later. Maybe I could find it and be ready when they came for it.

"Turn right at the next intersection," I said.

"Why?"

"You said we needed a plan. We're going to split up. You stay at the hospital in case Joy or Joe comes around. I'm going back to The Garhole and get my truck."

"Why?"

"When I was giving Joy CPR after she overdosed, Jake came out of the bathroom with the duffel. He slid it under the bed."

"So?"

"So...when Luther Bourdain came in, Jake jumped out the window. If the bag had been there when you and I went into the bedroom, I would have noticed it."

"So Jake took it with him?"

"Or Joy moved it before Luther showed up. Either way it's around there somewhere."

"But the cops searched for it."

"They searched Green's house, not the marsh? It's a big area, thick with cord grass and thorn bushes."

"So how are you going to get to The Garhole if I stay at the hospital?"

I grabbed Clementine's cell phone out of her purse. "How do you use this thing?"

She showed me. I got the number I wanted from the operator and pressed it in. Bully Stout answered. I explained about Joe Stubbs and what I wanted. I terminated the call and stuffed the phone back into Clementine's purse.

A. Hardy Roper

"Bully said he'd meet us at the hospital in 20 minutes. He didn't know about what happened to Joe. Wants to see him."

"Who's Bully?" Clementine asked.

"My uncle more or less."

"What?"

"Step on it, and I'll tell you."

I hung on to the dashboard while Clementine roared through the intersection at Broadway, narrowly avoiding a car coming from the beach.

"Bully Stout was married to my mother's sister. When my aunt died, I was in Germany. Bully needed a place to live, so I let him move into an old camper behind the bait camp. When I came home from Iraq, he helped me turn it into The Garhole Bar."

"Good friend, huh?" Clementine said.

I had to think about that. Bully had hung around a lot, drinking free beer and generally ragging me about anything and everything. But he'd also been there on the rare occasion when I needed him. I had just never thought of him as a friend.

We arrived at the hospital before Bully and made a quick check on Joy and Joe and found no change in their condition. We were standing outside Joe's room when Bully stepped off the elevator. Clementine's pupils grew big as coffee cups, as though she couldn't believe what she was seeing.

The stub of a fat cigar hung from Bully's lips. He stood well over six feet with a huge gut that hung over his belt. He wore a tattered Garhole Bar T-shirt and shorts. A hand-carved piece of ebony driftwood, he'd found on the beach, replaced his left leg below the knee. A black patch over his left eye and a full head of white hair and beard completed the portrait of the island's best-known pirate look-a-like.

With his one good eye roving over Clementine's body, Bully churned out his usual couth. "My God, Parker. You did good."

"Clementine Garza, meet Bully Stout," I said. "And the comment you just heard was a compliment."

Clementine recouped from her initial shock at Bully's appearance and stepped forward with her hand out. "Nice to meet you Bully Stout."

Bully grinned. "I get to approve all Parker's women. And by God, you'll do just fine. If I were 30 years younger..."

"Yes," Clementine said, a teasing smile on her lips.

The big man's face turned red.

Bully and I left Clementine at the hospital to monitor Joy and Joe and headed for The Garhole in Bully's old pickup.

The bag of meth had to be somewhere around Green's house or in the marsh. And if Jake knew the meth's whereabouts, the kidnapper had to come back for it. It was the only thing that made sense. I only hoped he would bring Jake with him. And that it wasn't too late.

A. Hardy Roper

Chapter Fifty-One

Clementine felt she was making good progress with the Morgan Stanford mystery. She realized she'd gone further than Stanford's original charge, but she figured he must have finally acquiesced to her pleadings because the $10,000 check in her purse wasn't a mirage.

After Parker and Bully left, she popped in to check on Joe Stubbs and Joy Green. She found Stubbs asleep, the side of his face still swollen and bruised from the trauma.

She walked one flight up to Joy's floor. If Joy was awake, Clementine figured she might get something out of her. Anything would help. She and Parker were desperate for a lead. A "No Visitors" sign hung on Joy's door. As she started to push open the door, she glanced down the hall. A nurse stared her down. Clementine walked to the nurses' station.

"Hi," she said, flashing her most innocent smile. "I am Joy Green's sister. I saw the sign on the door. Is there any way I can slip in for a quick visit? I—"

"No visitors, means *no visitors*," said the nurse, cutting Clementine off in midsentence. Her nametag read Charlene Morrow. Her short butch haircut, thick glasses and round face sat atop a hefty frame.

Clementine didn't hesitate. She rolled into Manipulation 101. She batted her eyes and said, "Oh, I am so sorry. I realize my sister is going through a difficult withdrawal, it's just that I drove in from Houston and..." She let her voice trail off for effect.

"You'll have to wait for the doctor," Nurse Morrow grumbled, "and he won't be back until late this afternoon."

Clementine put her hand to her mouth. "Oh my," she said. "Well, it was a long drive. I'll just check back later."

Clementine headed to the elevator. She considered returning after a few minutes, hoping to find Morrow on her rounds. But when she glanced back, the nurse had her arms crossed against her chest, her eyes focused on Clementine's departure.

Clementine went to the cafeteria and called Agent Matthews on his cell phone. She entered the food line, skipped the vegetables, and headed straight for the chicken fried steak, cream gravy and mashed potatoes. She reached the cash register just as Matthews answered. She held the phone with her cheek, all the while fumbling in her purse for her billfold. The checker frowned and the woman behind her in line cleared her throat. Clementine ignored them both.

"Any luck at police headquarters?" she asked.

"We went straight to the chief," Matthews said. "Everyone agreed Oliver's theory is bunk. Jake Green was kidnapped."

"Good," Clementine replied. She collected her change, ignored the checker's smug stare and moved to a table. "Parker is convinced the bag of meth is still around Green's house. He went back to look for it."

"Cross a 'police line'? We didn't hear that," Matthews said.

"What's your next step?" Clementine asked.

"Put a blast on radio and TV about the kidnapping. Amber alert. Get more patrols out with a special watch on all the exits from Galveston. Do you have a picture of Jake?"

"Doubt if he's ever been photographed. Shuffled around—in and out of school. Lived with a tweaker and meth cooker."

"We'll need you to work with a sketch artist."

"Can we meet me at the hospital? There is a chance Joe Stubbs may be awake. He's seen Jake more than I have."

"Good idea," Matthews said. "The police department doesn't have a full-time artist. We'll have to round one up. Shouldn't take long. Let's say we meet in an hour. We also plan to interview the Green woman. She has to know something."

Clementine polished off the steak and potatoes and pushed the plate away. She craved a cigarette, but no smoking signs hung all over the walls. She blew out a breath trying to control the urge. Then she quickly ran through in her mind what she knew. Parker had said the kidnapper had to be someone who knew about the meth, someone local or from out of town. The thought gave her an idea, but she needed cash.

A. Hardy Roper

Chapter Fifty-Two

During the drive to The Garhole, I brought Bully up to date about everything that had occurred from Lake Charles to the attack on Joe and Jake's disappearance.

We got out of the truck in the parking lot and Bully hobbled toward the front door, ranting all the way.

"Forkin' mess," he said. "I leave here for a few months and you're back to your old tricks. Always trying to save the forkin' world. Doping mother and—"

"That's enough," I said.

Bully droned on. "Joe Stubbs is a good man. Lying up there in that hospital, maybe dying. I swear if that sumbitch that hurt him comes around here I'll—"

"Joe is tougher than a chained dog," I said. "He'll be okay. The best way to find Joe's assailant is to find Jake. Whoever kidnapped him is still on the island."

"Well if you're right, let's split up," Bully scowled. "Check every house west of the seawall."

I shook my head. "We don't have time. We have to find the meth, so we'll have something to bargain with."

"Bargain with who?"

"Whoever has Jake. The dope has to be around here someplace. Eventually Jake will tell the kidnapper where it is, and they'll come back for it. If we find it first, I'll trade the stuff for Jake. It's our only chance."

"What about the cops or the FBI?"

"I'm not waiting on anybody."

"Okay," Bully said. "What if Jake doesn't know where the dope is? What if Green found the bag and dumped it into the bay? Worse yet, maybe the old man sold it?"

Bully's comment hit hard. Slim Green wouldn't have had the contacts to sell a bag of meth. So if he did take it, there was a good chance he had dumped it into the bay. And I knew if that happened, we didn't have anything to trade for Jake. That also might explain why Jake was kidnapped. If Jake knew Green destroyed the meth and he told the kidnapper, the kidnapper would have had no reason to keep Jake alive. Jake might have figured that out and decided to stay mum, stalling for time. Maybe try to escape.

The more possibilities we tossed out, the bleaker the outlook. I had to hang onto the possibility that Jake did know and that he would eventually tell. Jake was a tough kid. He'd suffered through horrendous torture from the sadist, Luther Bourdain. But Army survival training had taught me no one can hold out forever.

I'd had less than two hours rest in the last 24. My eyes fell to the concrete floor. I went up to my bedroom and put a fresh dressing on the cut over my eye. I could see much better now, and that was at least something.

I went back down to the bar to tell Bully I was leaving. It is not a good idea to catch Bully Stout without his eye patch. He dug his glass eye out of his blown-out eye socket wiped it with his shirt and stuck it back in. My stomach rolled. I headed for the front door holding back a barf.

"Wait," Bully yelled. "Where are you going? What's your plan?"

I waved behind me not wanting to turn around.

Bully kept yelling, "You spent 20 years in the Army. You G2 guys had nothing to do but plan. Don't tell me you don't have one. What do you want me to do?"

I turned at the door. "I know you want to help, Bully. But you'll just slow me down. Might get that wooden leg stuck in the mud."

"Parker, I ain't no forkin' invalid."

"I want you here. Clementine is at the hospital hoping to talk to Joy or Joe. I need you to answer the phone in case she calls."

"Come on, Parker. I can do more than that."

"Did you bring your shotgun?"

"Damn well know I did?"

"Keep it handy."

A. Hardy Roper

Chapter Fifty-Three

Clementine found a satellite location of the bank she used in San Antonio. After some discussion she convinced the manager to give her $2,000 immediate credit against the $10,000 check from Higginbotham and Perry. The teller gathered 20 banded packets of five bills each and placed them on the counter. Clementine slipped several packets into her purse and put the rest in a bag. She stored the bag in the trunk, chastising herself for not getting the flat tire fixed. She made a mental note to look for a tire shop and backed out of the parking lot.

It didn't take long to find the area of town she wanted. She knew every city had a dividing line to the other side of the tracks. In Galveston, the demarcation line was Broadway Boulevard, the main traffic thoroughfare.

Clementine drove the area slowly, observing paint-bare homes and shuttered stores. Many of the homes had open windows and doors, the resident's desperate attempts to cope with the sticky, salt-laden humidity. People sat on front porches in shorts and undershirts or no shirts at all. Clementine knew every eye of every person was trained suspiciously on her as she passed.

At the next corner, she saw a young black kid jiving to something coming from a plug stuck in his ear. The kid's eyes flashed constantly in every direction, studying every car that passed. Clementine figured he was the runner. It was safer for the dealer to use a kid. With the courts and CPS facilities overloaded, it was likely that a juvenile caught holding an illegal substance would get off with a slap on the hand.

Clementine watched the kid's eyes drill on her as she passed. For the right price, she knew she could score anything she wanted.

Clementine idled through several blocks and was beginning to despair thinking the hour was too early. Then she spotted two females at the next corner. A tall, skinny black girl with orange hair stood next to a short, plump white chick with tattoos on her neck. Both wore skimpy, low-cut, midriff blouses and short-shorts. They were young, maybe not even legal.

Clementine stopped short and surveyed the area looking for the ever-present pimp. Her hand automatically went to her waist feeling for her equalizer. Then she remembered the missing baton. She eased close to the curb and lowered the convertible top. She slipped the gearshift to neutral but kept the engine running. She removed a packet of twenties from her purse and waved the bills at the girls. The girls laughed. She waved the bills again.

The tall black girl with orange hair sidled to the curb. As she leaned in toward the Mustang, the girl's boobs jiggled underneath the skimpy top.

"You a cop?" she said.

Clementine shook her head. "Buying information."

Orange Hair backtracked to the white chick and they talked for a moment. Then both girls stepped to the curb. They looked around nervously, studying the approaches.

"What you want?" White Chick asked.

"A name."

"You sure you ain't no cop?"

Clementine pulled out her P.I. card with her photo on it. She extended her arm but held the card firmly in her hand. The girls moved closer to read the words. They glanced at the photo and stepped back.

"Private Investigator," Clementine said in case the girls couldn't read.

Saving Jake

"Show some faith," Orange Hair said.

Clementine handed the packet out the window. Orange Hair fanned the bills and stuffed the money into her shorts. She looked around again. Clementine did the same. Then she pulled out the remaining packets and held them for the girls to see.

"A woman and a boy showed up in Galveston a few days ago. The woman used to be a working girl here, but her local man sent her to New Orleans for a gig. She didn't like the Louisiana man, so she took off with her kid and some of the man's stash. The man followed them here. He got himself killed, and the woman was shot. Someone took the boy."

"What you want from us?" White Chick said.

"I want the name of the woman's pimp. Her Galveston pimp."

Clementine realized the two hookers were not much older than Jake. The chance of them knowing anything was slim. But they knew others, probably everyone in the working girl sorority. It was worth a shot and time was running out.

"I don't give a rat's ass who's selling what, you understand. Nobody gets in trouble. This is strictly personal. I'm looking for the boy."

"Hey," Orange Hair said. "We ain't got no mo time for jiving. What's the ho's name?"

Clementine slipped a business card from her purse and handed it to Orange Hair.

"You don't get the woman's name. You gotta tell me that. That way I know you're not jiving *me*. Pass the word around. Remember, I want the woman's name and the pimp's name. Anybody knows anything, there's 500 in it for them and another 500 for each of you."

The girls faces lit up. They glanced at each other and smiled. "Now you spoofing our ass, girl," Orange Hair said.

"Hey," Clementine said, putting the car in gear. "You don't like money, I'll find someone who does."

"No, no. It be all right," Orange Hair said.

"My number's on the card. But I gotta know today or the deal's off."

Just then the black girl shifted her vision to the back of the Mustang. She jumped back from the curb and disappeared around the corner. The white girl's eyes grew big as saucers. She mumbled something that sounded like "Jumbo" and quickly followed the black girl. Clementine checked the mirror too late.

A voice beside her car door said, "What you want here, bitch?"

Clementine clinched her teeth, kicking herself for not being more careful. Pimps were never far away from their stable, and she'd let this creep sneak up on her. She leaned toward the console to gain operating room and craned her head back toward the door. A giant of a black man, six four or five with weight to match, scowled through two gold teeth clamped on a toothpick. One of his hands rested on the top of the windshield frame, while the other gripped the top of the door ready to yank it open.

Clementine kept her eyes wide and her mouth open looking as frightened as she could hoping to distract the monster, while at the same time easing her left hand to the door handle and her right to the gear shift. She'd dropped her guard and let the creep approach, but at least she'd kept the engine running.

"I'm a realtor," Clementine said. "Just checking out the neighborhood. A client of mine is moving to Galveston."

Jumbo nodded. He checked both ways on the street. "That right," he said. "I be lookin' for a place to stay myself. Gimme your card. I'll call."

Saving Jake

Jumbo dropped his arm from the windshield and stretched it across Clementine's body reaching for her purse on the passenger seat. Clementine reacted in tandem. She unlatched the door with her left hand and shoved it into Jumbo as hard as she could while at the same time jamming the car into drive.

When the Mustang leaped forward, Jumbo's hand scrapped along Clementine's chest. She felt a surge of pain as his fingernails dug into her breasts, ripping her blouse open. Fat fingers latched onto her bra forcing her to the door.

With only milliseconds to react, Clementine jammed the steering wheel hard right and hit the gas pedal. The sudden lurch caused the big man to lose his grip on her bra. He fell to the side of the car.

The Mustang hit the curb and bounced across the corner sidewalk. Clementine glanced into the mirror catching the sight of the giant on his back struggling to get up. She floored the accelerator and spun out. She surged around the next corner hitting 60 as she crossed Broadway. She drove three more blocks and stopped on a side street. She rested her head on the steering wheel to calm her racing pulse. She glanced around and seeing no one, she raised and latched the convertible top. She grabbed a tissue from her purse and blotted the blood oozing from the scratches on her breasts, winching at the pain, holding back the nausea building in her throat. When she'd done all she could, she opened the car door, leaned out into the street, and retched.

Then she remembered her meeting with Agent Matthews and a sketch artist at the hospital. She steeled herself, tried to repair her blouse and bra, but it was no use.

Clementine parked on the side street next to Deborah's Boutique. She held the torn blouse and bra to her chest and called the store on her cell phone. The voice that answered sounded like the clerk who'd helped her before.

"Hi," Clementine said. "I was in earlier today and purchased a black bra and some panties and a couple of outfits. Do you remember me?"

"Yes," the woman said.

"I am parked outside your store," Clementine said. "I am having a problem and can't come in. Could you please come out? I'll give you the money and a list of items I'd like to purchase."

The clerk didn't respond.

Please," Clementine said again, waiting. "I need your help."

Saving Jake

Chapter Fifty-Four

Vinnie got out of the cold shower and wiped himself with a wet towel he found on the bathroom floor. He slipped into the same speedo underwear he'd put on two days earlier in New Orleans. He looked for something to put in his hair and found nothing. He wet his strands of thick, black hair, combed it straight back and hoped it would hold. When he had every hair in place, he put the comb in his back pocket and ran his thumb and forefinger over his short mustache and beard.

He flashed his teeth in the mirror, checking the latest bleach job, thinking it was time for another application. He raised his arms out to the side and flexed his biceps. Not bad, he thought. But he could do more. He missed his daily gym workout. He went into the bedroom and sniffed the purple pullover, noting the slight odor of dried perspiration. He slipped into the pullover, the matching pants, and the expensive Italian loafers. As much as he loved his clothes, he couldn't wait to trash the whole grimy outfit as soon as he arrived back in New Orleans. He picked up the automatic off the bedside table, checked to make sure a round was in the chamber and slipped the gun into his waistband. All ready now, he puffed his chest and ambled into the living room.

Codger sat by the police scanner fumbling with a knob.

"Anything," Vinnie asked.

"A fire downtown. Nothing more about the kid."

Tomasso sat at the table smoking, his pompadour swept up on the sides. He smashed the butt into the overloaded ashtray and reached for another cigarette. He crushed the empty package and tossed it across the room.

Jake was still trussed in a chair, his head resting sideways on his shoulder, the blanket on the floor beside him. He sat with his mouth open, shallow breaths sliding past his drooping tongue.

"Gimme your keys," Vinnie said to Tomas.

Tomas scrunched his forehead, "You ain't taking the Cad."

"What you want me to do...walk?"

Tomas shrugged.

Then Vinnie said to Codger, "What kinda wheels you driving?"

Codger took a quick hit off the shot stub of a joint and quickly blew it out. He reached into his shorts and pulled out a set of keys. "Camaro," he said. "Out back."

After Vinnie left, Tomas told Codger he was going out for cigarettes, telling him anything was better than staying in the hot box. Codger asked him to get some beer. When he heard the Cadillac leaving the driveway, Codger filled another glass with water and brought it to the table.

He scooted a chair close and noticed a grayish tint to Jake's face. His breathing was even shallower now, each exchange coming with total exertion as though the lungs were void of air. His head rested on his chest.

Codger clapped his hands hard. Jake's eyes opened, his head moved upward. Codger held the glass while Jake guzzled the water. When the glass was empty, he sat the glass on the table.

"I'm gonna get you something to eat," he said.

Codger removed a can of soup from the cabinet, poured it into a heavy ceramic bowl and added water. He heated the mixture of noodles and bits of chicken in the microwave and set the steaming bowl on the table.

He turned to Jake and said, "I'm gonna trust you, boy. Don't do nothing stupid."

Codger untied Jake's hands. Jake's atrophied arms dropped to his sides. Codger scooted the table closer. He got behind Jake, raised his arms and placed them on either side of the bowl.

After a moment, Jake picked up the spoon and gingerly sipped the broth. He kept at it slow but steady until the bowl was empty. Then he lowered his head onto his arms on the table.

Codger sitting beside him said, "You're gonna have to work with us, boy. If you know where the *ice* is, you'd best tell us. Tomas will be back soon. Don't know what he'll do to you."

Jake didn't respond.

Codger had held back telling Jake about Vinnie, but when Jake didn't answer, he felt he had no choice. He leaned closer to Jake and whispered, "Vinnie's gone to visit you mama."

"No," Jake screamed. He grabbed the heavy soup bowl and struck Codger hard across his nose. Codger fell back. Blood gushed from the cut. The bowl hit the police scanner and knocked it off the table. The scanner hit the floor with a thud. Jake staggered out the door before Codger regained his balance.

Codger pulled up his T-shirt and wiped the blood from his nose. He lurched to the door in time to see Jake rambling ahead, his gait slowed from his weakened legs. He watched Jake fall and struggle to rise. Codger cursed himself for untying the kid and hustled out after him, blood splattering his shirt and shorts as he ran, his long strides rapidly closing the gap.

Then he saw Jake slow and glance back. He seemed weak, almost stumbling, legs moving like rubber. But the boy kept going, trudging off the road into a mesquite thicket.

Codger followed, catching glimpses of Jake moving through the bramble of low hanging bushes. Mesquite thorns tore at Codger's shirt embedding into his skin. Blood whelps appeared as his shirt turned to shreds. He caught Jake a few yards ahead and shoved him to the ground.

"You little shit," Codger yelled.

Jake squirmed on the ground. He raised his hands defensively and scooted back on his butt.

Codger grabbed Jake's skinny arm and yanked him to his feet. He put his hand to Jake's throat and forced his face up, screaming, "Look what you did to me. Look, damn you!" He pointed to the cut on his nose and the whelps on his body. "You're going back into the blanket."

He held Jake's arm and slapped him hard across the face. Blood spurted from Jake's mouth. Seeing Jake's blood reminded Codger of his own cut. He removed the tattered remains of his T-shirt and pressed it against his nose. The scratches from the mesquite thorns still oozed blood and the pain from the nerve endings sent shivers through his body.

Codger held Jake's arm like a vise and half drug him back to the mobile home. He tied Jake to the same chair and wrapped the blanket around his body.

Codger stood in the shower letting the cold water soak into the scratches and cuts. The water soothed the pain. He stepped out and dried himself with a dirty towel. He rubbed Vaseline onto the scratches and the cut on his nose. He dug a pair of shorts and T-shirt out of the closet and slipped them on. In the living room, Tomas was at the table moving the dials on the police scanner.

"I found it on the floor," Tomas said. "Don't wanna work."

Codger moved to the scanner and tried the dials. Nothing but static. He looked at Jake. "Damn you kid."

Tomas glanced at Codger's face. "What happened to you?" he asked.

"The little bastard untied himself. Hit me with something and made a break for it."

"You dumb shit," Tomas said.

Codger's nose throbbed and the scratches on his arms and chest burned. He was long past caring about the kid. He went back to the scanner, moving the dials again, trying to make it work.

Tomas stepped close to Jake and bent to eye level. Jake's nose was so swollen all his breaths came through his mouth.

Tomas lifted Jake's head with his hand. "Ready to squeal now, kid. Vinnie's on his way to the hospital to see Joy. Tell me where you hid the stuff, and we'll call Vinnie off."

Jake raised his head, tears streaming down his cheeks. They had finally broken him. "No please," he cried. "I'll tell. Stop the man. I'll tell."

Tomas had no way to contact Vinnie. He couldn't have stopped him if he wanted to. And he didn't want to. Two shots at finding the meth were always better than one. Vinnie would find out what he could at the hospital, and the kid was coming around. Perfect, he thought.

A. Hardy Roper

Chapter Fifty-Five

When the sales clerk exited the store, Clementine noted the wary expression on her face and wished there was something she could do to make the woman feel safe. The woman studied the scene around the Mustang while slowly approaching the car. Clementine lowered the window. The woman stood back from the car as she bent to peek inside. Clementine held one hand over her torn blouse and bra and pushed her other hand out holding a list of items and two stacks of twenties. The woman glanced around the car again.

Clementine forced a smile and said, "I appreciate your help."

The woman didn't respond. She stayed as far from the car as she could and still reach Clementine's hand.

Clementine drove to a fast food restaurant on Broadway. She entered the restaurant holding a shopping bag high across her chest to block the view of her torn blouse. She went into the restroom and locked the door. She stood at the mirror and checked the scratch marks on her chest. The smell of Jumbo's fingers made her stomach roil.

She rinsed her mouth, splashed her face with water and dried her cheeks with a paper towel. She tossed her shredded blouse and bra into the trash bin, then wet another towel and gently dabbed the dried blood from Jumbo's fingernail marks. The new blouse buttoned to her neck to cover the scratches. Her new bra felt soft against her wounded breasts. She repaired her hair and face as best she could and stepped back from the mirror. Not bad, she thought. She opened the restroom door and strode out to her car thinking she was late for the meeting with the sketch artist at the hospital.

As she climbed behind the wheel, her cell phone buzzed. She didn't recognize the number. What now she thought? She pressed receive.

"It's Shanika," a voice said.

"Who?"

"The hundred dollar Ho on the corner. Got the honkies name you wanted. The ho too. I'm at the bus station. Bring the money."

"Where is the station?"

"Broadway and 29th. Hurry, I can't wait long."

Three minutes later Clementine wheeled into a strip center on Broadway. She glanced at the iron bars stretching across the windows of the convenience store and the two homeless men passing a paper sack back and forth. Inside the nail salon next door, two Asian women jabbered at each other while a customer sat with her feet in a tub of water. Just past the salon was an empty suite with a "For Lease" sign taped to the window. On the other side of the vacant space Clementine spied a small storefront with a bus station sign hanging in the window. Behind the sign were several cheap plastic chairs and a counter. A man stood behind the counter, working a computer. Shanika was pressed against the wall in the corner, looking out through the storefront window, studying the parking area.

On the sidewalk in front of the storefront, a sign fastened to a pole read "No Parking-Bus Loading Zone." Clementine backed into a space across the parking lot from the sign.

Saving Jake

Shanika peeked out the glass door and surveyed the area before stepping out. Her orange hair glistened in the sun as she scurried across the lot to the Mustang and leaned her tall, slim body down to Clementine's window.

She held a tissue to her bloodied lips and said, "Got the money?"

Clementine winched. Shanika's right eye was puffed and closed. Even with Shanika's cold black skin, Clementine could see shades of purple surrounded her eye socket. An egg-sized lump protruded from her cheek.

Clementine checked in all directions. She stepped out of the car and opened the trunk. The bank bag lay next to the lug wrench and the flat tire she'd forgotten to get repaired.

She put her hand on the bag and looked back at Shanika, "The names?" she said.

"Ho's name is Joy. Pimp is Codger," Shanika said, splitting blood into a tissue as she spoke. "Codger Moss. White boy. Runs a few girls and sells weed. Stays out on the west end someplace."

Clementine raised the bag as if to hand it over, but kept it tight in her hand. "How do you know this?" she asked.

"Girl I know used to work for him."

As Clementine handed the bag to Shanika, she sensed someone closing in from behind. Jumbo! She wasn't about to let the big ape touch her again. She grabbed the tire wrench and turned smashing the iron bar into Jumbo's kneecap. The big man collapsed to the pavement screaming in pain. Clementine brought the iron down hard on the big man's collar. Bone snapped.

As Shanika dashed into the bus station, Clementine slammed the trunk and jumped into the car. She cranked the engine and pulled to the middle of the parking area between Jumbo squirming on the ground and the front door of the bus station. She intended to get Shanika in the car and take off. But just then, a Greyhound bus pulled in and stopped at the door, its air brakes hissing across the parking lot. A moment later, the door to the bus opened and then closed again. As the bus eased past, Clementine caught a glimpse of Shanika, sitting at the window staring straight ahead, a defiant expression on her swollen face.

Clementine peeled out in the opposite direction. She wanted to stop and calm herself, but she knew someone had called 911. The police would be searching the area for a yellow Mustang. She didn't have time to be stopped and interrogated, maybe even hauled to jail.

She scrolled through the recent calls in her phone until she found the number with the 713 area code. She pushed send and the call immediately went to voice mail.

"This is Special Agent Maurice Matthews with the Houston office of the FBI. Please leave a message."

Clementine screamed into the phone, asking Matthews to call. She made a quick U-turn and sped down Broadway. She roared through the red light at 25th trying to remember which street cut over to the hospital. A few blocks later, she turned left with one hand on the wheel, barely missing a car traveling in the opposite lane. With the other hand, she hit the speed dial number for The Garhole. Bully answered.

Clementine screamed into the phone, "Where is Parker?"

"He's at Green's house. What's wrong?"

Clementine pulled onto the Emergency Room ramp at UTMB. She slammed the brakes and stopped in the "No Parking Zone" at the entrance. She jumped out and yelled the only thing she could think of into the phone.

"Tell him I have the name."

Chapter Fifty-Six

The trick, if there is one, is to not allow guilt to become remorse. That is possible only if the deed for which you felt culpable, the one that tears at your heart and leaves you full of self-reproach, has not completely passed by. To stave off a lifetime of regret, the act for which you feel the guilt must be recoverable. And that can only happen if you act quickly before the event has passed. In my case, I could only hope the time left for restitution had not expired. I had to find Jake alive and hopefully unharmed.

On the way to Green's house, I remembered every detail about Jake from his stringy, dirty hair that poked out from beneath his ball cap to the veil of forlorn hopelessness that enveloped his face, the perfect portrayal of a forgotten human being.

It was as though I'd just spun out of a time machine, and I was standing in Jake's body looking out, forsaken and alone feeling what Jake must have felt. That he'd already witnessed the total of life experiences not able to imagine or care about the future. I realized then how deep into my consciousness I'd pushed the same feeling. Jake and I were kindred souls, but it had taken Jake's kidnapping to awaken me.

I'd had plenty of opportunities to rise out of my own self-denial and save Jake. At the first meeting with Agent Matthews at The Garhole, I could have told him about the boy. As an officer of the court, he would have either pushed me to report the abuse or done it himself. Either way, Jake would now be safe. I could have said something to Sergeant Martinez, head of the Drug Enforcement Division, or called him back as I told Joe I was going to. Failing that, I should have called CPS when I saw Joy on the deck at Green's house, high on meth.

It wasn't that I hadn't been thinking about Jake. No matter how hard I pushed, he was never far from my thoughts. And then when Jake told me his mom was in the bedroom sexing herself...what more did I need? I saw the burn marks on Jake's arms and the fear in his eyes when he exposed them to me. He was adamant Luther was coming back, and I did nothing.

When Jake tore off his shirt and displayed the burn scars, he was showing me he trusted me to stand with him. He was willing to face the future, unafraid, because for the first time in his life, he felt someone had his back.

And then when Joy overdosed, I'd let old man Green take Jake home from the hospital. Even then I still had a chance at redemption. And later, when Jake wanted to go in and see his mother, I should have been the one to take him instead of Joe.

There was no way to know the amount of meth in Joy's duffel bag or its value. All I knew was that it was enough that Luther Bourdain lost his life trying to retrieve it, and Jake's kidnapper risked life in prison.

To a normal person, no amount of crystal meth or even cold cash is worth spending the rest of your life in jail. But the universal truth is...everything in life is relative. In the slums of big cities and even in Galveston, there are people who will cut your throat for a pack of cigarettes. What would those people do for a sack of meth?

Joy had the duffel when she left my truck at Green's house. Judging by the death grip she held on the bag, she would have kept it close. Probably not out of her sight. For that reason, I doubted Slim Green could have gotten his hands on it.

Still if he had, and realizing the potential money involved, would he have dumped it in the bay or hid it? There was no way to know.

I drove through Bay Harbor and parked in the driveway of a vacant house across the street from Green's. The kidnapper didn't know my truck but Jake did. If he returned, maybe Jake would see it and know I was around.

The yellow crime tape still guarded the gate and the house. It was too late to worry about breaking the law. I ripped the tape off the gate and entered the yard. The tarp, which had covered the boat, lay on the ground, reminding me the entire place had already been thoroughly searched by both the kidnapper and the cops. Still, I felt I had to try.

The sun baked down hard as I hustled the stairs. The afternoon temperature had to be close to a hundred. Sweat poured from my forehead. The cut over my eye burned from the salt. I had forgotten to bring water or even a hat.

I stepped past the torn crime tape and entered Green's house. The inside temperature hit me like a blast furnace. It was hard to breathe. The interior was just as we'd left it—ransacked cabinets and open dresser doors, the mattresses cut open and searched. I concentrated on Slim Green's bedroom, hoping to find a secret compartment. I searched the closet, looking for a cut in the wall or floor. I found nothing. I went outside to the upper deck and surveyed to the fence line in all directions. I made a quick trip around the yard, looking for recent diggings and found nothing. A wave of hopelessness shook my chest.

I had no time to search a mile of shoreline and the boggy estuary. The only option left was the animal trail Jake had taken the night he'd escaped from Luther Bourdain, the trail I'd already partly searched. But this time I would be more careful, fan out and look under every bush on both sides of the trail. I made a quick trip around the outside perimeter of the fence, searching fifty feet out in all directions. And then I started down the trail, my heart sinking fast, hopes fading.

Chapter Fifty-Seven

Clementine slammed through the revolving doors and dashed through the ER to the elevators. A minute later the doors opened, and Clementine stormed out toward Joe Stubbs' room. She shoved through the door, hoping to find Matthews and Hebinck with the sketch artist. She found Stubbs sitting up in bed, a nurse helping him drink through a straw.

"Where are they?" Clementine shouted.

"Just left," Joe whispered.

Clementine turned rapidly and rushed out to the hall. She glanced in both directions but saw nothing. Then she remembered Matthews had said they would interview both Joe and Joy Green. Clementine raced to the next floor. As she cleared the door, she glanced toward the nurse's station. Empty. Clementine realized the nurses were making their rounds. She hoped Agent's Matthews and Hebinck were still in Joy's room with the sketch artist.

Clementine rushed toward Joy's room. The "No Visitors" sign still hung on the door. Just as Clementine pushed open the door, she glimpsed the nurse rounding a corner. The nurse quickly backtracked to her station and grabbed the telephone.

Matthews and Hebinck sat in the cafeteria, drinking coffee with the sketch artist, disappointed Joe hadn't gotten a look at the perp. An announcement blared over the intercom, mentioning the fourth floor. A uniformed security guard hustled toward the elevator. The agents were closer and entered at the same time as the guard.

Matthews flashed his FBI credentials. "What's the problem?" he said.

The guard said, "Unauthorized entry to a patient's room."

Clementine pushed the door open to find a man standing over the bed struggling with Joy, her eyes wide with fear. He had one hand over her mouth and the other on Joy's throat. The muscles in his arms and neck were large and powerful. The man noticed someone behind him and started to turn, but Clementine was quicker. She grabbed his neck in a chokehold.

Vinnie Calzone spun to his right. Clementine felt his elbow connect solidly to her jaw. She collapsed to the floor, dazed. She shook her head trying to regain composure. The man looked down on Clementine, a sadistic grin on his face, as though it was all a game.

Just then, Joy Green found her voice. She screamed, the sound carrying out to the hallway. Vinnie pivoted and slapped her hard across the face. Then he turned backed to Clementine still on the floor.

"You're next, bitch?"

Clementine didn't answer. A sharp pain radiated across her jaw and into her neck. She put a palm out in surrender, trying to buy time, to adjust, to prepare.

The man's arms loomed even larger now, and his chest muscles bulged against his shirt. She knew her 120 pound frame was no match for Mr. Universe. That only meant muscle man had a surprise coming. She rubbed her jaw with her left hand and turned her right hand into a fist behind her body, waiting for big boy to shift his focus.

Vinnie leaned over, staring hard into Clementine's face. Then he straightened and moved his hand along the edge of his hair, pushing back a wayward lock. Clementine grabbed her chance. She gritted her teeth and with everything she had, launched a fist first directly into Vinnie's family jewels. A whoosh of air and sickening grunt came from above her.

Vinnie bent over and grabbed his groin area. He stepped back, giving Clementine the chance she needed to regain her footing. As she struggled to rise, Vinnie recouped and hit Clementine square on the nose. Blood squirted. She collapsed to the floor.

And then Vinnie's arm was around her chest, lifting her to her feet. When his arm shifted to her neck, she felt his lips at her ear and his hot breath across her face.

"Having fun, bitch?"

Clementine felt the cold steel of a weapon pressed against her cheek. She smelled the oil from the gun and felt his grip tightening on her throat, cutting her wind, consciousness fading.

Just then, the door opened and agents Matthews and Hebinck stood side by side, their standard issued .40 mm Glocks aimed at Vinnie's head.

Clementine felt the man twist her body, trying to shield himself from the agents. She felt the gun barrel pushing harder into her cheek. She did the only thing she had the strength left to do. She dropped her head to the side.

Matthews and Hebinck fired simultaneously, the noise reverberating through the open door and along the hallway. One round hit Vinnie at the top of his forehead, blowing off part of his skull. The other shot hit his right eye and exited through the back of his head.

Blood splattered across Clementine's cheek. Behind her, Joy mumbled incoherent words, trying desperately to free herself from the straps cutting into her body.

Clementine sat on the edge of the bed with a strange hand on her throat.

"You'll have some bruising," the doctor said. "Nothing a little makeup won't hide. Other than that, you're fine. You're lucky you're nose isn't broken." The doctor removed his hand and sat back on his stool.

"Thanks, Doc," Clementine replied. "But I don't feel too fine. My throat aches like I've just been cut down from the gallows. And my new, $200 outfit is trashed with blood."

She glanced at the white hospital gown covering her body. She slipped off the bed and looked around the room. "I've got to get out of here, and I have no choice but to put those rags back on. Where are they?"

"Evidence," the doctor said. "Police took everything."

"That's just great," Clementine said. She put a hand over her eyes and steadied herself. She felt Vinnie's arm around her throat, his weight dragging her to the floor, and Vinnie's blood and gore on her face.

The doctor put his hand on her shoulder. "You okay?"

Clementine sighed. "No choice," she said. "I have to be okay."

A light rap came on the door and Agent Hebinck walked in.

"Codger," Clementine said. "Codger Moss...we've got to—"

"I know," Hebinck said. "You told us."

"What..."

"You screamed his name all the way to the ER. Agent Matthews and Galveston SWAT are organizing the raid now. Lieutenant Oliver is leading the assault."

"Oliver? That weasel."

The door opened and Jenny Hillbro stepped in holding an armful of clothes. She rushed to Clementine and hugged her tight. "Thank God you're all right," she said. "Let's get you dressed."

"How did you—?"

"I came to see Joe. Saw what happened and rushed home to get you some clothes. I hope they fit."

Moments later, Clementine, Hebinck, and Matthews rolled out of the ER parking lot in Matthews's FBI sedan. Hebinck was driving while Matthews talked to Oliver on his cell phone.

"Garza wants in on the bust," Matthews said. "I think she deserves to be there."

"No way," Oliver said.

Clementine, leaning close from the backseat, overheard the comment and grabbed Matthews' phone. "Look short-stuff," she yelled. "I'll be there and there ain't nothing you can do about it. Just be glad you still have my baton, or I'd cram it up your dirt chute."

Clementine terminated the call before Oliver could retort. She grabbed her own phone out of her purse and called The Garhole.

"Bully, where is Parker?"

"I told you, he's at Green's."

"Get over there and tell him we're going after Jake."

Clementine slammed the phone back into her purse. "Some Intelligence Officer," she said. "He's gonna miss the whole goddamn show."

She sat back in the seat, squirming, uncomfortable in someone else's clothes. "Screw it," she said. She reached under her blouse and unhooked the bra Jenny had brought her. She yanked the bra free and dropped it on the floorboard.

Hebinck swerved to avoid a signpost. "Jesus, lady," he said, slowing to the speed limit. He blew out a breath.

"Sorry," Clementine said. "A 32B just don't cut it. Now either shove those wingtips to the floor or let me drive."

Hebinck slammed the pedal and flipped on the emergency lights and siren, speeding along Broadway weaving among the cars. He swerved left onto 61st, running through the tail end of a yellow light.

"Look for Stewart Road," Clementine yelled.

"Next light," Matthews said.

Hebinck cut through the corner gas station, avoiding the cars at the intersection and peeled out on Stewart Road. He spotted the emergency lights of the SWAT van several blocks ahead. They caught the caravan and hugged the van's bumper.

They screamed past the last subdivision and hit a plat of open fields. The SWAT van slowed to negotiate a big 'S' turn in the road and came to a stop past the curve. Hebinck stopped behind the van. Lieutenant Oliver and several heavily armed SWAT officers got out and gathered in the road.

"What are you doing here?" Oliver said as Clementine approached.

Clementine scowled. "Somebody had to keep you from screwing everything up."

Oliver blew out his breath trying to keep his composure and turned to the SWAT team. "No more sirens or lights. Codger's doublewide is a short ways up the next turnoff several hundred yards back in the trees. We don't know how many bad guys are in the house. And—"

Clementine interrupted, sounding off at Oliver's back. "Matthews and Hebinck took care of one of them for you at the hospital. Maybe you should let the FBI handle the assault."

Oliver's turned, his face glowed red. He started to speak, but Matthews stepped in.

"Perp at the hospital was named Vinnie Calzone, out of New Orleans. Has a brother named Tomasso. Couple of bad hombres. Don't know the connection between Calzones and Moss yet, but we figure Vinnie Calzone came for the dope. He must have known Jake's mother was in the hospital. Went there to get the location of the stash."

Oliver's cell phone vibrated. He answered, listened intently and terminated the call.

"They found Codger Moss' Camaro in the UTMB parking lot. No sign of him."

"Vinnie Calzone must have used it to get to the hospital," Matthews said. "That ties them together."

"If Codger is in the mobile home, Jake must be with him," Clementine said.

"You're assuming Tomasso Calzone and Moss are the only two bad guys," Matthews said. "There may be more."

Oliver turned to his men. "Let's roll," he said.

A. Hardy Roper

Chapter Fifty-Eight

I was nearing the end after searching more than a mile of trail between Green's house and The Garhole Bar, exploring both sides 30 yards out, looking for the duffel that I'd seen with Joy or even a freshly prepared mound of dirt indicating a recently dug hole. I had found nothing but pieces of debris washed into the marsh by the last hurricane—various cans and bottles, a rusted bait bucket, a crab trap.

I was still convinced whoever kidnapped Jake would have to return to find the meth. I needed to find the duffel, get my hands on it. Using it as a bargaining chip was my only hope.

The relentless August sun had sucked the last vestige of moisture from my body, leaving me cotton-mouthed and weak. I stopped to rest a hundred yards short of the oak motte. It was as though I didn't want to take the last few steps, the emptiness in my gut telling me when I reached the bird pond the search would be over, failure complete.

I was closer to The Garhole than to Green's house. I decided to continue on and get Bully to take me back to my truck. Maybe Clementine had returned or at least called. Maybe she'd learned something.

I passed the oak motte and the bird pond and was halfway to the bar, when I saw Bully hobbling out to his truck. I yelled his name and he looked my way squinting. I wasn't sure he saw me. I hustled ahead.

"Just coming to get you," he snapped. "Clementine called. Said they were on their way to get Jake."

"What?"

"You heard me right."

I ran inside to the telephone and called Clementine's cell. She answered on the first ring.

"You found Jake?"

"We ain't been sleeping out here."

"How?"

"Don't have time to tell you. Just before that big 'S' curve on Stewart Road turn toward the bay. You'll see the SWAT van a few blocks up. Hope you make it, big boy. We're not waiting."

I turned to Bully. "Give me your keys."

"I'm coming with you."

"No, stay here by the phone."

I peeled out in Bully's truck, hoping the heap would stay together, pushing it to the limit. I didn't know what was going on, but I wasn't about to miss the play.

Chapter Fifty-Nine

Clementine and the FBI agents followed the SWAT van. The van turned right onto a gravel road and proceeded in slow motion. They passed a grove of salt cedars and an old corral and windmill. The van stopped beside a thick stand of oleander bushes that fronted the road. Clementine and the FBI agents got out and approached Oliver and the SWAT team at the roadside.

Oliver pointed to the entrance almost totally hidden by the bushes. "This is it," he said.

Oliver spoke to Matthews and Hebinck. "I'm sending two officers through the trees to the back of the house. We'll keep one here to secure the entrance and the rest of us will approach from the front." Oliver pointed a finger at Clementine and said, "You stay here with the officer."

"Screw you," Clementine said.

Oliver started after her, but Matthews stepped in front of him. "Let's be civil," he said to Oliver. "Let her go with us. I'll take responsibility."

Clementine didn't care what Oliver decided, she was going anyway. The officer designated to remain at the road stepped forward ready to take action on Oliver's orders. No one moved.

"Okay," Oliver said to Matthews. "She's yours. Put a rope around her fat ass and hold her close."

Clementine raised her middle finger as she stepped aside to let Oliver and the SWAT officers pass. The two FBI agents and Clementine trailed behind.

A few yards up the lane, two SWAT members peeled off into the mesquite thicket to work their way to the rear of the mobile home. The officer working point in front of Oliver hustled back toward the group.

"No one in the house will be able to see us until we pass over a rise about two hundred yards ahead," he said. "No vehicle in front. Windows are open. We'll have to be careful about noise."

Oliver nodded. "We'll proceed to the knoll and hold until we hear from the assault team in back."

Oliver's radio vibrated. A soft voice said, "Team two in position. No vehicle in back. Windows open. No movement inside."

Oliver ordered the rear team to hold while the front team moved into position. The SWAT officer and Oliver split to either side of the home. They approached to the front corners and held.

Clementine and the FBI officers trailed close behind Oliver. A scrambling noise came from within the mobile home as though someone was running across the room. Instead of rushing in, Oliver seemed frozen, unsure what to do.

Seeing Oliver hesitate, Clementine grabbed the Glock out of Matthews' holster and stormed through the front door.

I saw the road before the 'S' curve barely in time to slam the brakes and make the turn. The truck slid across the gravel into the ditch, hitting the barbed wire fence bordering the road. I peeled out, tires spinning. I spotted the SWAT van by the turn off. A cop stepped to the middle of the road with his arm up signaling me to stop. I cut past the cop, causing him to leap into the nearby ditch. I skidded into the lane to Codger's house without slowing, scraping a bush and almost blowing a tire. I reached for my .45 automatic in the glove compartment and cursed, realizing I was in Bully's truck, not mine. I jumped out of the truck and ran forward, clearing the knoll in front of Codger's house at full gallop. I saw no one and realized everyone was already in the house. I hoped I wasn't too late.

Clementine scanned the empty living room, quickly noticing the open door to the bedroom. She moved to just outside the bedroom entrance. She took a deep breath and let it out. She charged in, gun extended. Something hit her hand, knocking the gun loose. An arm grabbed her around her neck. She smelled unwashed hair, perspiration and marijuana. The arm was thin, the man tall, towering over her. And then she felt the edge of a knife at her skin close to her jugular.

I picked up speed, running downhill. I hit the door, blowing past Matthews and Hebinck, past Oliver and the SWAT officer, straight to where they were staring.
"You don't have to do this," I said to the tall man with the knife at Clementine's throat. "Put the weapon down. We'll talk."
The man's eyes seemed glassy, hazy, as though he wasn't all there, unable to concentrate. Then I caught the marijuana scent. I hoped he was not over the top, deluged by paranoia, past rational thought.
The knife was perfectly poised at Clementine's jugular, one slip, one inadvertent movement, would send blood pumping out at a rate difficult to stop. I'd witnessed a soldier in Iraq bleed out with the same injury.
Clementine's eyes seemed to be pleading, asking for something. Look behind you the eyes said.
I glanced back. Oliver and the SWAT officer were at the door, their weapons extended, aimed at the man's head.
Oliver screamed, "Drop the knife, Codger. Now!"
Codger. At least I had a name. "Whoa, whoa," I said to Oliver, my palms up pleading. "Back off, please—

I turned to Codger. "It's okay," I said. "We'll talk. Just put the knife down."

"The boy's okay," Codger said. "He's okay. I took care of him."

"Good," I said. "That's good. You don't know me, Codger. My name is Parker. I'm just here for Jake. You don't want to see Jake hurt do you?"

Codger shook his head. His eyes closed. Then he opened them quickly, as if fighting sleep, the marijuana taking over.

"Put the knife down, Codger. Tell me where Jake is. That's all we want."

Codger's eyes closed again and flashed open. The knife slipped off Clementine's throat. Clementine jammed her elbow into Codger's stomach and twisted away.

I grabbed Clementine and shoved her aside. The SWAT officer rushed through the door, weapon extended.

"No, no," I screamed.

The rounds pierced Codger's chest, slamming him backwards across the bed.

I ran to him, my ear close to his mouth, "Jake," I said. "Where is Jake?"

His lips moved, but I couldn't hear. Then he breathed in again, I thought this was it, he would tell me. But his breath came out slow, almost painful it seemed, and he was dead. I gave Clementine a big hug and stepped into the living room.

Matthews and Hebinck, along with Oliver, and a SWAT officer were standing by a chair, looking down at a blanket on the floor surrounded by several pieces of rope.

"They tortured the boy," Matthews said. "Sons of bitches."

Clementine punched Oliver in the stomach. "I hope you're proud of yourself, you little Napoleon shit. See what your delay caused."

Oliver folded over. Matthews grabbed Clementine and pulled her away.

Oliver screamed, "You're under arrest, Garza. Assaulting an officer."

"Good," she shouted back. "Hope your pension's vested. Your next job's gonna be with the sanitation department picking up dog turds off the beach."

Clementine started toward Oliver, but Matthews twisted her away.

"Let's keep calm heads," Matthews said. "Jake's still missing."

A SWAT officer stuck his head in the door. "We're searching a 100 yard perimeter for any sign of a grave. Gonna take a while."

"But Codger said Jake was okay?" Clementine said.

"They have to check every angle," Matthews said.

Another officer came in from the bedroom and announced that the articles in the bedroom indicated there were three of them.

Hebinck broke in. "Here is what we know," he said. "Vinnie Calzone drove Codger's car to the hospital. Vinnie didn't come in from Louisiana on the bus. Tomasso Calzone is here."

Matthews opened his cell phone and dialed the number for the New Orleans Lieutenant he had spoken to earlier. He asked a few questions and then took a pen from his pocket and wrote a number on his note pad.

"Tomasso drives a new Cadillac Deville."

Oliver called dispatch and ordered an APB for the car and Tomasso Calzone.

I took Clementine's arm and whispered that we needed to talk. We slipped outside.

"It's all clear now," I said. "The Calzone brothers had a deal with Luther for the meth. When he didn't deliver, they went after the meth themselves. They attacked Joe, ransacked the house and kidnapped Jake, thinking he knew where it was. Jake wouldn't talk so they threatened Joy. Jake confessed to save his mother."

"Makes sense," Clementine said. "Codger said Jake was alive. He has to be with Tomasso.

"Right," I said. "And they're probably on their way to The Garhole, Green's, or somewhere in between. I'm going to The Garhole and work my way through the marsh. You take the rest to Green's."

Chapter Sixty

With Jake slumped in the passenger seat, Tomasso Calzone slowed the big Cadillac Seville for the turn into Bay Harbor.

"Not yet," Jake said, motioning with his hand. "Keep on the highway."

Tomas pushed ahead. "You wanna see your mother again, kid. You best not be jacking me."

A mile down the road at a sand lane, Jake said, "Turn here."

Tomas spotted The Garhole Bar, the parking lot empty. He removed the .380 Ruger from his waistband screaming at Jake, "What is that?"

"Just an old bar," Jake said. "Don't stop. Follow the sand road this side of the building."

Tomas followed Jake's directions, peeling off about 30 yards from the bar. He hated the sand and salt on his new car, already thinking about a detail job back in New Orleans. Tomas scowled, "Where you taking me, kid?"

"It's just ahead."

Bully Stout had been inside the mobile home, sitting on the bed cleaning his glass eye when he heard the phone ring. By the time he'd reattached his wooden leg, put his eye in, and stumbled down the wheelchair ramp, he'd missed the call. He hoped it wasn't Clementine calling with bad news.

He stayed by the phone hoping for another call. He picked up the double-barreled 12 gauge off the bar, opened the breech, and checked the load—two high-velocity number four shells he'd owned since the days when he'd hunted the sand hill cranes that wintered on the island. He wondered if the 30-year-old shells would still fire.

He heard the hum of a car engine and hobbled to the front of the bar, hoping Parker or Clementine had returned. He held the shotgun to his side and opened the door, surprised to see a Cadillac driven by someone he didn't know, easing up the lane past the parking lot. Bully put his hand to his forehead to block the sun and get a better look.

An arm came out of the driver's side of the Cadillac with a gun in it. Bully saw the gun fire and heard the bullet smash the Garhole Bar sign over his head. He quickly raised the shotgun and fired at the retreating car. The first shot missed, but the load from the second barrel shredded the back tire of the Cadillac. He knew the heavy sedan couldn't go far in the loose sand without a tire. He reloaded the shotgun and considered going after the car, but was afraid he couldn't maneuver in the soft sand. He waited by the door, hoping for another shot.

Bully Stout didn't scare easily. He'd lost a leg and an eye during the Battle of the Bulge, stepping on a mine while carrying his wounded Lieutenant to safety. He'd been shot at many times and by a trained enemy. He wasn't about to let some pistol-shooting flunky get the best of him.

The Cadillac came to a halt. Tomas looked back at the building. He was out of range of the shotgun, but the old man was still standing in front of the door, the shotgun over his shoulder. At least he wasn't advancing, Tomas thought.

Tomas got out of the Cadillac and studied the rear wheel buried to the axle. He worried he'd never get the Cadillac out of the sand. He ordered Jake out of the car.

"Where to?" Tomas demanded.

"A pond up this road," Jake answered.

Saving Jake

Tomas first had to get the meth, then he'd figure a way out. He'd put the kid down as soon as he had the stash and kill the old man. Then he'd hike up to the highway and flag down a car. He couldn't think of anything else. He only hoped the old man hadn't called the cops.

A. Hardy Roper

Saving Jake

Chapter Sixty-One

A pistol shot echoed across the marsh. And then two shotgun blasts roared from the direction of The Garhole. I raced past the entrance to Bay Harbor and down the sand lane to The Garhole hoping I wasn't too late.

Bully stood at the front door waving at me to stop.

"Some sumbitch in a Cadillac took a shot at me," he yelled. "I knocked his back tire out. He's up the road toward the bird pond."

"Did you see Jake?"

"Jake? Was he in the car?"

I hit the gas pedal and surged up the lane until I reached the Cadillac stuck in the sand. I ran past the car to the bird pond and spied Tomas Calzone at the top of the berm, looking down at the water. He said something and disappeared down the inside slope.

I was halfway up the outside of the berm, when I heard Jake's voice. And then everything centered. How could I have not thought of it? For the past 60 years the weatherproofed concrete box at the bottom of the blind had been the perfect hiding place. Jake had remembered the story of my grandfather building the box so his bootlegger friend could hide contraband whisky there during prohibition.

Jake had remembered, but I had forgotten. And then it hit me. Jake had picked the spot because he knew I would think about it. If only—

No time to dwell on that now. Jake was in trouble. I crawled to the top of the berm and peeked over. Jake was bent over the blind, reaching into the concrete vault. Tomas Calzone stood on the edge of the bank facing Jake, a gun by his side. I glanced around for a weapon, a stick, a rock, anything, but found nothing.

Then Jake straightened, standing tall on top the blind, the duffel in his hand. He tossed the duffel to Calzone's feet. Calzone unzipped the bag.

"It's all there," Jake yelled down. "What about my mama."

When Calzone raised the gun, I took off on a dead run down the incline yelling, "Jump, Jake, jump."

Jake heard me screaming and stepped off the back of the blind into the water. The shot smashed the steel stanchion close to Jake's head and ricocheted across the pond. I gathered momentum, charging down the berm, and hit Calzone in full stride just as he turned toward me. We tumbled into the pond with me on top. The fall momentarily stunned us both, but I recovered first, reaching for his hands, trying to grab the weapon. The gun was somewhere in the mud. No time to worry about it now. Calzone regained his strength and used his weight to roll me over, pushing my face under the water, hands around my neck. I was fading fast, losing strength and consciousness.

Jake leaped from the top of the blind and knocked Calzone off me. I pushed up, sucked in a big breath, and hit the bastard hard in the face, then hit him again. I leaped onto his chest, wrapped my hands around his neck and held him under. He thrashed and squirmed, trying to push me off. But I had him good, my knees holding his arms in the mud. I held on tight, the events of the past few hours flashing through my mind— Green dead, Joy hurt, Joe with a broken jaw, and worst of all, Jake's torture at the hands of Luther Bourdain and the bastard I had my hands on.

I pressed harder beginning to lose strength from the effort. I had to hold on, give maximum effort. And then I felt the body beneath me begin to still. I felt no compassion, no sense of right or wrong, only an overwhelming desire to end the threat, to save someone I cared about, a boy who'd suffered beyond measure, who'd missed the good things, all that was right, all that should have been. A few more seconds—

A scream rocketed down the embankment. Clementine stood at the top of the berm shouting down at me, her mouth moving in animated motion. She was yelling something, but the words were lost, the noise in my head drowning out everything but my heart beat.

And then they were all there, agents Matthews and Hebinck and Lieutenant Oliver, their weapons drawn and aimed down the slope.

A. Hardy Roper

Saving Jake

Epilogue

One month has passed since the showdown at the bird pond. Agent Bernard Hebinck is back at FBI headquarters in Quantico, Virginia leading another kidnapping seminar. Except now he has added a new chapter to his presentation.

Agent Maurice Matthews announced his retirement from the FBI. A major cruise line immediately created the new title of "Master Host" and offered Matthews the job training the dance hosts on all its ships. He will also serve as the assistant security officer. At last count, over 30 Houston area women and another 20 from around the world had registered for his first cruise. Matthews is now somewhere in the Caribbean, fretting about his overdue Viagra order.

Tomasso Calzone remains jailed without bond, awaiting trial on torture and kidnapping charges, totally distraught that he has not been allowed to keep his diamond pinkie ring and 50 peso coin necklace in his cell. He spends his time reading the New Orleans Picayune, fuming that the Bastone gang has successfully taken over the drug trade in New Orleans.

The local American Legion chapter is holding a special award ceremony, honoring Bully Stout as the most decorated WWII veteran in Galveston County. Bully was also selected to serve as the Grand Marshall of next year's Mardi Gras parade.

Joe Stubbs is back at The Garhole, recovering from his broken jaw. He and Jennifer Hillbro are now an item, with Jenny spending more time in Joe's mobile home than her apartment in town. With Jenny's encouragement, Joe has signed up for the new titanium prostheses procedure and is awaiting approval from the VA.

Lieutenant Dan Oliver was promoted to Captain for his courageous efforts in solving Jake Green's kidnapping. He is now in charge of the Homicide Division of the Galveston Police Department. Go Figure.

Jake has made new friends at school and seems happy living in Joe's trailer and running the crab traps morning and evening. The results for the DNA comparison among Jake, Morgan Stanford and Kurt Dussair were completed in record time thanks to Jenny Hillbro's influence and Reginald J. Stanford's money. The results indicate a 99.6% match that Morgan Stanford is Jake's biological father. Lou Dussair seemed delighted at the news.

Old money bags Reginald J. Stanford has finally acknowledged his grandson. And although, Reggie baby, as Clementine prefers to call him, has yet to see the boy, he has set up a substantial trust fund for Jake. No one knows if he has also changed his will. Higginbotham and Perry will manage the trust with Jenny's father at the helm.

Everyone involved is hoping Joy Green can progress to a normal life and regain custody of Jake. She is out of the hospital and two weeks into her three-month stay at Galveston's premier rehab facility, her stay funded by daddy Warbucks himself. All reports indicate Joy's attitude is good and she is progressing on schedule.

Buster, the German shepherd, died at the veterinarian's office. Jake and his mother had Buster cremated and his ashes mixed with Slim Green's. Jake and Joy scattered a few of the ashes around Green's yard and buried the rest behind his house. We all gathered at The Garhole Bar for Slim and Buster's Celebration of Life. Clementine and I served fried shrimp and oysters, Harry brought cupcakes, Bully drank beer served by Joe and Jenny, and Joy and Jake stood hand in hand enjoying just being together.

Maggie called wanting me to come in for a checkup with Doc Kennon at the VA. I managed to avoid an appointment, but I did buy a new bottle of Famous Grouse to replace the scotch Clementine drank. I poured half of it out and positioned the bottle on the same shelf beneath the bar. I need it to be there. I need to see that half-bottle of scotch every day.

Today, I put clean sheets on my bed, cleaned the bathroom and brought in several bottles of expensive wine. Clementine Garza is on her way to The Garhole after a trip to San Antonio to catch up on her bills and buy more clothes. I can visualize her now, top down on that fiery Mustang and Madonna, whoever she is, blaring away on the radio. With her new connection to Higginbotham and Perry, Clementine is considering moving her office to Houston. She plans to spend a night or two with me before meeting with Jenny's father.

Fall is approaching, the time when songbirds begin their seasonal trek south to their native lands. Soon the bay waters will cool, and the trout will return to the shallow bays. A fresh pot of crab gumbo sits on the stove sending out beguiling aromas of roux and garlic, bay leaf, thyme and filé.

The Garhole Bar crew is gathered on the dock to watch the sunset—Joe in his wheelchair, Jenny and I beside him on the bench, Jake sitting on the dock, his feet dangling off the bulkhead. We sit mesmerized. The fading ball of light and energy is a balm to the soul, offering hope and redemption. As the sun settles to the horizon across the bay, my mind travels to the generations before me who witnessed the wonder of its continuance.

For hundreds of years past, roving bands of Karankawa Indians, drawing their sustenance of oysters and crabs from the life giving waters, viewed the scene from the grassy shorelines of West Bay.

A. Hardy Roper

Jean Lafitte and his band of cutthroats observed from the decks of pirate ships, and early Galveston residents in tall hats and hooped shirts watched the sunsets from skiffs and sailing sloops.

The world continues to turn at The Garhole Bar. Friends drop in to visit, talking about everything and nothing. All is right with the world. As the sun slips below the horizon and evening shadows covert the water, the refrain from an old Robert Earl King tune drifts softly through my head—"the road goes on forever and the party never ends."

Reviews for "The Garhole Bar"
From the Galveston Daily News
"Captivating and Engrossing"
By Margaret C. Barno "story weaver"

How long has it been since you've stayed up to the wee hours of the night so engrossed in a book so that you could read just one more page? It happened to me last night, or rather, this morning.

The Garhole Bar is a thriller, full of suspense, unexpected turns and many of these events unfold on the West End of Galveston Island. Its author, A. Hardy Roper, who called that location home for over twenty years, sets the novel, his first, at a bar owned by Parker McLeod. Named after the skeleton of an alligator gar jaw he had found and pried open, it is displayed prominently, hanging from the ceiling behind the bar counter.

The story's plot is complex; depth of character development, covering a sixty-year time frame. The scenes initially shift from Germany and Galveston, eventually covering three continents.

Parker McLeod, a 19 year veteran, is struggling to get his life back together. While attempting to help an old friend and his granddaughter, Parker discovers skills learned during his military service come in handy in his new career as owner of a small bar on the west end of an island in the Gulf of Mexico off the coast of Texas.

The story is well presented and kept my heart thumping to the last page. I hope that next thriller involving Parker McLeod is ready for press soon. My hunch is that A. Hardy Roper has a new venture as author that will keep him busy and his books in demand for years to come.

A. Hardy Roper

Reviews for "The Garhole Bar"

Review Written by wilhelmlette (Houston, TX USA)

Well done...riveted my interest from start to finish!
Having been to Galveston Island many times, this book was especially fun to read. This novel will clearly be just as much of a page turner for those who don't know the island at all. A. Hardy Roper does a nice job of character development and successfully weaves the various storylines into a truly entertaining novel of intrigue. The book was an easy and entertaining read.

By Richard W. Lake on January 6, 2013

Roper paints an excellent picture of the Galveston and Fredericksburg TX area. He does a great job of character development. Also, it is a page turner. I would recommend this book to any one, especially those people familiar with the Galveston area.
Great

By Paul A. Schumann Jr. on October 27, 2014
Format: Paperback

Great novel!

Saving Jake

Review for "Assassination in Galveston"
From the Galveston Daily News
December 3, 2011

"Island thriller is a page-turner."

by Margaret C. Barno, story creator

Military veteran and former spy Parker McLeod had all intentions of settling in Galveston's West End to fish and run a quiet restaurant, The Garhole Bar, after his medical retirement resulting from the Gulf War.
    Those plans have been only partially realized. He has gotten involved in solving crimes. This book is another of those unanticipated adventures when a dear friend and lover Of Kemp's ridley sea turtles is murdered and her home set ablaze. The plot is multi layered, involving assassinations initiated and orchestrated by Fidel and Raul Castro, of Cuba. The long-range goal is instigating an uprising in Venezuela, resulting in a coup in which a friend and ally hopefully will become ruler, enabling the flow of much-needed oil to go to the desperately impoverished nation of Cuba.
    Where there's life and danger, there's usually romantic intrigue. The author has placed a realistic variety of such interludes throughout the book. The scenes are descriptive yet not graphic. For that I was grateful.
    It's another page-turner that, on a couple of evenings, I set a chapter limit to read no further before going to bed. Roper's characters are well-developed, like the "bad guys" to the folks at the VA hospital and residents on Bolivar Peninsula and Galveston's West End. Perhaps the best descriptions were the Galveston landmarks, particularly the areas around the ferry landing. I could hear the waves hitting the boat, the ever-

A. Hardy Roper

hungry gull cries and occasionally see the dolphins racing the ferry no matter who was going where for whatever reason.

I've deliberately not mentioned the ending. If Ii had, you'd not read the book. You'd miss a thriller by doing so. I'm going back to read it again to see what I missed during the first time through.

"Assassination in Galveston"
By Saucer

This is another of the Parker McLeod thriller series I couldn't put down until finished. The author's descriptive writing style puts you right in the Texas Gulf Coast area. The beaches, seasonal storms, old restored homes, and other sites bring Galveston alive right at the seaside.

The protagonist, Parker McLeod, is an ex-army Intel officer who inadvertently gets involved in a plot to murder a South American presidential candidate. When a good friend of Parker's is murdered, he begins his own investigation and meets a cast of nefarious characters and a beautiful Cuban ex-patriot who he teams with to attempt to solve the mystery.

W. Clyde Hull

"Assassination in Galveston" by Linda Dussair

Exceptional! Meticulously plotted, with superb character development, this fascinating thriller is destined to be a best seller. The fast-paced story of Parker McCloud will keep you riveted until the very end. Roper has captured the essence of Galveston and woven it into this highly charged second novel of suspense and intrigue....a MUST read!

Saving Jake

About The Author

As a fourth generation Texan and Galveston resident, A. Hardy Roper writes from a wealth of knowledge about the island's storied past and vibrant present. Mr. Roper's great grandparents arrived from Germany in the 1840's and entered through the Port of Galveston, at the time, second only to New York for immigrant destination.

A. Hardy Roper

Today's Galveston is an eclectic mixture of 'old money' and Victorian mansions checkered among indigent neighborhoods of African Americans and Hispanics, all weaved tightly together, as if huddled against the onslaught of the next storm like the epic 1900 hurricane that claimed 6,000 lives.

From its 19th Century past of pirates and buried treasures, to its 20th Century lifestyle of bootlegging, bawdy houses and gambling, Galveston Island offers an endless setting for mystery and intrigue.

A. Hardy Roper has studied its culture and its history. His Parker McLeod mysteries weave an intricate path of deceit and mayhem as the city struggles to balance its colorful past with the inevitable collision of sleepy 'island life' and the hurried weekend rush as the playground of Houston's wealthy baby-boomers.

Contact : Hardy@assassinationingalveston.com